FALLING FOR THE GOVERNESS

Historical Regency Romance

THE DUKES' LADIES
BOOK 4

ABBY AYLES

STARFALL
PUBLICATIONS

Starfall Publications

ABBY
AYLES

Clean Historical Romance Tales

PRAISE FOR ABBY AYLES

Abby Ayles has been such an inspiration for me! I haven't missed any of her novels and she has never failed my expectations!

-Edith Byrd

The characters in this novel have surely touched my heart.

Linda C - "Melting a Duke's Winter Heart" 5.0 out of 5 stars Reviewed in the United States on December 21, 2019

This book kept me on the edge of my seat and I could not put it down.

Wendy Ferreira - "The Odd Mystery of the Cursed

Duke" 5.0 out of 5 stars *Reviewed in the United States on April 13, 2019*

Oh this was a wonderful story and Abby has done it again! This storyline was perfect and the characters were developed and just had you reading to see if they get their happily ever after!

- Marilyn Smith - "Inconveniently Betrothed to an Earl" 5.0 out of 5 stars Reviewed in the United States on April 8, 2020

The sweetest story, with we rest abounding! I especially liked the bonus scene - totally unexpected engagements. Well written with realistic characters. Thank you!

Janet Tonole - "The Lady Of the Lighthouse" 5.0 out of 5 stars Reviewed in the United States on December 27, 2022

I just finished reading Abby Ayles' The Lady's Gamble and its bonus scene, and I wanted to tell other readers about this great story. I love regency romances and I believe Abby is one of the best regency writers out there!

Carolynn Padgett - "The Lady's Gamble" 5.0 out of 5 stars Reviewed in the United States on March 16, 2018

Such a great Book! So enjoyed the characters....they felt so " real"....and loved the " deleted" scene. Thanks Abby, for your gift of writing the best stories!

Marcia Reckard - "Entangled with the Duke" 5.0 out of 5 stars Reviewed in the United States on May 22, 2021

I loved this story. It took you through all of the exciting ups and downs. The characters were so honest. I could read it again and again.

Peggy Murphy - "The Duke's Rebellious Daughter" 5.0 out of 5 starsReviewed in the United States on December 3, 2022

I am never disappointed when reading one of Ms. Ayles stories. They have strong characters, engaging storylines, and all-around wonderful stories.

Donna L - "A Loving Duke for the Shy Duchess" 5.0 out of 5 stars Reviewed in the United States on December 23, 2019

A thoroughly enjoyable read! Love the complexity of the intelligent characters! They have the ability to feel emotions deeply! Their backstories help to explain why they behave as they do! The subplots and various interactions between characters add to the wonderful richness of the story! Well done!

Terry Rose Bailey - "A Cinderella for the Duke" 5.0 out of 5 stars Reviewed in the United States on October 8, 2022

ALSO BY ABBY AYLES

The Keys to a Lockridge Heart

Melting a Duke's Winter Heart

A Loving Duke for the Shy Duchess

Freed by the Love of an Earl

The Earl's Wager for a Lady's Heart

The Lady in the Gilded Cage

A Reluctant Bride for the Baron

A Christmas Worth Remembering

A Guiding Light for the Lost Earl

The Earl Behind the Mask

Tales of Magnificent Ladies

The Odd Mystery of the Cursed Duke

Falling for the Governess

Saving Lady Abigail

Secret Dreams of a Fearless Governess

A Daring Captain for Her Loyal Heart

Loving A Lady

Unlocking the Secrets of a Duke's Heart

The Duke's Rebellious Daughter

The Duke's Juliet

SCANDALS AND SEDUCTION IN REGENCY ENGLAND

Also in this series

Regency Loves of Secrecy and Redemption

Forbidden Loves and Dashing Lords

Fateful Romances in the Most Unexpected Places

The Mysteries of a Lady's Heart

Regency Widows Redemption

The Secrets of Their Heart

Lovely Dreams of Regency Ladies

Second Chances for Broken Hearts

Trapped Ladies

Light to the Marquesses' Hearts

Falling for the Mysterious Ladies

Tales of Secrecy and Enduring Love

Fateful Twists and Unexpected Loves

Regency Wallflowers

Regency Confessions

Ladies Laced with Grace

Journals of Regency Love

A Lady's Scarred Pride

How to Survive Love

Destined Hearts in Troubled Times

Ladies Loyal to their Hearts

The Mysteries of a Lady's Heart

Secrets and Scandals

A Lady's Secret Love

Falling for the Wrong Duke

GET ABBY'S EXCLUSIVE MATERIAL

*B*uilding a relationship with my readers is the very best thing about writing.

Join my newsletter for information on new books and deals plus a few free books!

You can get your books by clicking or visiting the link below

https://BookHip.com/JBWAHR

PS. Come join our Facebook Group if you want to interact with me and other authors from Starfall Publication on a daily basis, win FREE Giveaways and find out when new content is being released.

Join our Facebook Group

abbyayles.com/Facebook-Group

FALLING FOR THE GOVERNESS

Isabella Watts' life of privilege is about to come crashing down.

Her wealthy lifestyle, as the daughter of the adventurous Baron Leinster, is swept away when her father is unexpectedly killed, leaving her with a debt she cannot possibly overcome.

Not only that, but her father has turned the estate over to the vile Mr. Smith, a man whose advances Isabella has already once refused and who is now out for revenge.

. . .

Fleeing from the repugnant Smith and his desire to humiliate her, Isabella finds work as the governess of a young ward at Wintercrest Manor.

There she meets the Marquess of Bellfourd, recently returned from the navy to take his place by his father's side following the death of his elder brother.

But there are deep and possibly irreconcilable rifts at Wintercrest Manor. Wounds so deep they may never be healed.

Can Isabella help the family to overcome their woes while staying out of reach of the clutches of her nemesis? Or will her past catch up with her even there?

PROLOGUE

My dearest Louisa,

I fear my heart is broken. It is with the saddest news I find myself writing to you today. Just yesterday I received a visit from Mr. Jenkins, my father's lawyer.

As you know, my father was on a ship set for Cayman Island in relation to his import business. As I had mentioned a few times at our last meeting, I was becoming exceedingly concerned since his vessel had not yet returned. Without any ill news, I hoped that they had only been delayed by poor wind and calm waters.

Unfortunately, this is not the case. While in the tropics, father contracted a most dreadful fever. His most experienced sailors fell ill.

To prevent the sickness from spreading, ill people were to be left behind to recover and return home with another vessel. My father was too prominent of a figure to just leave behind, and the MHS Poseidon decided to stay in Cayman Island for a fortnight to allow him to recover.

I am told the fever passed. For that I am grateful, but why did my stubborn father have to push himself? I don't know how to feel. You are aware of how much I disliked him going on these journeys to begin with.

Having gained his strength back, father sailed Poseidon homeward, but his health took a turn for the worse.

The ship's surgeon did all he could to help, but in the end, it was not enough. My father passed away a little over a month ago in the middle of the Atlantic Ocean. There's nothing I could have done, and I resent myself for that.

Mr. Jenkins, having been informed himself just last night upon the arrival of the ship, came to bear me the sorrowful news this morning. He assured me that my father had the most lavished and honorable burial at sea that could be mustered for the situation.

I am so overcome with confusion and sorrow. It is a wonder that I can compose myself to scribe such a letter to you.

Though father was always very busy with his business and adventures, he was a loving and attentive man. I feel my life vastly emptier without the assured knowledge that though he may be away, he will always return home here to Rosewater house.

Mr. Jenkins has also informed me that I will need to come to his offices on the morrow to discuss my father's estate and I suppose, to some effect, what is to become of me.

I cannot even imagine being able to subject myself to conversations of financial and worldly status when my heart is so full of turmoil.

It is for this reason that I must offer my deepest regrets to inform you that I will not be able to accompany your excellent mother to tea. Please tell Lady Gilchrist that I send my deepest regrets.

I hope that I will see you very soon, my dear Louisa, so that I may receive comfort from the words of wisdom you always seem to use so deftly.

With humble heart,

Isabella

The next evening Isabella received a return letter from Lady Lydia in the five o'clock post.

My Dearest Isabella,

It is with the heaviest of hearts that I give you my deepest condolences on your loss.

I have informed her Ladyship of your necessity for absence from her humble event tomorrow afternoon. Though you will be greatly missed by not only my mother but all those who are to attend, we all understand your need for time to quietly reflect and compose yourself.

Please do not fear for your well-being. Your father was a

good man, and I am confident that he will provide for you even after the untimely event of his death.

As soon as you are able, I invite you to my residence so that I may be able to comfort my dearest friend in her time of need.

Your humble friend,

Louisa

1

*I*sabella's eyes wandered lazily as she sat in Louisa's comfortable drawing room. It was the smallest drawing room of her dear friend's London residence, used for the entertaining of very intimate friends of the ladies of the house.

Isabella was struggling to collect her thoughts or even know where to begin after the events that had transpired over the last two days. She did her best to keep her trembling hands clasped in the lap of her dark black cotton dress.

Her hand rattled the teacup just slightly when she took it from Louisa's loving hands. Isabella was happy for the privacy such an intimate setting provided. She wasn't sure if she would be able to hold her composure as she retold Louisa all that transpired.

"I scarcely know where to begin," she said after taking a small sip of courage.

She didn't have much appetite at the moment but felt the tea might help to clear her head. The last few nights had been restless and anything but rejuvenating.

"Start with when you arrived at Mr. Jenkins' offices yesterday. I am quite sure we will find a way to untangle any mess you may now find yourself in," Louisa responded calmly.

She was just two years older than Isabella but not the slightest in comparison to physical beauty. Where Isabella had rich, shiny black locks and emerald-green eyes, Louisa had mouse-brown hair, which rarely plaited as it should, and ordinary brown eyes.

It did not prevent them from finding an inseparable bond as young girls at the prestigious Mrs. Mason's School for Exceptional Young Ladies.

Louisa had always been a quiet child who often kept to herself. Isabella, on the other hand, was openly pleasant to be around and was commonly found at the center of the conversation, entertaining the other ladies of the school with wild tales heard from her father's adventures.

Louisa, at first, had listened quietly to her tales, but Isabella saw more to Louisa than her shy exterior. Much as Isabella had expected, Louisa was the most kind and giving young lady she had ever met. Her friendship and confidante was something she treasured all through her youth and young adulthood.

"I suppose you're right," Isabella responded with a steadying breath before setting the tea down.

"I arrived at Mr. Jenkins office yesterday morning. I was surprised when I was shown in to find Mr. Smith already there."

"Mr. Smith? Your father's horrid business partner," Louisa clarified, and Isabella nodded in agreement.

"I had done my best to avoid him at all costs since that dreadful event four years ago. It gave me quite a shock as it had not been mentioned to me that he would be there.

Though now looking back on it, it was certainly reasonable that he should be there as we discussed my father's estate."

"Of course, you are not expected to have the clearest of minds in such a time," Louisa said attempting to erase any guilt Isabella might feel on her state of propriety.

"That awful man," Isabella stated, now with her green eyes full of anger. "He didn't even stand at my entrance, and in truth, I didn't see him at all from his chair at the back of the office till Mr. Jenkins motioned to him during the conversation."

Isabella thought back to that horrible meeting four years earlier. She had been barely seventeen at the time, having completed her schooling and finished her first season out among society.

It was a small dinner party that her father was having at their very own Rosewater house. She had been all aglow with the excitement of her season and the joy of having her father momentarily home with her.

Mr. Smith was there, of course, since he was Baron Leinster's closest friend and business partner. Isabella had not paid him much attention as he was even older than her father and she could never imagine him having interest in such a young girl.

As the evening transpired, however, Mr. Smith found a chance to enter into a private conversation with Isabella. It was then he requested that she should consider him a suitor and accept his proposal of marriage.

Isabella was so shocked by the declaration that all she managed to say was "but you are so old." It was probably not the most polite thing for her to say, but so often when she was shocked, she tended to speak truths without thinking.

Isabella was young and full of spirit. She had received much attention from various social gatherings of the season. She was not so conceited enough to think she was above those outside the peerage. Isabella had always assumed that with her father's honorary title she would find herself a gentleman in the society she had been raised to be a part of.

Of course, having affection for her future husband was a necessity for her, his status had not been. Even so, she would never have imagined marrying such an older, coarse man at such a young age.

She did her best to regain her composure and thank Mr. Smith but politely decline. He became enraged by her very respectable but negative answer and made quite a scene of it.

From that day on, Isabella had done everything in her power to not be in the company of Mr. Smith. It was not always an easy task when he had such close financial relationships with her father.

"Mr. Jenkins informed me that my father had left his import and export business to Mr. Smith."

"I suppose that seems reasonable enough," Louisa said. "After all, as partner, it would only be right that he inherit the whole of the business. And I suppose you are to be left Rosewater house and a living?"

"That is the worst of it. Mr. Jenkins informed me that all of my father's estates had been specifically put in the charge of Mr. Smith, having no other male family member. He then informed me that my father had also collected a large sum of debts," she lowered her voice, "gambling."

"Oh dear. Had you any idea of these debts?"

"I was aware of his enjoyment of gentlemanly horse races. I suspected the thrill of it was much like that of a boy crossing the sea. But I had no idea that he was in such a poor situation."

"What does this mean?" Louisa asked with fear in her soft eyes.

"Well, Mr. Jenkins said that he had been in conference with Mr. Smith all morning and had made several arrangements."

That moment, when she finally looked over her shoulder to find Mr. Smith sitting behind her would most likely haunt her the rest of her days.

He had stood then and walked forward, wholly unearthing himself from the morning shadows that the windowless office provided.

He was much older now than would be expected for the four years that had passed since his proposition. His hair was long and straggly on the sides and completely missing on top. Instead of choosing to wear a wig, he tied the straggled strands back with a ribbon.

His face was worn and marked by the years he, himself, had spent as captain on a merchant ship before striking business with Baron Leinster.

Though his clothes were of a gentlemanly style, they were outworn and dusty. The edges of his coat were stained with dirt.

Undoubtedly, his lifelong bachelorhood had led to the inferior care of his outward appearance. He smiled smugly, showing his blackened tooth, something she remembered quite clearly from her first encounter with him.

Quite awkwardly Mr. Jenkins had fiddled with some

paperwork on his desk. He was a rather young man for his position, only recently taken on by her father. Her interactions with him, however few, had always been enjoyable ones.

Usually, he had a jolly expression to his eyes, especially since the birth of his first child.

Isabella wasn't sure she had ever seen Mr. Jenkins so uncomfortable, even when he had informed her of her father's passing.

"As the benefactor of your father's estate, Mr. Smith here has decided to sell all assets in order to pay off the debts incurred, including Rosewater house and everything in it."

"But that is my home!" Isabella said with a raised voice. "Where am I to live?"

Isabella could not bear to take her eyes off Mr. Jenkins to turn to the scoundrel behind her. Most certainly he was enjoying the destitute situation he had put her in.

"I have spoken of this very concern with Mr. Smith at length," Mr. Jenkins replied, obviously understanding her fear. "He feels, as sole proprietor, he is, and I rightly agree, responsible for your safety and security."

Isabella stood up from her spot, forgetting all dignity, "I won't marry him!"

Mr. Jenkins looked at her apologetically, whether from the necessity of marriage between a senior man and a young lady of one and twenty years or other less favorable options she wasn't sure.

"Though I suggested such an arrangement, for the sake of your comfort, I was informed that such arrangements were no longer...no longer..." he hesitated to try to find the words, "no longer a possibility unless..." Mr. Jenkins gave a horribly painful sigh. "He would like you to ask him to take you in."

"Absolutely not," Isabella stated still standing, trembling with fear and embarrassment.

She could hear the tone of disgust behind her but refused to turn to look at him.

"Before you speak Miss Isabella, I encourage you to consider your situation. Mr. Smith does intend to sell all valuable possessions. Even so, it will just barely cover your father's debts. Without such an arrangement I cannot imagine how you will see to your comfortable lifestyle.

"Then I shan't live as I have thus far. I am willing to be more frugal with my life. Am I not allowed some sort of income from my father's business?"

"I did discuss such matters with Mr. Smith in the event that you did not want to...um...abide to his requirements. He agreed a yearly income was only fair since, after all, he was named your protector. The sum he agreed on was... well...it was fifty pounds a year."

"Fifty pounds a year?" Isabella now turned to face Mr. Smith.

"It is half his yearly wage, though you wouldn't know it by the way he lived, and it is quite generous considering I will most likely need to take on another partner," Mr. Smith spit back indignantly.

He had quite the smug look on his face as he rocked back and forth on his heels, hands pleasantly clasped in front of him. What was torturous to say for the lawyer, and unbelievable to hear for Isabella, was quite enjoyable for this horrible man.

He had positively backed her into a corner. With such a small amount, there was no possible way for Isabella to live alone. It wouldn't even support a house staff of just one or two servants. He had meant it to force her to beg before him for that which she had denied him all those years ago.

"Good heavens, Izzy, what did you do?" Louisa asked as she listened, horrified and enraptured by the retelling.

"Well, I refused to give in to his boorish demands. I told him I would find a way to settle on such low income and that was the end of that. I will starve to death before I give that man the benefit of seeing me grovel at his feet.

"But Izzy- without a home or any possessions of your own, how will you do it?"

"Well, after I announced I would not give in to the wretched blackguard, Mr. Smith stormed out of the room, slamming the door quite loudly behind him. Mr. Jenkins, the poor man, began apologizing profusely, saying that if there were anything he could do to help me, he would."

"Well, what is there to be done, Izzy?"

"I thought on this fact for the better part of last night. I have come to one conclusion. I will need to find myself some sort of employment."

"Certainly not?" Louisa asked with surprise, though Isabella could already see the wheels turning in her head that this was the likely alternative.

"I think we both know that this is how it must be," Isabella said with a defeated tone.

"It is either that or giving in to Mr. Smith. My pride, however sinful to keep, will not allow such a thing. I will not be offended at all if at such a declaration you find your-self unable to keep my company."

"Absolutely not!" Louisa said using a firm tone.

"You are my dearest friend. You were the only one who cared to spend time with me when we were together at school. I would never abandon you, no matter the cost."

"Not even if I am a lowly scullery maid?" Isabella asked, tears welling in her eyes.

In all honesty, she had spent the whole night not just thinking about a life of employment, but terrified of the fact that she had no idea what employable skills she had.

Though she may have been born on the lower side of the peerage, her father had never spared her a comfort, and she feared she could not even dress on her own, let alone take on tasks.

"You will be no such thing," Louisa said firmly. She

placed her own small, delicate hands in Isabella's lap and began to ponder.

"I understand now why you have come to me. We will most certainly find something that would be suitable for your position."

"But I don't have a position; I am free of status now and completely destitute, without any skills at hand."

"Of course you have skills," Louisa encouraged. "Why, you were always one of the top performers in our school! Do you not remember? Mrs. Mason would have you stand and recite your French lessons before prospective students. Why, that is it!" Louisa said with the light of a plan. "You could easily find employment as a governess."

Isabella thought this new idea over for a bit. She unquestionably had loved school and took to it quickly.

She was accomplished enough in her educational knowledge as well as music and other various genteel talents. She could certainly teach such things to young lords and ladies.

Of course, it was a definite step down from being one of the peerages to serving and educating them. It was not as low as the serving class but somewhere in between.

Between her employment and her small allowance, Isabella would most certainly be able to manage on her own.

"Do you think I would be hired as such? Mr. Jenkins did

offer to help me find employment when I found myself in need of it."

"Of course. I am quite sure that Mrs. Mason would also be happy to give you a shining reference. You could most likely find a home here in London to instruct pupils at and we could still be close friends."

"Oh, my dear Louisa, I fear wishing so much good fortune to happen at this time in my life,is much like wishing to catch a star. I will be quite satisfied with any position and your continued friendship, even if through correspondence only."

"Have faith, Izzy," Louisa said, reaching across the small table of tea and taking Isabella's hands.

"We will find a way to overcome this hurdle together. Certainly, it isn't something to worry about now. The Season is almost upon us. Mr. Smith certainly won't put you out till after. It will give you an opportunity to more earnestly search a match and perhaps escape all the necessity for such talk."

"I hope you're right, Louisa," Isabella responded, giving her a grateful squeeze of the hand in return.

"I was frightened by his rage upon my declaration not to heed his request. I am almost certain he will do everything in his power to hinder my progress at every turn."

2

*T*he following week, Isabella made her way back to Mr. Jenkins's office after receiving a note that he had found a suitable position for her. She had been reassured by Louisa that she would have at least the season to see if she could come up with a better course of action before settling on being a governess.

It was not to be the case.

Sadly, no more than a week after finding out about her father's untimely death, Mr. Smith had visited Rosewater house. There he had informed Miss Isabella that she would have a month only to collect items and vacate her home.

He then proceeded to boldly go through the house, solicitor in tow, informing her of what things he planned to sell.

Isabella hadn't informed the servants yet of the

impending liquidation of her father's estates. Mr. Smith even went boldly into Isabella's own room and rifled through her belongings. Mr. Smith announced he would be procuring all her belongings including dresses and jewelry.

The solicitor, embarrassed, hastily suggested that such tactics were not necessary to the closing of the amount owed.

Mr. Smith reluctantly allowed Isabella to keep her clothing but still required all jewelry be turned over to him for selling. She didn't have much in the way of fancy jewelry.

Therefore, she didn't care much for giving it up if it meant not allowing Mr. Smith the satisfaction of seeing her beg him for marriage.

Her hardest items to part with were the silver comb her father had stated her mother wore on their wedding day, the small gold band that was her mother's wedding ring, and a silver chain with a locket of her mother's hair which she wore around her neck always. It had been a gift from her father on her sixteenth birthday.

Having never met her mother, for she had passed in childbirth, any stories or items her father shared with her were cherished.

After taking all belongings worth selling on the spot, including the ring and comb, and informing Isabella that they would be back in a month, for the third time, to take possession of the house, Mr. Smith set his evil eyes on the locket around her neck.

Isabella defiantly clasped her hand around it. This was one thing Isabella would not allow to be taken from her.

Would Mr. Smith really stoop to such a level of evil?

Luckily the solicitor interjected, "I believe we should allow Miss Watts to collect herself. I am sure it has been a very tiring day for her. We can always come back to collect any other items upon the sale of the establishment."

Mr. Smith had reluctantly agreed and left. Not a minute after the front door shut on the two men, Isabella crumpled to the hall floor in a heap of sorrowful tears.

Her kind maid, who must have also been beside herself to learn that she would be without a situation in a month's time, helped Isabella up to her room to lay down.

It was clear that she would not have time to find a better end to her situation. The next day, Isabella inquired of Mrs. Mason for a letter of character reference and delivered it to Mr. Jenkins that same day.

She wrung her hands for the next week, waiting for word from Mr. Jenkins. She had no idea if anyone would ever accept a governess at her age without any prior employment references.

Mr. Jenkins had assured her that he would do everything in his power to see her well settled. She had felt so blessed to have such a willing friend to help her in her time of need.

The time had come when a letter arrived stating that Mr. Jenkins had found her a station of employment. She made it to his office the following day in haste.

Isabella was dreading and desperate to know what establishment she would be employed at for the remainder of her days.

Would she find herself teaching in a girls' establishment just as she, herself, had attended? Or would some member of her peerage take pity on her and take her on for the benefit of his children's private education.

She sat nervously across from Mr. Jenkins.

"I must confess I had a harder time finding a situation for you than expected. You see, most of the lady schools in London were well staffed. Mrs. Mason did express in her letter, had she the room, she would have happily taken you on."

It was something that Isabella had expected. There were often more ladies seeking employment than available opportunities for suitable work.

A part of her wanted to feel slightly shocked or betrayed that not one of those in her acquaintance here in London had tried to take her on for employment. She was no longer a member of that society, however, and would not be seen as someone to have around.

"I am sorry to say that the situation I found for you is far outside of London. I know you had expected to stay in the area, and I did my very best to do so but..." he trailed off.

"It is quite alright. I know you did your very best, Mr. Jenkins, and I am very grateful of all your efforts. I am sure that no matter the location, I will find my situation quite adequate."

"I am glad to hear your brave words. The position is for the Duke of Wintercrest. He has taken on a small ward over the last year, a young woman I believe, and is seeking a governess for her. He specifically asked for a lady of London breeding to prepare her for society, as well as provide her with a strong understanding of the French language."

Isabella, of course, knew of the Duke and Duchess of Wintercrest, though she had never had the honor of making their acquaintance. She was aware that they were relatively older in age with children of their own, and therefore questioned who this young ward might be. Perhaps a relation they willingly took on.

"It seems that it might be an ideal position for me."

"Just as I thought when I was told of it. The Duke is also willing to give a much more significant pay than often given for a governess, forty pounds a year. I had assumed that you would be willing to take the position since they were in need fairly soon. I took the liberty to tell them that you would accept the position. I hope that is fine?"

"It is quite alright. I suspect it is more than I could

otherwise hope for and I thank you for all your hard work on my behalf."

"I am glad to hear it," Mr. Jenkins said relaxing into his normally happy face. "As I said, they are in need of a governess right away and have made transportation for you. You will travel by public coach in two days' time. I must warn you to pack relatively lightly as there is not much room in such situations, and dress comfortably, for that matter. You will be spending two nights on the road during your travels."

"A three-day travel? Forgive me, but where exactly do the Duke and Duchess of Wintercrest live."

"Yes, that. It is quite far north. Just a day's ride south of Edinburgh."

"Is it in Scotland, then?" Isabella asked, a little shocked. She had not dared to hope that she would stay in her beloved London, but to leave England altogether seemed terrifying to her.

"No, not quite. Just short of it. I do believe the vast lands of Wintercrest come into contact with the country, but the manor itself is still on English soil."

"I see," Isabella said trying to accustom herself to her new lot in life. "I thank you again, Mr. Jenkins, for not only your work with my father but for the help you have given me and your continued friendship. I will hurry home now and begin my preparations for travel."

Isabella did just that. She did her best to pack a

minimal amount of clothing into her chest and prepared anything she might want to keep safely tucked inside.

Luckily, her maid, Sally, was there to help her with the work. All the time she wondered how she was going to make do on her own.

Her last step was that of utter defiance. The night before she was set to leave, she took her small sewing kit and sewed her silver locket into the hem of her dress.

She certainly couldn't be seen leaving the house wearing it, for Mr. Smith might come after her, demanding the property. That would be no way to start her new life.

At the same time, she refused to leave it behind in the house that was once her home, for that wretched man to handle so roughly and sell like nothing more than a worthless trinket. She hoped that by the time Mr. Smith learned of her deceit, she would be far away and out of his reach.

If there was one good thing about having to travel so far away from the city she loved, it was that she would also be far away from the man who sought to destroy her life at every turn.

Her three-day journey up north was not entirely uneventful. She was very uncomfortable having been placed inside a carriage with five other people. There was scarcely room to sit, let alone adjust one's position.

She had to count herself lucky, though. After all, the fare was paid by her employer, and he had given her the kindness of a seat inside the carriage. There had been two who could only afford to sit on the roof of the carriage out in the elements.

Many of those in the carriage were friendly enough and made small talk. As the days progressed, each got off in their turn till she was left alone with one other man.

She noticed quite quickly that the scene outside her window changed from the warm sunshine of spring air to dark and gloomy clouds, as she progressed northward.

The final morning, just before he took his leave, Isabella asked the portly gentleman across from her, if grey weather was the norm in the north.

"My dear Miss Watts," he said with a gruff, mustache filled voice, "I have lived here my whole life and can only boast of seeing full sunshine a handful of times each year. You are lucky that you have come for spring and summer first. It will help you acclimate before the harsh winter falls. I, myself, choose to stay in town for the dreary months, now that I am able, and only return for these warmer seasons."

Isabella looked out her window again and contemplated how he could have possibly counted her view outside as a warmer season. She had decided to wear her simple light brown traveling dress. It was relatively without frill, which also meant it wouldn't show wrinkles as much in her travels.

Though there was beautiful, lush green land as far as she could see, the sky had been nothing but grey. A hard, bitter wind bit back against the carriage and, from time to time, it even drizzled down on them.

Isabella had also learned from her companions on the ride that she would be staying just east of Northumberland along the coast. From the description of the estate, it sounded astonishing. Isabella supposed she would just have to get used to not only coastal fresh air and beautiful greenery, but also grey skies and damp weather.

Finally, as dusk was beginning to settle on the third day, Isabella saw a long stone wall along the road. The driver had informed her earlier that this was the edge of Winter-crest estates and when they came to it, he knocked on the roof to silently point it out to her.

Her excitement reached its limit as the driver slowed to a stop before the main gates. She got out and took a moment to stretch her limbs. The driver was already down and removing her trunk. Watching him struggle with it, she wondered if she had perhaps packed more than she should have.

He set it down on the ground next to her at the gate and dusted his hands off, looking up at the expanse of the property. Isabella followed his gaze and admired it as well.

Turning back to the driver, she was surprised to see him retaking his place on top of the carriage.

"But wait," she called out. "Please sir, what shall I do now?"

"Can't say, Miss Watts. All I am to do is drop ye right here."

With a flip of his reins, he made his way onward, leaving Miss Isabella Watts utterly alone and confused at the threshold of Wintercrest Manor.

3

Isabella looked down the way leading to the manor house. She couldn't say for sure, however, since she could see nothing in the dimming light but the road before her. She tugged at her trunk, unable to lift it from its grassy resting place.

She supposed that most people seeking employment here, only brought the clothes on their back and another outfit for Sunday attire. If the six gowns she had foolishly packed weren't too much, then the books from her father's small library surely were.

She had convinced herself that she could use these beloved stories as part of her pupil's education. Of course, the Duke of Wintercrest had enough of a library on his own that bringing books of her own was a silly, selfish move on her part.

A cold wind whipped her and she tightened the simple shawl she had wrapped around herself. Isabella suddenly wished that she had thought to bring a pelisse in her chest. Certainly, they knew she would be arriving today. She waited a few moments, considering that the coachman who was to meet her was just a bit late.

After a period of ten minutes, she was convinced that at least a footman would eventually come to fetch her. Finally, as her ability to see in the cloudy, dim light was almost impossible, she determined that no one was coming and began to drag her trunk down the road.

Had she been in the right frame of mind, she might have left her chest at the gate and walked on only to have it fetched at another time by someone more capable. She, however, was not in a good state of mind. She was shivering with cold and had no idea what she was to expect or have expected of her in her new lot in life.

Luckily, the moon was full, and as clouds parted, she was able to get brief views of the way forward. When clouds obscured her only illumination, though, she did her best not to panic as she could only see a few feet in front of her. Hopefully, the lights from the house would begin to show in a parting of the hedge trees, that ran along the road.

Finally, in a glimpse of momentary light from above, she saw a gentlemanly figure walking toward her up the road. He stopped upon also spotting her form.

"Oh, thank heavens," she called out, assuming him to be a servant sent to receive her. "I feared I was all forgotten about. Please, would you kindly help me with my portmanteau."

She straightened from her crouched, pulling position. The figure across from her, no more than ten feet ahead, didn't seem to move. She couldn't make out his features in such dark lighting but assumed that no one but a footman would be out, at such a late hour.

"Certainly," a sure, deep voice called back to her. The hurried figured met her and bent down to pick up her chest.

"Pray, do tell me though, why exactly are you dragging a chest down this road so late at night," the man asked as he began to walk forward easily with chest in hand.

"Oh, forgive me. I thought you were the footman sent to retrieve me. I am Miss Isabella Watts. I have been employed as governess for His Grace. I do not mean to impose on you, if your intention was not to come fetch me," she added quickly.

"Well, I don't think I could leave you here to continue dragging such a large item," he said, shifting smoothly the weight in his hand.

"I just assumed. You looked from a distance to be a footman by your stature, sir," she hesitated on her last word, pointing out that he had yet to give his own name.

"Beg your pardon, Miss Watts. I am Captain Grant. I

had just stepped outside for a walk in the fresh air. Sometimes things can get quite stifling inside."

"Captain. Well, no wonder you have the stature of a footman," Isabella said, realizing it might be quite forward of her.

"I just mean, my father was a sailor as well. I suppose I found kinship with your nautical air."

"Was he also in the Royal Navy?" Captain Grant asked as they continued on their way. He seemed to know the direction by heart and walked at a steady pace through the now almost complete darkness.

"No, he was on a merchant ship as a boy, and had his own set of vessels later in life. He had quite a taste for the adventurous sea life," she added with a bit of nostalgia.

"Pray, what was his name? Perhaps I met him on my journeys."

Isabella was quite unsure of what name to give- his Christian name or his title. Certainly, to have a titled gentleman's daughter in the house might raise some animosity when it came to fitting in with other servants.

Since Captain Grant was unquestionably a guest and not a member of the staff, Isabella risked the chance of giving her father's proper title, as he would have liked.

"My father was Baron Leinster. He unfortunately passed a few months back."

"I am so sorry to hear that," the gentleman looked

down at her in the little light and held a tone of sincere sorrow. "My deepest condolences."

Isabella thanked him for his kindness, and they walked on a few more minutes in silence. She pondered to ask him about his service in the Royal Navy, hoping to make a good transition in the conversation, when she saw the lights of the manor up ahead.

She gave a grateful sigh of relief. She had done her best to hide it, but her thin traveling dress and shawl had not been much to protect her from the wind that sliced between the hedge trees. She noticed immediately that her companion made his way to the head of the house.

"Oh, if you please, Captain Grant, I would find it more appropriate for me to find my way to the servant's entrance. If you could just point me in the right direction, I would happily part company with you with my full thanks for your service."

Captain Grant seemed to hesitate a minute.

"I couldn't possibly leave you to take the portmanteau yourself," he finally said. "I am certain the household will find you a welcome guest."

As much as Isabella would have liked to enter the vast manor in front as a guest, she knew that was no longer her station in life. It was time for her to divide the line from who she had been, to who she was now.

"I appreciate your kindness, but I am quite sure the housekeeper will expect me."

"Alright then," Captain Grant seemed to resolve to her reasoning, "I shall escort you there. You are lucky you came upon me, for I know the servant's entrance well."

"You do?" Isabella asked, surprised.

"Yes," he replied with a soft chuckle. "I lived here in my youth, and as a young boy I was quite gangly and always in want of something to eat. Usually sweets," he continued with that same flow of storytelling that Isabella had enjoyed so much from her father.

She smiled and wondered if all seamen were expert folk-tellers. "I would often make my way through the kitchen by way of the service entrance, to sneak a sweet cake from under the cook's nose. She, of course, knew exactly what I was doing and kindly turned a blind eye to it."

"She sounds like a very considerate chef."

"She is that, not to mention the best in all of the county."

"How fortunate His Grace must feel to have her here under his roof."

They had finally arrived at the side entrance door, and moving the trunk to one hand, Captain Grant unceremoniously opened it and gestured for her to enter. Isabella was startled, when she entered the room, to find a well-lit hall with three long tables all filled with servants, no doubt eating their evening meal. They all stared at her in silent shock until the Captain entered the room behind her. Instantly, the whole hall stood up.

An older woman with a tight-fitted blonde bun and keys jingling at her waist came rushing forward. Isabella had no doubt that she was the housekeeper of the manor.

"Lord Bellfourd, can I be of service to you, sir?"

She was frantically looking between the new lady stranger and the Marquess of Bellfourd, son of the Duke of Wintercrest.

"Mrs. Peterson, please let me introduce Miss Watts, our new governess. I was out on an evening stroll when I found her in some distress."

Immediately, at Mrs. Peterson's request, a groomsman came forward and took the portmanteau away. He left the room with it, Isabella hoped to her own room. She, however, noticed that Mrs. Peterson had not addressed her or even looked at her directly.

"I do apologize for your inconvenience, Lord Bellfourd. The governess was meant to arrive much earlier in the evening. Mr. Larson and I were just discussing sending out someone to inquire after her only a few moments ago."

It was a little irritating to Isabella that she was being treated like a child and discussed without any acknowledgment of her presence.

"I was left at the entrance, Mrs. Peterson, with no one to see me to the house," Isabella chimed in, tired of being ignored.

Mrs. Peterson looked at her in shock, like she had just noticed her for the first time. Finally, she turned back to the Marquess.

"Thank you again, Lord Bellfourd. Is there anything else I can get for you before you return upstairs?"

Isabella could see his countenance sink at the mention of his proper place above the servants' quarters. The situation was confusing enough on its own, but why had he given her a false name? Why hadn't he told her that he was the Duke of Wintercrest's son?

She may not have been entirely well-versed in all the peerage, but she had certainly done her research before leaving and had learned that the Marquess of Bellfourd was the oldest son and heir to the Duke of Wintercrest.

Lord Bellfourd turned to her and, giving a slight bow, began to bid her goodnight, probably something he should not have done. His eyes stopped at her feet though, maybe coming to his senses she thought, and looked up at her questioningly.

"Miss Watts, there seems to be something coming out of the hem of your gown."

Isabella looked down in fear to see the chain of her locket sticking out and dragging along the ground.

"Oh dear," Isabella said, crimson with shame.

She pushed her skirt with her folded hands in front of her, as if the act would hide the charm dangling below. It was bad enough that she had obviously made a fool of herself, calling the Marquess a footman, but now she had the added shame of showing the jewelry she had sown into her dress for safe keeping.

No doubt, in the short time they had been together, he had surmised she was not only naive and rude, but also very odd.

"It is very dear to me and I feared to lose it in traveling," she stammered, most embarrassed.

Much to her horror, and the horror of everyone in the room, Lord Bellfourd bent down and removed the last of the chain from her hem. He stood and held it out for her to take. Without looking him in the eye, for fear of crying, she let the chain fall into her gloved hand.

"Thank you, Lord Bellfourd," she said softly, with the most profound curtsy she could manage.

"I will bid you goodnight, then," Lord Bellfourd responded, not wanting to make the young Miss Watts any more embarrassed. "Good evening, Mrs. Peterson."

The whole room waited till he was out of the hall, before resuming their seats and whispering amongst themselves.

Isabella finally met the gaze of the housekeeper, who seemed to be measuring her, once the room went back to hushed speaking and clanking of dishes. Without so much as a word, she turned on her heels, pausing only once to beckon, in an irritated fashion, for Isabella to follow.

Utterly put in her place, Isabella did her best not to

look at the side glances around her as she followed Mrs. Peterson out of the servant dining hall.

4

*I*sabella listened silently on her hastened tour from Mrs. Peterson, the weight of her locket heavy in her hand. Mrs. Peterson insisted that the trip must not be a quick one, since she had arrived much later than expected.

She cared not for the fact that Isabella had been left on the side of the road, with no help getting to the manor.

"You will be situated in the west wing of the manor in the extra servants' quarters in the attic. Your student's room, nursery, and school room are also located on that side of the manor. There is no reason for you to venture outside that wing without permission, is that clear?"

"Yes, of course," Isabella responded, now leaving the lower levels of the servants' quarters and up to the main floor. Not stopping on the main floor, Mrs. Peterson immediately turned and went up the second set of stairs, then a third, and finally, a fourth.

By the fourth set of stairs, the ascension was steep and narrow. The final floor was, no doubt, the attic space used for overflow staffing. The ceiling was scarcely tall enough not to rub against Mrs. Peterson's high bun.

She walked two doors over and bade for Isabella enter. The room was unquestionably smaller than the one she had at home, but not at all displeasing to look at.

The footman had kindly deposited her trunk at the end of a small, but comfortable looking bed. It was dressed in a simple quilt, decorated with embroidered flowers.

The footman had also been kind enough to light a fire in the small fireplace that was to the right of the bed. To the left of it was a little, round port window in the pointed arch of a spire.

In front there was a small table and one plush, but ragged looking, chair. No doubt, it had been moved up when no longer suitable for the main house.

Aside from that, the only other furniture was a small table, for basin and water pitcher, and a petite cabinet closet. Though none of the furniture matched and the walls were only a pure whitewash, the room was warmed by the fire and cozy.

Isabella was grateful to see the space she could call her own,after the long trip with such close quarters.

Mrs. Peterson waited, arms folded in front, while Isabella inspected the room. When Isabella turned back to her, she didn't have a moment to speak before Mrs. Peterson began.

"Your breakfast and basin of water will be brought to you every morning. You will eat your breakfast here, luncheon and tea will be served with Miss Jacqueline and her nurse, and dinner will be brought up to you here, promptly at nine o'clock."

"Won't I be taking my meals downstairs?" Isabella asked, a little surprised that she would be expected to hole up in her room any time she was not with her student.

"Of course not. You are not one of the staff, you are the governess. Your meals will be taken here, where it is good and proper."

It was easy to see that Mrs. Peterson found propriety very important.

"I was told that your father was Baron Leinster," she continued.

Isabella was slightly disappointed that her upbringing was already well known.

"Yes," was her simple reply.

"Well, I am sure you understand that things are different now. You are not a guest of His Grace, but a paid worker. You are expected to do your job to the best of your abilities. You will not have a lady's maid. I trust you expected this and can take care of yourself." It was more of a statement than a question.

"Of course, I would never have presumed otherwise."

"Very well, then. As I said, warm water and your breakfast tray will be brought to you in the morning at seven and seven-thirty, respectively. I will come and get you at a quarter to eight to meet Miss Jacqueline. At ten, you will be presented to His Grace and introductions to the rest of the family will follow, as he dictates. He will tell you what duties are expected of you while you stay."

It wasn't hard to miss that Mrs. Peterson was not pleased that Isabella had already acquainted Lord Bellfourd before the designated time.

"You have from three o'clock onward to yourself, as the nurse will take her duties then. You may explore the grounds outside, as long as you are not infringing on the family. You are expected to accompany Miss Jacqueline to church with the family every Sunday morning, and then you are free to use the afternoon as you wish. Many of the servants use the opportunity to go into town, which is about a mile's walk. All other expectations will be given to you by His Grace in the morning."

"Thank you, Mrs. Peterson," Isabella said, now feeling very exhausted from her journey. "Could you also please tell me how I might post mail?"

She seemed to think this over for a minute, undoubtedly weighing what was proper for such a situation. Of course, mailing post along with the members of the household would not be acceptable. She wasn't quite sure whether leaving it in the servant's hall, as the other staff members did, was quite right for her either. Finally, though, it was what she settled on.

"There is a basket on a small table next to the service entrance. Letters may be left there to be posted."

She bid Isabella a crisp goodnight and left the room. Isabella sat for a few moments on her bed, taking it all in, before finally opening her still-gloved hand and replacing the locket around her neck.

Feeling like herself again with her treasured locket adorning her neck, she set about unpacking her belongings. It took some effort to get all her gowns into the small cabinet and she realized again how ridiculous she must have seemed to the Marquess, forcing him to lug so many belongings.

For lack of a better place, she lined up her treasured novels along the wall between the cabinet and the metal headboard of the bed.

With most of her last possessions in their places, Isabella managed to get herself undressed, only the third time she had done so on her own, and slipped beneath the soft cover of her bed. She was grateful for a room with a fireplace.

She stared dreamily into its dwindling embers, as she wondered if that was why she had been placed in a room so far away from the other staff. Had it been for the extra comfort of the fire? Or was it for the access to her pupil's side without interfering with others in the house? Or simply to give her a physical reminder that she was neither one of the lords and ladies who lived in such a lavished manor, nor one of the staff that served them?

Her last thought as she fell asleep was if this had been how her father felt when out to sea. Adrift, with land in front and land behind and nothing but a lone ship to carry her. Would she spend the rest of her days lost out at sea as a solitary island, or could she find a way to make it to shore, no matter the one she chose?

The next morning, Isabella woke early to the darkened grey sky greeting her, through the small porthole window. She was surprised how well she had slept, no doubt due to exhaustion from the long journey. She was afraid that she might have overslept, as she was not used to waking up early. She got up hastily and quickly tip toed over to the small clock that alone adorned the fireplace mantle.

She poked at the fire, finding a few coals warm beneath the ash, and did her best to use the fuel provided to get it going again. Once there was a small flicker of flame, Isabella turned, hearing a slight knock at her door.

She opened it to find a maid standing with a pitcher of

steaming water and basin. She stood aside to let the girl in to set it down on the small stand next to her bed.

"Thank you, that looks lovely, miss..." Isabella trailed off waiting for the girl to introduce herself. She was very young, not more than sixteen.

"Just Betsy, Miss Watts," she said with a thick Scottish accent and a curtsy.

"Are you Scottish, then?" Isabella asked.

"Aye, most of the lower staff is, Miss Watts."

"Please call me Isabella," she encouraged. "Shall I bring my basin down when I am done?"

"Oh no, Miss...I mean Isabella. I shall come and fetch it up when I brin' your breakfast tray."

"That is very kind of you; I am sure it is tedious work to go up and down so many stairs."

"Dinna fash. I dinna mind it one bit. It's a much more enjoyable task than the others." Betsy turned to leave after another short curtsy, but paused just a moment. "I dinna mean to be a bother, but I was a'wonderin' if you happen to need help with your things, dressin' and hair, I mean to say. I would be happy to help you."

"That is very considerate of you, Betsy, but I would hate to ask more of you than you already do, or give you additional tasks. It may take some practice, but I believe I will soon learn to do it on my own."

"You see, you would be doin' me a favor if you let me," Betsy continued. "I want to be a lady's maid one day for a fine house. May'haps even this one. I need the practice first, you see. I heard that you were raised as a lady, so I thought you might help me. Tell me if I was doin' somethin' wrong and the like."

"Well, I suppose I could use some help to make something simple with my hair."

"Aye, that would be great practice for me if ye would allow it."

"Mrs. Peterson won't be mad? I had the feeling she didn't want me speaking with others very much."

"It's not like that. She is just verra particular that all are in their place and none try to be more than they are. It makes it pretty impossible for a lass like me to make much more o' herself. But what she dinna ken won't hurt her much."

"Well, if you are sure we won't be caught," Isabella hesitated. "I suppose it would be fine. I would love to do what I can to help you."

Isabella meant it sincerely, too. It was the first friend she had made in the house and any way she could help Betsy she was willing to. It reminded her of something her father used to say, "a small act of kindness can open the door for great friendships."

Isabella used the warm water to wash and freshen herself before dressing. She found a soft green colored cotton morning dress that she paired with a dark, velvet green spencer jacket. Though the dress was very modest in cut, she still fretted over its look as a practical dress.

She was, after all, hoping to put the right foot in front of His Grace, after clearly blundering things with the Marquess the night before. She smartly tucked a fichu into the top of her green gown, before putting on the spencer jacket.

Though she had the fire going relatively well, she feared she would never get used to the chill that always seemed present in this northern country. Tucking a cream handkerchief into her long sleeve, she finished just in time for Betsy to knock at the door again.

She came in and set the tray down on the small table beside the port window. Before eating, Isabella sat in the only chair facing the window while Betsy pulled her hair back into a tight chignon. She left a few of Isabella's dark ringlets out to frame her face. Isabella did her best to feel around to assure Betsy she had done a fantastic job, as there was no mirror present in the room.

Seeming happy to have gotten some practice in, Betsy thanked her again, then took the water basin and left Isabella to eat her breakfast alone.

She had just finished her toast and rejuvenating cup of tea when a knock came to her door again. This time, it was Mrs. Peterson, and she was very accurate with her timing. Without so much as a good morning, she turned on her heels, expecting Isabella to follow after.

Isabella supposed that this was a common habit of Mrs. Peterson. Not only did she feel everyone had their place to be, but also the use of words that didn't need to be spoken were a waste of time. She quickly walked to catch up to Mrs. Peterson for the second time in two days to start her new beginning as governess.

5

*I*sabella made her way down the narrow stairway and ended on the second floor of the main house. She followed Mrs. Peterson along the Turkish-rugged hall listening to the soft pads of their feet on the ground and swishing of skits.

She was surprised that, for such a large house, filled with not only the family of the house but at least a hundred servants downstairs and not all the tables were even full, it was so quiet.

Where was everyone else? She had expected to see maids bustling around and hear the clank of breakfast silverware in the distance, but it was complete and utter silence as she walked. *Perhaps it was just that the west wing of the manor was far off from the rest of the house*, she thought.

The wing was basically a rectangle shape with a

walkway that outlined the rectangle. Off the walkway, numerous doors sprouted along the walls.

The middle, however, was open, with four enormous chandeliers hanging down from the ceiling. Isabella took a second to look over the railing on their walk and saw the most magnificent ballroom she had ever set her eyes on. It took up the whole of the bottom floor.

The chandeliers, as well as at least a dozen standing candelabras dotting along the floor, were all covered with sheets, as was a section in the far corner that was no doubt used for a live orchestra. She imagined royalty might very well dance in that hall on occasion.

As she walked, she learned that her quarters were the farthest west and left edge of the manor, her small port window looking out at the left side of the property.

She had gotten so mixed up walking the downstairs corridors that she hadn't realized which way she was facing. She remembered seeing the front of the manor in the dark and pictured mentally the three sections. Her left side held the grand hall and a significant amount of what she assumed were guest rooms above it.

The middle section was, no doubt, the main part of the house with studies, libraries, sitting and drawing rooms. Most likely, in a house this size, it also boasted a smaller hall for more intimate affairs and the various dining rooms.

Then, lastly, she pictured in her mind, the east wing of the manor. She wondered if it shared a similar large hall and rooms that housed the family or if it was completely different from the beauty she was walking along.

Finally, they made their way from the bottom of the attic stairs along the straight walk, to the other end of the wing. Here, there was a small half circle alcove that led to two rooms on either side of the end of the rectangle and a grand staircase that lead down to the lower floor of the central portion. It was a sensational foyer, with painted ceilings squares, another large chandelier, and marble floors. Isabella stopped for a moment to look at the grandeur of it all.

She saw the large double doors that lead from the outside into the foyer, as well as an exquisite matching staircase opposite her. She did see a single maid dusting one of the vases that adorned the great room along with several marble statues. It was unimaginable to Isabella that this house was lived in. It looked like a royal estate, more magnificent than any she had ever seen.

"Miss Watts, if you please," Mrs. Peterson said with impatience. She motioned to a third door from the small half circle alcove.

No doubt these rooms, closest to the main house, were meant for children. They were far enough away as not to be a bother to the lords and ladies that graced the house, but close enough to come when needed. Isabella smiled at the thought of how many little eyes had spied over the walkway banister to lavish balls below.

Mrs. Peterson opened the door without knocking, and Isabella followed in, after her. She found herself in a large room with a small library of its own on either side of a crackling fireplace. There were comfortable chairs seated near the fire, no doubt for reading.

There was a long wall facing outside to the back of the estate. Lush curtains in velvet green draped between the windows that showed vast, manicured gardens and even a large pond. Next to the windows were a small table and four chairs, probably for lunch. And all the way to the right side of the room was a child-sized table where one timid little girl was sitting quietly with her hands folded on top.

Next to the girl stood a woman just past middle age. She was wearing the cream-colored dress and apron of a nurse, as well as a bonnet with large ruffles framing her kind-looking face. She motioned for her charge to stand at the women's entrance and the little girl did as she was told.

"Mrs. Murray," Mrs. Peterson started, "I am pleased to introduce you to Miss Watts, our new governess. She will be relieving you of your duties during the day."

"Ach, they are not much of duties with this little angel," Mrs. Murray said in a thick Scottish accent.

The little girl smiled up at her nurse with affection. It was clear she didn't understand much of what she said. She was a young girl and seemed small for her age. Very petite and thin. She had golden blonde ringlet hair and still had the round face of a small child. She looked shyly at the newcomer.

"Miss Jacqueline De'belmount," Mrs. Peterson said a little louder than before, "this is your governess, Miss Watts."

Mrs. Peterson, ever the proper lady, made the formal introduction to the child. Isabella laughed a little to herself. The child spoke a different language; she wasn't hard of hearing. Isabella stood before the young girl, then kneeled down to Jacqueline's level.

"Enchante. Je m'appelle Mademoiselle Watts."

Jaqueline's little face lit up. "Parlez-vous français?"

"Oui," Isabella answered with a small smile.

This poor little girl had probably felt so alone and isolated in this house. Indeed, she was well loved by her nurse, but Isabella couldn't imagine leaving one's home and being surrounded by a new culture and language.

Mrs. Peterson cleared her throat, "Though all members of His Grace's family are fluent in French, the duke would prefer if the child learns English."

"Of course," Isabella said, standing back up.

The young girl slipped her hand into Isabella's and Isabella smiled down at her, giving her hand a gentle squeeze.

"If you please, I would like to meet with my pupil and see what she already has learned."

"Of course," Mrs. Peterson said, already leaning toward

leaving the room. Surely, she had much more pressing matters at this time. "I will return to escort you to His Grace."

Isabella nodded in understanding and waited for Mrs. Peterson to leave. She turned to Mrs. Murray who hadn't gone yet.

"Mrs. Murray, if you have a moment before you go, would you please share with me how you and Miss Jacqueline have been spending your day?"

"I dinna mind at all. Miss Jacqueline is a verra sweet child. Sadly, she doesn't know much to say. She does enjoy playing with her dolls. We go on walks after luncheon to enjoy some fresh air. I expect His Grace will desire her time in nature to continue."

"That would be fine. It would give us some time to explore natural science. I understand that Mrs. Peterson wants Jacqueline to focus on learning English, but I hope you will allow me to discuss what she knows thus far from her previous education. To do so, we would need to speak in French."

"Och, don't you worry about that. Mrs. Peterson is a stickler for the rules. What she dinna ken won't hurt her. I will sit right here," she said as she took a spot in a chair by the fire. "I've been working on some winter mittens for the wee lass. I'll be able to hear when Mrs. Peterson comes up the hall and give ye warnin'."

"Thank you, Mrs. Murray," Isabella looked down into

the little hand still clasped in hers, "Shall we find some dolls to play with then?" she asked in French.

Jaqueline's small eyes lit up. Tugging on Isabella's hand, she took her past the table and through a door that lead into a nursery. She collected some dolls and brought them before the fire at her nurse's feet, something she had apparently done on a regular basis.

Isabella followed along and took her place next to the child on the floor. While they played, they discussed where Jacqueline grew up and what she liked to do.

She was just five years old when her mother told her that she would be leaving France and spending time with her grandparents. She spoke lovingly of her mother, but from what she said, her mother seemed to be of a certain profession.

"Grandparents?" Isabella asked.

"Oh aye, Jacqueline is the daughter of the late Marquess of Bellfourd" Mrs. Murray said not looking up from her work. "Lord James, God rest him, was an honorable man. I ken him since he was a young boy of twelve. He could be a bit free-spirited, but not any more so than others of his upbringing. Two years ago he came home from a hunting expedition that had taken a turn in the weather. He never recovered from it," she finished softly.

"Papa?" Jacqueline asked softly of Mrs. Murray, only understanding a few words of what her nurse said. She nodded to the girl.

"Your Papa was a verra good man, lass; no kinder heart could be found. You see," she said turning back to Isabella, "about a year after his passing His Grace received a letter from a Madame De'belmount of Paris. She claimed that Lord James had fathered a child by her and had been giving her a living. She asked that the child continue to be provided for, as she struggled to do so on her own. His Grace agreed under the condition that she be brought here and raised as a proper young lady."

"What a kindness considering her...her..." Isabella didn't want to say with the child present, whether she understood the words or not.

"I suspect that after the heartache of loss; you see, His Grace was verra close to his eldest son, he was hoping for a chance to have a bit of 'im back."

"And certainly he feels blessed to have her here," Isabella said, looking down at Jacqueline who was softly singing a French lullaby to her doll.

"Many of us do," Mrs. Murray said without explanation.

It left Isabella wondering who wouldn't be happy to have such a polite little girl in the household. She supposed that her parentage might cause some discomfort. She would never be considered a lady of the peerage, but growing in the duke's house and having an exceptional education, she would be a fine lady someday.

Isabella spent the remainder of the morning playing with the child asking her questions here and there to see what amount of instruction she had thus far. She didn't expect much at the tender age of six, but was surprised that the girl's mother had spent every night reading to her from quite beautiful books.

She felt a pang of sorrow for this little girl who too had lost her mother, even if just by the separation of land. She couldn't imagine having such happy memories with her own mother and then being forced to leave her.

"Have you written to your mother since coming here?" Isabella asked her in perfect French.

"Yes, Aunt Abigail is kind to me. She writes letters for me, and reads back what my mother sends me."

Isabella was happy to hear that she was able to keep correspondence with her mother, at least.

"Soon, I can show you how to write your own letters and words and then you may write to your mother, all on your own."

Of course, Isabella knew writing fluent letters, even in French, was a way off for a girl of six, but it was at least the start of a goal they could make for her education.

"Miss Watts, I believe I hear footsteps. I suspect it is Mrs. Peterson coming for ye. It is mid-morning, and I am sure His Grace is ready for you now."

Isabella stood and made sure her skirt was in proper order. Jacqueline came to hug her waist before she left. Already, in just a few short hours, this child was endeared to her.

Isabella was out the door just as Mrs. Peterson reached the top of the stairs, much to her surprise. Without many words, however, she merely turned around, expecting Isabella to follow. Isabella shook her head with a soft laugh. She wasn't sure if she would ever understand the complexity of Mrs. Peterson.

6

They made their way down the stairs and along the marble hall through to the back end of the central part of the house. Isabella did her best not to look so shocked by the extravagance of everything around her. Some large oak doors were closed, others open, showing a breakfast room, a vast library, and a morning sitting room. Isabella couldn't help but wonder what was behind the other doors. If she could only explore the winding corridors.

They stopped at a closed door, just to the right of the library. Mrs. Peterson knocked and when bid to enter, she opened both doors. It was a massive office with its own grand fireplace burning warmly along the longest wall. Next to the hearth was a door that Isabella was sure it was connected to the library. Why His Grace would need access to that library when he had three walls covered in books here in this room, Isabella didn't know.

The room itself was covered in a dark navy wallpaper with gold trimming. All along the walls, where books weren't found, were various paintings of the previous owners of this office.

Isabella wondered why every room she had seen, thus far, in the main house was draped in such a dark manner. Surely, with the gloomy weather outside bright, vibrant colors would help to warm the large estate.

She had to remind herself, again, that she was no longer a lady and that she didn't need to waste her time wondering about things she had no business thinking of. Her sole purpose now was education, and that was what needed to occupy her thoughts.

She stood in front of the desk and waited for the elderly man, bent in work, to notice them. When he set his writing down and looked to her, she followed Mrs. Peterson's lead and gave a polite curtsy.

"Your Grace, I present to you the new governess, Miss Isabella Watts."

Isabella did her best to ignore the gentleman who was directly behind the duke, and had apparently been discussing whatever work His Grace was doing before the women entered. One quick flash of a look at the Marquess of Bellfourd showed a broad, bright smile as he presently looked back at her.

It was infuriating to Isabella. This man had made a fool of her only the night before in front of the whole household of servants, and here he stood smugly about it. He probably had even shared his story with his father. The ridiculous governess who treated her employer's son like a footman.

The Duke removed the pair of wired spectacles he had been wearing and inspected Isabella up and down.

"I was informed you had an extensive education? That you would be quite capable of teaching a pupil, though you have no references or experience?"

Isabella caught a questioning look from Lord Bellfourd. He must not have been informed that she was without experience. The Duke looked to be getting on in years and health, and Lord Bellfourd was, of course, here to help him in preparation for his own turn as manager of the estate. Would she be out of a job upon this occurrence?

"No experience? Are you sure this is the best we can do for little Jackie?" Lord Bellfourd asked his father, right in front of her.

"I studied at Mrs. Mason's School for Exceptional Young Ladies. I enjoyed my studies and kept them in practice over the years," Isabella stated, jutting her chin out just a little.

"The child is lucky to have a governess at all. I did as you and Abigail requested and hired a lady from London. I do not doubt that her qualifications will be suitable for the child's situation. Also, you are well aware that I do not like it when you call her by that name."

Isabella didn't like standing there and being spoken of in front of her for the second time in two days. It also didn't escape her attention that Lord Bellfourd had been the one concerned for Jacqueline and the duke himself had refused even to speak her name.

She wondered if this was what Mrs. Murray had alluded to. Certainly, it was the duke who had allowed the child to come to his home. Was he unhappy with her presence now that she was here? Isabella couldn't imagine how such a sweet young thing could upset him, though.

Perhaps the memory of the lost son, though desired at first, had turned into a constant painful reminder. Isabella understood well the feeling of loss, and the complicated emotions it brought out.

Turning back to Isabella, "I am sure you will be well suited, Miss Watts. I do, however, have a few conditions before you proceed in regards to how I want her educated."

"Of course, Your Grace. I will be happy to meet any requirements you see fit."

"Good. Foremost, I want her to start learning English right away. I am aware that you are fluent in French?"

"Yes, Your Grace."

"Please, use your talents to transition her to the language of her new home. I don't want any more encouragement of her native tongue now that you are here to teach her otherwise properly."

Isabella could see that last comment was meant for the Marquess and not herself.

"Of course, father," Lord Bellfourd said with slight irritation.

"Perhaps," Isabella chimed in, seeing that this was a subject at odds between her current employer and potential future one, "it might be beneficial for her to keep the native language. Of course, I will do as you wish, Your Grace, and begin immediately to develop her English, but we could also have a short time each day for her to have a French lesson. Having a second language is an important tool for any young lady, and it could bring her comfort to be able to write to her mother in such a way."

Isabella heard Mrs. Peterson clear her throat behind her, obviously not happy that Isabella had suggested something that had just been contradicted by the duke.

"I rather think that would be a fine compromise, Father," Lord Bellfourd chimed in.

"Well," the duke faltered a bit, "I suppose it will be fine if she only speaks it during specific lessons for the language."

"Of course, Your Grace."

"Now, other requirements for the child. She is to spend a portion of her day outside for lessons and exercise, and twice a week you will present her to me so that I may assess her progress."

"Of course, Your Grace," Isabella repeated.

She could see the duke's spectacles were being put back on and guessed that meant that was the end of the discussion.

"I already have a vast library of resources for the child in the schoolroom, but should you need any others you are welcome to the library just over that way," he waved to the door. "You, yourself, may borrow any book you wish from the collection, as long as you sign the servant roster found within."

"How very kind of you, Your Grace."

"I suspect you have reading material sufficient for your needs at the moment, judging by the weight of your case," Lord Bellfourd chimed in with a knowing smile.

Isabella's eyes hit the floor as she flushed red. She heard an indignant puff from behind her.

"What are you talking about, Christian?" The Duke said, lowering his spectacles to look up at his son.

"Nothing, Father," he said with a jolly smile.

Isabella was irritatingly embarrassed but also relieved that Lord Bellfourd had chosen not to share the events of the night before with the duke.

"Mrs. Peterson, I am sure you are quite busy with household business. I will be happy to escort Miss Watts back to the school room as I have not yet seen my niece today."

Mrs. Peterson hesitated. Of course, she would not argue with the request to leave, but she also questioned allowing such a thing to happen. With no apparent objection from the duke, who was back at his work, she made one last curtsy and left.

Lord Bellfourd gave his father a hand on the shoulder and the duke waved him off without looking up from his work. Coming across the room, Lord Bellfourd motioned for Isabella to go on ahead of him. She waited till they were out of the office and well past the doorway before speaking.

"I don't think I ever got a chance to apologize for my mistake last night," she finally said, not looking at him.

"There is nothing to apologize for. I am just glad I was there to help. I can't imagine dragging such a heavy load all the way from the main road."

Isabella looked up at him to see if he was teasing her again. She took a moment to study him. He was much taller than most men she knew and broad of shoulder.

He had thick, strawberry blonde hair that was tied back with a simple ribbon. His eyes, which looked down at her with a joking glint, were of the most transparent blue. They reminded her much of the little girl she had just spent the morning with, though everything else about his features was much different.

In a way, he resembled a much younger version of the

duke with a square jaw and long pointed nose. She decided that he couldn't be more than twenty-six years old. She had noticed that, not only did the Duke share the strawberry red hair, though the duke's was mostly grey, but many of the portraits on the wall in the office did too.

"I'm glad to see your charm made the trip safely," he added with a wicked grin and motioned with his eyes to the locket around her neck.

Isabella quickly clasped her hand over it, hiding it from him. She heard the rumble of a chuckle from inside his chest and she could bear the embarrassment no longer.

"I changed my mind; I don't apologize for the mistake. In fact, one might say the situation was all of your making, since you gave me a false name and all."

Lord Bellfourd stopped at the bottom of the steps leading up to the west wing and gave a hearty laugh at her moment of rage. It was a fantastic, deep sound, something she could tell his Lordship used often.

"My dear Miss Watts," he finally said, regaining his composure, "I am so sorry I have upset you. Forgive me, I am told by my sister I do tend to be a teaser. I meant nothing by it. Though, I must inform you that I didn't lie to you. My name is Captain Christian Grant, formerly of the Royal Navy. It has just been a little over a year that I have been anything besides this."

Isabella thought this over in her head. It made sense, of course. He was the second son of a duke, so an employment in the Royal Navy was undoubtedly fitting. Upon his brother's untimely death, he was most likely called back home to take his place.

"Oh, well…" Isabella stammered, feeling her brazen attitude may have gotten her in trouble again.

"Don't concern yourself, Miss Watts. How could you have known?" he said reassuringly. "Perhaps, though, you could gratify my curiosity and tell me what exactly you had in that trunk of yours and why that simple locket is so important to you."

"Well, you were right on the first part. I brought with me some of my favorite books, not realizing I would be allowed to borrow others. And the locket…" she said smoothing the silver she still held in her hand as they made their way upstairs, "It was my mother's. My father gave it to me for my sixteenth birthday with the lock of hair she gave him the first time he went out to sea."

"I can see now why that might be so cherished."

"Yes. She passed in childbirth, so it gives me a sort of closeness to her."

"It seems your life has been full of hardships," he said back.

"Not more than others," Isabella said as she scrunched her nose in thought. "I imagine many have much more heartache than myself. Life seems to be equally unfair to all in one way or another."

"Well said," he agreed.

They had made their way up the stairs, and without ceremony, Lord Bellfourd entered the school room.

"Uncle Christian!" Jacqueline squealed with delight as she hopped up and wrapped her arms around him.

She began spilling out the morning's events in quick French to her beloved uncle. It was clear to Isabella that he was beloved by this little child. Though his teasing had put her off a bit, she couldn't help but enjoy his company as she watched him interact with his little niece, more like a child than the future Duke of Wintercrest.

7

*M*y Dearest Louisa,

I hope that this letter finds you well. I have missed you and your pleasing companionship since leaving London.

I have now settled into my new station here at Wintercrest Manor. I have never seen something so spectacular as this house. The gardens, too, are vast and intriguing. The house is so large that I have been here almost a week and have only seen a portion of the servants and half of the household. It is hard for me to imagine a child growing up in such a large and looming house.

My pupil is a beautiful little child. I told you in my last letter of her upbringing and what resulted in her residing here. She is such a kind and sweet little girl. We spend each afternoon walking the grounds, per the Duke of Wintercrest's request. This is a cherished time for both Jacqueline and myself.

It is clear to me now that she was raised deep in the city of Paris and never spent much time even in parks. Every new side garden we take or walk along a wooden path is a glorious adventure for her. I, too, have grown to love our afternoon walks. Though the air is almost always chilled, even as spring approaches, I have thoroughly enjoyed the open beauty that this country has provided me.

I told you before of my disastrous first meeting with Lord Bellfourd. I had hoped, after that first day, I would not see him much at all. Unquestionably, he is very busy helping his father with the estate and learning all that comes with it. Much to my surprise, he finds a moment almost every day to spend with little Jacqueline. Often, he sits and listens as she tells him of the adventures she has had or stories she has learned that day.

One day, in fact, he insisted that Mrs. Murray and I make ready and send Jacqueline and her afternoon tea down to him in one of the sitting rooms. He treated her like a proper lady coming to attend him for afternoon tea. Jacqueline could barely contain herself when she came back to us. She genuinely felt like a princess that day.

Despite his early teasing, I have found Lord Bellfourd to be a kind man who loves to dote on his little niece. I can't help but hold a high regard in my mind for someone who could be so incredible to a small girl, that has already overcome so much in her young age.

I have learned from Mrs. Murray today that the youngest member of the household, Lady Abigail, will be returning home today from a visit to her relatives. I will have the opportunity to meet both her and her mother this evening, as I have been informed that I will be presenting Jacqueline for her first inspection to the duke after their evening meal.

I am not sure what worries me more, meeting such fine ladies of such a lavished house, or presenting Jacqueline before her grandfather. We have spent the better part of today's lesson practicing her introductions in perfect English, and have also taught her counting from one to ten. I feel this is a great feat for such a young child who, up until last week, knew almost no English at all.

It is clear that her uncle's lavish attentions also prevented her from picking up the new language, as he has only spoken to her in French, as far as I have seen. This is in spite of the duke's evident dislike of it. I confess that I am happy that this child's transition over the year had been all the less traumatic with the familiar words of her homeland.

I hope that you are doing well and receiving my letters. I am quite aware that this is the second I have sent in a week's time. I am so very used to talking to you every day, even passing our notes when we do not see each other. I suppose I will have to get used to the long travel each letter must take to reach you, my dear. It is an excellent opportunity for me to exercise patience, something you, of course, know I am not altogether good at.

Your friend,

Isabella

8

Isabella was pacing her room, occasionally stopping to recheck the clock. She was to pick up Jacqueline and take her down to the duke and the rest of the family precisely at eight o'clock to be inspected. As this was her first time ever doing this, she had no idea what to expect.

She, of course, knew that Mrs. Murray, who had to take charge of the child that afternoon as she always did, would take special care to make sure Jacqueline looked her very best.

What scared her even more was the prospect of meeting the duchess for the first time tonight. Of course, the duke had been the one to hire her, but if she didn't find favor in the duchess' eyes, then assuredly the employment would be terminated. What was Isabella to do then?

She certainly would never go back to Mr. Smith to beg for his mercy. She touched the locket around her neck. How had he reacted when he found it missing? She hoped he had left it alone. After all, it wasn't really worth much, but at the same time, she knew it wasn't about the money or her father's debt. All Mr. Smith wanted to do was make Isabella's life miserable as a punishment for turning him down all those years ago.

The clock chimed the quarter hour, and Isabella stopped her pacing. She straightened her skirts one last time. She had wracked her brain over how to dress. Should she wear the one velvet green dinner gown she had left, or continue to wear her more plain and simple cotton dress she had worn during the day?

She had no idea what would be more proper in this situation. She had finally decided on the dinner gown. It was at least dark in color, such a deep forest green that, in the evening light of candles, it could take on a hew of black. It seemed most fitting for a governess.

Isabella made her way down the long walkway toward her pupil's nursery where she was to pick her up from Mrs. Murray. She entered the room with a soft knock to find Jacqueline sitting on the floor playing dolls with another young lady. Mrs. Murray was sitting in the corner rocker, knitting another pair of gloves. The lady stood upon Isabella's entrance and she knew that this must be Lady Abigail.

She was a young girl of no more than ten and seven.

She was wearing a beautiful, soft blue silk dinner dress with white pearls decorating the bodice. She shared her brother's same crystal blue eyes, but her hair was a rich red, almost startlingly so.

"I beg your pardon, Lady Abigail," Isabella said with a curtsy, "I was asked to take Jacqueline to His Grace."

"Why, you must be Miss Watts, then," Lady Abigail said with a sweet smile. "For a second, I was worried you were that horrid Mrs. Peterson coming in. She shan't have liked to see me sitting on the floor playing dollies. She is quite a strict one, isn't she?" Lady Abigail asked like she was talking to a friend.

Isabella was uncertain how to respond. Naturally, she would not share her personal opinions of Mrs. Peterson to a lady of the house; it would have been most forward of Isabella.

"Mrs. Peterson does seem very devoted to her duties. She seems to have a good feel for such a large estate," was all that Isabella could come up with.

"She hasn't been here with us long, you know." Lady Abigail continued, as if she was speaking to a close confidante. "Only the last year, just before we got our sweet Jackie here. I suppose father was hoping to find someone who would tighten the reins on us children a little more."

Mrs. Murray cleared her throat from the corner. Abigail smiled at the action.

"Nurse Murray, on the other hand, has been here so

long she took care of not just myself but my brother Christian, as well. I believe she thinks I am too much of a gossip. It is a bad habit of mine, I must admit. I apologized, Nursie," Lady Abigail said affectionately while turning.

"You dinna need to apologize, Lady Abigail. Perhaps you best be off though, so as not to keep yer father waiting, aye?"

"Nursie?" Jacqueline giggled under her breath at Lady Abigail's nickname for her nurse.

"Well, you see, I was very little when Mrs. Murray came and it was just easier for me to say," Lady Abigail told the child in French.

Jacqueline turned to Mrs. Murray and slowly asked in the best English she could muster, "I call you Nursie, uh... que puis-je vous appeler?"

What can I call you? Isabella's heart swelled at the question, as she watched Mrs. Murray connect with the little girl.

With tears glistening in her eyes, Mrs. Murray reached her arms out. "Yes," she whispered. "You can call me Nursie."

Jacqueline went to her quickly and they shared an embrace.

Mrs. Murray nuzzled the crook of Jacqueline's neck and her eyes lifted to meet Isabella's. "I expect that would be quite lovely," Mrs. Murray said after getting control of her emotion. "Now, off you go, my little lass, while your curls are still bouncing."

Of course, Jacqueline's perfectly curled blonde hair was always in immaculate ringlets, but Mrs. Murray fluffed them, all the same, before returning the girl to her waiting aunt. Jacqueline slipped one hand into Lady Abigail's and then reached out to Isabella with the other.

It was one of the things about Jacqueline that Isabella enjoyed so much. Her pure, innocent spirit. Of course, Isabella should follow behind the two girls as just an employee, but both Lady Abigail and Jacqueline stood ready. So, with a girlish giggle of her own, Isabella took Jacqueline's hand. The three of them happily marched down the broad stairway leading to the main house.

It wasn't until they got to the hallway leading into the large drawing room that the fun giggling stopped. Mrs. Peterson was in that hall. It was as if someone had opened a window and let a cold gust in. Lady Abigail took the lead with little Jacqueline in hand while Isabella slipped back, just behind them.

In this way, they entered the drawing room. Isabella found the rest of the family already seated. The duke sat in the large high back chair closest to the fire with a blanket over his lap. Isabella wondered if his health was not good. The duchess was sitting next to her son at a card table and got up to embrace her daughter at her entrance. Jacqueline gave her grandmother a very proper curtsy before giving her a light hug.

Lady Abigail shared many of her father's sharp facial features, but it was clear that her petite frame and lush, dark red hair was her mother's. Though she looked to be at least ten years younger than her husband, the duchess had some gray streaks running through the rich auburn hair that fell in little curls around a bandeau.

Isabella could see that Jacqueline was just as nervous as she when standing before her grandfather.

She gave a deep curtsy and, as clear as a bell, said, "Good evening, Your Grace. You are looking very well."

Isabella wondered at the sentence that she had encouraged Jacqueline to practice over and over till it was perfect. Upon closer examination, he didn't look well at all.

"And tell me what you learned, young lady," he said in response, no light in his eyes.

The whole of the room was watching this exchange with joy, and yet the duke didn't seem as moved as all the others by her angelic face.

Jacqueline looked back to her governess, who stood just behind her. Isabella gave a reassuring nod for encouragement.

"I have learned to count and recite the Lord's prayer."

"Well then, let's hear this," the duke said, putting aside the book he had been reading. He spoke with some skepticism, which discouraged the girl.

Isabella took a step forward and, bending down, encouraged the child onward. In Isabella's eyes, she did wonderfully. Lady Abigail and Her Grace even clapped when Jacqueline finished the Lord's prayer, though she had stumbled once.

The duke said nothing to the child.

"You seem to be making good progress, Miss Watts," was all he said before returning to his reading.

"Thank you, Your Grace," she responded, taking the child's hand and preparing to leave.

"Jacqueline, won't you come over here and show mother how you drew that pretty flower the other day," Lord Bellfourd said from his card table.

"Oh, yes. I would love to see a drawing," Duchess Wintercrest announced, putting her card game aside.

A servant produced a small writing desk with tools and Jacqueline went to sit by her grandmother. Isabella wasn't exactly sure what to do. She was told to keep charge of the child for the night but didn't know if she should stay or excuse herself. When Jacqueline had gone to the duchess, Isabella had been invited to sit. She had taken a wooden chair against the wall, so as not to intrude on the intimacy of the family.

After a few minutes, Lady Abigail had joined her mother, brother, and niece, at the card table and was attempting to teach little Jacqueline a simple card game.

"Miss Watts, do you play the piano at all?" Duchess Wintercrest asked.

"Yes, Your Grace."

"Would you play for us now?" she asked sweetly, motioning to a pianoforte just to the side of Isabella. "My daughter did not take to lessons, and I so miss the sound of music in the evening."

"Of course, Your Grace," Isabella said, taking a seat at the piano.

There was already sheet music laid out. Another servant appeared wordlessly and placed a small candelabra on the pianoforte to give her the best light.

"Thank you," she said to the man she hadn't met yet.

He nodded and returned to the corner of the room where he stood waiting. The music was simple enough, and Isabella recognized it as a sonata by Pleyel that she had learned in her youth.

She played softly in the background to amuse the duchess but not to distract them from their evening together. She got so lost in concentration over the notes, that she didn't even notice when Lord Bellfourd came to stand next to her.

She came to a part on the page that she couldn't quite see due to the previous page covering it partially. Before she even had time to react, a hand reached forward and fixed the offending page.

"I suppose you have come to tease me some more," Isabella said without stopping her playing.

She had become entirely used to his teasing manner over the week, during his various visits with his niece, and had found herself becoming quite comfortable around him.

"I would do no such thing," Lord Bellfourd said, faking shock. "I came to admire your wonderful playing. Perhaps you will teach Jackie to play as well?"

"I am not sure if she is old enough at the moment, but certainly, I would be happy to teach her in the future."

"I suppose you are right, though it is a pity."

"A pity? Why is that, Lord Bellfourd?"

"Well, I had hoped you could teach her and have a song ready for when I return in the fall."

"Return? Where are you going, Christian?" Lady Abigail chimed in, overhearing the conversation.

"To town for the season, of course," Lady Wintercrest answered. "Your father is not well enough to go this year for parliament. Christian will oversee what is needed."

"Can't I go as well, then? I know we agreed that I wouldn't go this year since you will be here with father, but if Christian is going?"

Isabella continued to play, but her heart went out to Lady Abigail. Indeed, any girl of her age would be dying to leave the country for the society of the season.

"I do not feel comfortable allowing you to go without a

chaperone," the duke chimed in not once glancing up from his book.

It was the final word on the matter. Lady Wintercrest took her daughter's hand in comfort and tried to encourage her with thoughts of summer in the country.

Isabella was surprised at how disappointed she felt, knowing that Lord Bellfourd would be leaving for the season. She wondered if it was perhaps just jealousy that he was going to enjoy the society that she had once had. She felt it was more than that, though. She would miss his company and the smiles he brought to not only his niece, but also Mrs. Murray and herself, on his visits.

"I can do my best to find something simple for Miss Jacqueline to learn in order to celebrate your return," she said as she ended her piece.

She looked up at Lord Bellfourd to see his bright blue eyes smiling down at her.

"I would appreciate that very much. I know Jackie would love it also," he said with gratitude that made Isabella's heart swell.

She was quite confident that he had asked purely because he knew that to do such a thing for her uncle's homecoming would make Jacqueline feel so dignified. It would give her a place as part of the family.

9

*S*unday morning, Isabella made ready to escort little Jackie, as she too had begun to call her, to church with her family. The estate had its own private chapel for the families and servants to attend.

Isabella had already found it once, tucked away in a grove of trees when walking with Jackie. It had looked spectacularly old and beautiful all at the same time. They had wandered around the small family graveyard next to it and even found Lord James buried there. The following day they collected some wildflowers to place on the grave.

Though Jackie had never met her father, Isabella thought it might be important for her to come and visit the grave site from time to time.

Isabella was also excited because, for the first time since she had arrived a week ago, the clouds had finally parted, and there was glorious sun shining down on God's beautiful, green earth. She was sure that, though it was only a half-mile walk to the churchyard, the family would be riding in a carriage. She decided that Jackie and herself would walk and absorb some of the glorious sunshine.

For this reason, she had opted to wear a light cotton walking dress instead of the more delicate gowns that she might have worn to church back at Rosewater. She put on a full brim summer bonnet and her only pair of sturdy leather half boots. Adding a light shawl, she felt she was ready for the brisk walk to church.

She came to pick up her little pupil from Mrs. Murray and found her to be just as adequately dressed. She wore a fine, cream colored cotton dress with patterns of bluebells in striped fashion. It did wonders to bring out the clarity of the child's azure eyes.

She too was wearing sturdy leather boots instead of silk slippers and even had a matching parasol for her and her little dolly, who sat by the window at the tea table to await their return.

Taking the child's hand, Isabella thanked Mrs. Murray for all her efforts and skipped along down the stairs and out to the church.

They arrived at the churchyard just as a fine Barouche came rolling up on the main road. It was gleaming in the sunlight with a Wintercrest coat of arms painted on the side. Two cream colored horses trotted along in front.

Inside, the duchess, duke, and their two children were sparkling in their most excellent wear.

Isabella heard Jackie give an audible "aw" sound as the carriage came around and pulled in front of the chapel.

"Doesn't Her Grace look just like a queen?" Jackie whispered to her governess.

"Well, if that is true, then I shall have to start calling you Princess Jackie," Isabella said in return.

The little girl laughed at the thought of being a princess and began to dance and twirl her small umbrella around the courtyard.

Isabella, however, watched as how Lord Bellfourd left the carriage first and then helped both his sister and mother in turn. After they were safely out of the transport, he grabbed a cane situated for his father and made sure that he, too, made it out safely. She studied Lord Bellfourd for a moment.

Today more than ever he looked like the real Marquess of Bellfourd. He was wearing high, dark brown boots, tan pantaloons, a dark navy waistcoat, and long black tailcoat. He looked dashing with his silk top hat; his hair pulled back with a simple, navy blue ribbon. It quite caught Isabella's breath to watch him. She had to tell herself to look away.

He waited till his mother was adequately placed on his father's right arm before taking Lady Abigail's in his arm and escorting her in. Both Lady Abigail and he were a vast contrast to the lady and lord of the drawing room just the night before.

Even Her Grace was much more poised and held an air around her. Sunday was an important affair, Isabella guessed, where their status as head of the house was put properly in its place before all the staff.

The duke, in Isabella's mind, seemed to be the one who put propriety first, and the others were only doing so on his direct wish. Sunday, apparently, was a day that no exceptions could be made, in the eyes of the duke.

In fact, on the walk over, Jackie had informed Isabella that this would be her first time attending services with the family. Without a governess to escort her, she had been instructed to stay home with her nurse. It was still a wonder to Isabella that the duke, who had evidently brought the child to help him grieve the loss of his son, could then push her away and ostracize her from the rest of the family.

———

The church service went quite well. The sermon was lovely and, though Jackie could understand but a little of what was said, she kept still in her place on the pew behind the duke, duchess, and family.

Once the service was over, the servants who had followed behind the family now began to make their exit.

The duke went up to the pastor to discuss that day's service while the rest of the family stood by. It was all so very proper, that Isabella had to mentally rub her eyes to distinct the lord before her, with the gentleman that gave little Jackie horsey rides in her school room.

Isabella hesitated, not sure if she should wait to present the child to the duke again. Deciding against it, she took Jackie's hand again and proceeded on their walk back to the manor.

She had scarcely left the churchyard when she heard the sound of feet quickly walking to catch up to her. She turned to see Lord Bellfourd coming their way, hat already removed and under one arm.

She curtsied respectfully to him, "Lord Bellfourd."

"Miss Watts," he said coming up to her. "I couldn't bear to ride, even in an open carriage, on such an exceptional day. Would it be alright if I accompany little Jackie on her walk back home?"

"Oui! Please, Miss Watts! May he?" Jackie asked, swinging her little arm in Isabella's.

"Of course," Isabella said, releasing the child and allowing her to hug her uncle.

Isabella watched them walk a few steps ahead before Lord Bellfourd stopped and turned back to her.

"Surely you will accompany us as well, Miss Watts?"

Lord Bellfourd had walked the gardens twice already with little Jackie and Isabella in the afternoons over the past week, but that was always with Mrs. Murray present as well. She wasn't sure if it would be proper to walk alone with him now.

"Oui! Yes please, Miss Watts. Uncle Christian will tell us l'histoire de pirates while we marche."

"Pirates?" Isabella asked, now too intrigued to care for propriety. She made her way up to meet them.

Without much thought to the action, Lord Bellfourd let out his free arm for Isabella to take and she slipped her hand into its crook. It felt nice to be treated like a lady again. It may have only been a week, but it had felt so long since she had been part of the world she had grown up in.

"I suppose I can tell you one tale of the high seas," Lord Bellfourd started as they walked, "but only if you promise you won't get scared."

"Oui, je promets."

"Bien," Lord Bellfourd said with a nod, then began to search his mind for a good story to share. "I will tell you of how I came to captain my own ship."

He spoke with a little squint in his eyes as he expounded on his daring tale of life on a ship. The hardships, the vast emptiness, and keeping the men from mutiny against their captain.

Finally, he motioned them over to a small grove of trees off the path, which opened to a lovely pond. Isabella was so entranced by his tales, she hadn't even noticed the divergence from the way home.

Without a blanket, Isabella and Jackie sat in the sun next to a large oak tree that Lord Bellfourd leaned on as he continued to weave his tale.

"But the ship you captained, Uncle Christian. Tell me of that," Jackie encouraged.

"Well you see, I had just been made a commander and was sailing on the Queen Elizabeth. She was the fastest warship yet built by the Royal Navy. We were sailing in dangerous waters between the coast of Spain and France. Napoleon had just started his reign and tension was high. Only after a few weeks out, we spotted another British ship, a merchant ship. She was low in the water with cargo, and we easily sped up to meet her. Only when we got to her side, did we see that it was the French flag flying at her mast. She had been taken over by villainous pirates and the British crew, well the ones left, had been arrested and forced to work the ship sails in chains."

Jackie's eyes were now as big as teacups and Lord Bellfourd smiled in pleasure. He was a fantastic storyteller, indeed.

"Of course, we opened fire on her determined to see her sunk or back in British hands. The battle was a fierce one. The sound of cannon fire was deafening, but there was no way for such a heavy ship to escape. Finally, we boarded her, myself included. With pistol and sword in hand, we finally took control of the ship."

He paused for dramatic effect. It wasn't lost on his audience.

"We learned that the ship had sailed from a Spanish port set for England. It was filled with rice and spices from India. With the French pirates under control, we took back the ship. Unfortunately, the captain and first mate had been among the first executed by the pirates. The ship had no one to lead the few sailors remaining back home.

The commanding officer, Captain Johnson, ordered myself and a few men of my choosing to stay on the merchant ship and see that she sailed safely home. He would navigate ahead, with the speed of the Queen Elizabeth, to prepare for our arrival. You see, the merchant ship was severely damaged from the fight, and assistance would be needed upon her arrival to port. It was my first command as captain of a vessel and I couldn't have been more excited about it.

We watched the Queenie sail on ahead and made ready ourselves, making any repairs as was needed. One thing that was particularly worrisome was a hole in the port side just at the water line. Water had been spilling into her. First, we stopped the hole as best as possible, fashioning a patch with one of the smaller sails. Then we began pumping out the water.

All seemed right and we set out on our way. By the middle of the night, though, we started to hear a curious groaning from below deck. Now, all ships groan and each one makes their own unique symphony, so we paid no attention to it. By morning, however, we noticed that the boards of the deck were moving. They had separated and swelled away from each other and began to sway with the rocking of the ship.

I thought, at first, that the sail had not held in plugging the hole and went to inspect it over the side of the vessel. Much to my surprise, I could not see any portion of the sail in the early morning light. We had sunk so deep that it was entirely underwater now. I had my men go back down to inspect the cargo and see if it was again flooded with water. If we needed to, we would pump water day and night to keep it afloat.

Though some water was dripping through the pressure of the canvas, it wasn't nearly enough to be flooding and weighing down the ship. Then I came down myself to inspect what could be the cause. I realized then that the bags of rice butted up to that particular wall of the ship. Do you know what happens to rice when it touches water?"

Jackie shook her head excitedly.

"Well, it soaks up that water and expands bigger, much like bread soaking up milk. Even though we had stopped up the plug well enough, all the bags of rice had been flooded with water and now were swelling and expanding; literally weighing the ship down and pushing on the walls of the hull.

I called all my men down and began to have them haul

the bags of rice away from the walls, up on the deck and over the side. It was better to get rid of the cargo than to lose the whole ship, you see. We worked for hours, carrying fifty-pound bags on our shoulders up and over the side of the boat.

After a whole day of this, we seemed to be making no progress. The ship was still swelling under the weight of all the rice expanding below. The vessel had already sunk so low into the water, that one could almost touch it from the deck.

It was then we discovered something much more sinister. Under one of the bags of rice, along the haul, was a second hole that had been spilling in and pouring on to the bags of rice. So low was it, though, that all the water was soaked up before it even made it out past the piles of grain.

I determined, at this point, that there was no hope to save the ship. We had to abandon ship in the middle of the sea with little hope of being rescued. I piled my men, the merchant sailors, and the imprisoned French pirates onto three lifeboats. I had been captain for only twenty-four hours before having to give my post to the depths of the sea."

"What happened to you?" Isabella asked, forgetting herself. She was so enraptured by the tale, she had forgotten he was telling the story for the benefit of Jackie, not herself. She blushed, "Sorry."

"No, don't be," Lord Bellfourd said with a soft smile. He

turned back to Jackie to finish the story but now glanced at Miss Watts from time to time. "We were in our lifeboats for three days. We tied them together to keep from losing each other. I had taken the boat with the prisoners to keep them from revolting. On the night of the third day, a great storm came and blew us around like a cork in a bottle all night long. By morning, we were still together but had no idea where we were. Did we get pushed back toward France? Had we blown south toward the tip of Spain? Or perhaps, did Poseidon himself give us this storm to hurry us on home?"

"Which one was it, Uncle?"

"France, sadly," he said, to both of our audible gasps. "We had just spotted the coast, maybe twenty miles in the distance, when a French ship made its way from a port, no doubt spying on us.

Fearing capture ourselves, I did the only thing I could think of- I cut my boat with the prisoners loose, hopped on a boat with my own men, and rowed for our very lives in the opposite direction. Certainly, our only hope was that the French would take their own men and leave us be.

We weren't entirely sure we would be so lucky when out of the west came Queenie herself, back for another round of patrol. They had expected us to be in port with the merchant ship by then, and were surprised to find us floating so close to France in nothing but little row boats.

They scooped us up and we were again in the safety of Queen Elizabeth's belly."

"And so, for one day you were captain of a ship?" Isabella said with awe.

"Well, technically four, because I captained the rowboats as well," he said with a twinkle in his eye.

Both girls giggled at this.

"The commanding officer of the Queenie so appreciated the care I took of the men on the ship, that he recommended me for captain on our next port call. A year later, it was made official."

"I can imagine so. To keep such a clear head in the midst of one travesty after the other," Isabella said in awe.

"Did you find any mermaids?" Jackie asked on an entirely different train of thought.

"Loads," Lord Bellfourd said, standing and helping little Jackie out of the grass. "Only you had to stay away from them. They would sing you into a trance until you sailed your boat onto unseen rocks."

"Mermaids don't do that," Jackie said quite sure of herself.

"Oh, pardon me. You're right. They were sirens," he said, offering a hand to Miss Watts as well.

"Sirens, you say," Isabella retorted skeptically, taking his hand.

"Yes, I always seem to find myself entranced by beautiful women raised under the influence of the seas."

Isabella blushed immensely as he pierced her with his eyes.

Finally, he turned to little Jackie and whispered, "The green-eyed ones are, by far, the hardest to ignore."

She giggled, "Uncle Christian, I think you are making that up. There are no such things as sirens."

"Oh, yes there are. You must ask your governess to tell you all about them next week," he said with a wicked grin in Isabella's direction.

10

*I*sabella had no idea what Lord Bellfourd had meant on that warm Sunday by the pond. Indeed, he was the teasing sort, but his words distinctly bordered on flirtation.

Before she really had time to address the matter, or even think it over much herself, Lord Bellfourd was off for London. In the end, she surmised it was for the best.

Lord Bellfourd was dashingly handsome with his sunny blonde hair and tall stature. She didn't imagine he would last the season without finding at least one lady who would be more than willing to attach herself to the future Duke of Wintercrest.

Isabella told herself once that happened, Lord Bell-fourd would turn his teasing attentions elsewhere, and she wouldn't have to ponder the confusing emotions she felt when he was near.

"Come, Jackie. Today, for our nature walk, we will be picking wildflowers in three colors of your choosing. We will be pressing them into a pattern for your arithmetic today."

"Oui, Miss Watts," little Jacqueline said as she picked up the woven basket they had become accustomed to taking on their walks.

Now that Isabella had been teaching her pupil for just over three weeks, Jacqueline was utterly fluent in understanding English and did her best to solely speak the language. Isabella was proud of how far she had come, and how quickly.

With spring now in full bloom around them, Isabella chose to extend their nature walks to much longer than the cold weather had allowed before.

Often, Isabella would bring a book with her, and they would find themselves sitting by the same pond where Lord Bellfourd had taken them before his departure. They would often spend an hour or two reading and making clover flower crowns.

Today, however, they would be traveling in the opposite direction of the pond, to a small meadow Isabella had discovered on one of her explorations of the property.

She found herself now wholly comfortable in the country life, more than she had ever imagined possible.

Though she wasn't sure she would ever be acclimatized to the chilly weather that seemed to persist as spring marched on, Isabella was willing to ignore it on account of the beautiful landscape that she never seemed to find an end to.

"Aunt Abigail!" Jacqueline exclaimed as she exited the school room.

Isabella gave a respectful curtsy to the lady as she too stepped out of the schoolroom.

"What are you off to do today, my sweet Jackie?" Lady Abigail asked of her niece.

"We are going to pick some flowers. Miss Watts is going to show me how to press them."

"How lovely," Lady Abigail said.

She had evidently come to the west wing of the estate to see the child.

"Would you like to join us, Lady Abigail?" Isabella asked.

"I would like that very much, if you don't mind, of course."

"Not at all. Both, Jackie and I, would enjoy the added company. Mrs. Murray has a bit of a cough and will be staying indoors today."

"Oh, how terrible," Lady Abigail replied, looking around to the rooms behind. "I hope she isn't too ill."

"Not at all," Isabella said reassuringly. "She assured me it was just a small cough and she would be right as rain in a day or two."

"Oh good," Lady Abigail said with a sigh of relief. It was clear she cared deeply for her old nurse. "If you would wait just a moment for me, I will change into more appropriate shoes." She motioned to the silken slippers under the hem of her cotton dress.

Ten minutes later Lady Abigail met her two companions in the foyer, booted adequately for the adventure. She had a rosy glow of excitement to her cheeks.

It had been so disappointing for Lady Abigail when her brother had gone to London without her, that for the first few days after his departure, she could do nothing but sit and feel melancholy. Isabella was happy to see the sharp look back in her blue eyes as they made their way out.

For much of the journey, the two ladies walked side by side in silence on the soft dirt path while Jackie skipped ahead. Once they were entirely out of view of the manor, Lady Abigail slid back her summer bonnet with a sigh of relief.

Her vibrant red hair looked almost brown in the grey shadows of the dreary sky. Isabella imagined her a great beauty at a London dance hall, her hair genuinely shining as it reflected red rays off the candlelight.

"Did you attend many events in London, Miss Watts?" Lady Abigail suddenly asked, as if reading Isabella's thoughts.

"I wouldn't say an excessive amount, but perhaps three or four a week during the height of the season."

Isabella could tell that Lady Abigail was again dwelling on all that she felt she was missing.

"But surely you have gone in years past? And you have many years yet ahead of you to go."

"I was able to travel with mother last year for the season. I was only fifteen at the time and mother didn't let me attend many events because of my age."

"I'm sure things will be better for you next year."

"Yes, I suppose so," Lady Abigail said sullenly.

"You must have some friends you can write to, to pass the time? Of course, you are always welcome to join us, too," Isabella added.

"I do have a cousin that I correspond with. She is a few years older than me. Probably about your age. It is my mother's sister's family."

"Was that who you were visiting before we met?"

"Yes. She is very close and dear to me. She is in London for the season and promised to write me all the details. I fear that will only sour my disposition even more."

The path opened to a clearing and the subject was dropped. Isabella laid out a blanket to sit on that she had carried in her own basket while Jacqueline pranced around the meadow like a fawn.

"Don't forget to find three different colors," Isabella called out to her student. "We will be using the flowers for our math lesson today," Isabella explained to Lady Abigail.

"Oh, how very smart to incorporate some lessons into the excursions."

"I know it is not the most popular method of education. I, myself, was trained as most children, with memorization and recitation. I had one particular teacher, though, Mrs. Wentworth. She always seemed to find a way to relate our studies to the world around us or even tales she told. I found that, in this manner, I was able to remember my lessons better."

"I would have certainly loved such a teacher," Lady Abigail agreed. "My governess was from London, like your-self. She, however, was very somber and talked so dully that I would struggle not to fall asleep." Lady Abigail giggled at the memory of her governess.

"One time, just before Christian left for his officer commission, he found a small brown mouse that a barn cat had caught. He stuck it in the governess' chamber pot! She screamed something awful, waking the whole nursery in the process. I don't think I had ever heard her speak above a soft whisper up until that point."

"Truly?" Isabella said surprised to hear that Lord Bell-fourd would do such a thing. "And you heard her scream all the way across the west wing?"

"What do you mean? The governess' room was just next to the school room. Is that not where you are staying?"

"Oh," Isabella said not realizing that she had been

treated differently than the governess' in the past. "Um, no. I am just above in the far tower."

"All the way over there? Why, that is an awful distance away from the rest of the household."

"I rather enjoy the room. It is a bit of a walk, but I find it to be good exercise. The window overlooks a beautiful view of the side of the estate as well."

"I shall talk to Mrs. Peterson about it, none the less. It is silly to make you stay so far away. I find her to be an utterly ridiculous woman."

Lady Abigail spoke as she twirled a lock of her auburn hair that hung to the side of her beautiful plaiting.

"Do you know, just last week, I heard her scolding my lady's maid?" Lady Abigail continued in her comfortable conversational tone.

"Nancy was just trying to be helpful when the poor chambermaid spilled a box of coal. Mrs. Peterson first yelled at the chambermaid for being so clumsy and then at Nancy for helping her! She didn't know that I was just in the other room in the bath when she did so. I can't stand the way that she speaks to the other staff, always telling them to stay in their place."

"She is harsh in her manner sometimes, but shouldn't the job of the housekeeper be to maintain order, especially in such a large estate?"

"I understand that. Of course I do," Lady Abigail agreed. "Things just didn't used to be so strict. Father has always been very prim and proper, and James was much like him, but Father really left Christian and me to our own devices. Things were much more comfortable and, honestly, happier here."

"I remember," Lady Abigail continued after a moment, "one summer, Mother had accompanied us on a walk after school. It was just the governess, Nursie, mother, and I. We were by the main road and found some of the kitchen maids struggling to carry baskets home. There was to be a large dinner party that night and the wagon they were riding in had been damaged. They were struggling to get the goods back to the manor in time for the meal. My mother," Lady Abigail continued with a smile, "simply grabbed a basket and beckoned for me to do the same. She always said we are all God's creation and, as such, should treat each other with the same love and respect that He would bestow upon ourselves."

"What a beautiful thought," Isabella encouraged.

They sat and watched Jacqueline for a few minutes and Isabella considered the story that had just been told to her. It wasn't a typical upbringing for the daughter of a duke. Usually, with such high status came a self-proclaimed distinction between any lesser than themselves.

From the few weeks that Isabella had already spent at Wintercrest Manor, she could see that such separation had not been the case here. Lady Wintercrest seemed, not only warm and caring to her own children, something not often a trait of an elegant lady, but from what Lady Abigail had just expounded, she shared that grace and kindness to all around her.

11

*A*s the weeks continued, Lady Abigail often visited Jacqueline during school. She also started to invite Isabella to tea in her private sitting room in the late afternoon.

Isabella wouldn't say no to such an invitation. She knew it was given purely out of loneliness and couldn't fault Lady Abigail for it. Often, Her Grace would join them in the afternoon.

Mrs. Peterson made it abundantly clear, with her looks and huffs, that she didn't approve of Isabella in the central part of the house, and most unquestionably not to social afternoons with the ladies of the house.

Nothing could be directly said against it, though, since Her Grace was present at these social encounters. Mrs.

Peterson, so prim and proper, though not agreeing, would never dream to go against the duchess.

Isabella was enjoying the company and friendship that came along with Lady Abigail being home. Isabella's first few weeks had been so secluded from any other person, she feared she would die of loneliness.

Of course, she had her mornings and afternoons with Jacqueline and was often able to chat with Mrs. Murray during lunch, but she was missing the companionship and social gatherings she had lived for in London.

Isabella also enjoyed the time because, as the ladies sat in the small drawing room, they worked on some embroidery. It was a favorite pastime of Isabella's since she was a child.

Isabella took the opportunity to walk to town, after a few weeks, and picked up some supplies to embroider. It didn't take long for her to decide what to make first.

She had sewn a small dress for Jacqueline's favorite doll and was making progress adding lace and small blue rosettes to decorate the garment.

Teatime with Lady Abigail was the perfect time for her to work on the dress while keeping it a secret from Jacqueline.

Jacqueline's seventh birthday was four short weeks away, in the middle of June, and Isabella wanted to give it to her as a gift.

"Do ye fash much if I try somethin' a lil more fancy

with yer hair today, Miss Watts?" Betsy asked Isabella one morning as she brushed out the long black locks.

"I don't want to make you late," Isabella answered with concern.

"It won't take long at all. Nancy showed me just yesterday how ter make a nice plait. I was hopin' to try it out. You have to take Miss Jacqueline to His Grace tonight. It might be nice to look a lil finer."

"Okay, if you are sure you won't be in trouble for the extra time."

Isabella enjoyed the mornings she spent with Betsy, who often talked about the other servants and things that happened downstairs. She was assuredly in the space of limbo, spending her mornings with Betsy discussing the servants' troubles and her evenings with the ladies of the house, talking over matters of the town.

After Betsy finished, Isabella did her best to feel around, still with no way to see.

"Oh here, Miss Watts. I brought this out of my own room," Betsy said, handing Isabella a small, round piece of mirror.

It was the first time that Isabella had seen her reflection since moving to Wintercrest. She examined the dark curls that were neatly pinned with small ringlets flowing down her left shoulder. It was as beautiful as any lady's maid might do.

Isabella also took a quick moment to steal a look at her

face. Though she had never spent much time in the sun in London without a bonnet, she was decidedly paler now. Her green eyes even looked a little grayer than usual.

Isabella stuffed down her feelings of altogether disappearing in this small room, so removed from the rest of the world. It didn't do any good to dwell on things that would make her unhappy. She gave back the mirror to Betsy.

"I believe this the finest job I have ever seen. I look ready to see the Queen, herself," Isabella complimented.

"Thank ye," Betsy said shyly, but with a bit of pride in her work.

"I suspect you will be a lady's maid in no time. Well, that is if the dashing Mr. Johnson you tell me so much about doesn't steal you away first."

Betsy blushed. Isabella hadn't met Mr. Johnson. He was the son of a tenant farmer near town. Betsy had met him once at the weekly market. Since then, he had waited by the road each week for Betsy. He would walk with her to the market and back again, stopping at his father's farm.

Betsy made him sound very handsome, and she was convinced that soon, he would start to court her in seriousness. Isabella loved to hear Betsy talk of him. It was that exciting chatter of someone finding love.

———

"How were Jacqueline's studies today?" Lady Wintercrest asked in the small drawing room over her own embroidery.

"She did very well," Isabella responded. "We practiced addition facts today. She is taking to them very quickly. I believe she will have a terrific knack for numbers, Your Grace."

"I thought I heard her small forte the other day, as well. Are you teaching her to play?"

"Yes. Lord Bellfourd requested that she play him a song upon his return."

"And is that going well?" she asked.

"As much as can be expected for a child of such a young age," Isabelle replied. "Our goal is to learn one song before Lord Bellfourd's return. I am hoping it isn't too high of an aspiration."

"As you said, though, she is very young," Lady Abigail chimed in. "Christian will just have to be satisfied with what he gets."

"Perhaps you will have her play for us tonight," Lady Wintercrest invited. "I don't expect it to be wonderful, but it might be nice for the duke to see her taking up the accomplishment."

"I would be happy to have her share all that she has learned thus far."

Isabella enjoyed the fact that she wasn't the only one desperately trying to encourage the duke to accept Jacqueline into his heart.

"I suppose the dressing-bell is going to ring soon," Lady Abigail said, leaning to look at the clock on the mantle over the small fireplace.

Lady Abigail wasn't one to enjoy sitting and doing needlework. In fact, every day that Isabella had sat to tea with her, she found that Lady Abigail went from reading a book to working on some embroidery, to working some lace, and back to reading a book.

Isabella agreed that the hour was getting late and it was time for the ladies to dress for dinner. She began to pack away her embroidery in the small bag she had brought along with her.

"Why don't you join us tonight, Isabella?" Lady Abigail blurted out without thought. Isabella enjoyed that Lady Abigail had taken her encouragement to call her by her Christian name.

"Abigail," her mother cooed in a warning, but soft tone, "as much as I know we would both enjoy Miss Watts' company at dinner, I don't think your father would approve."

"It's so silly, the way Father is acting, as of late. He never cared about such things before. Do you know, he has Isabella all the way at the end of the west wing up in the attic? It's a ridiculous walk for her."

"I really don't mind it at all," Isabella interjected before Lady Wintercrest might think she was ungrateful.

"I am sorry for this situation, none the less," Lady Wintercrest replied. Her soft brown eyes filled with sincerity. "As Abigail said, things weren't always like this. Since the situation with James and..." Lady Wintercrest paused, deciding against speaking of family matters. "Well, my husband feels that he let our younger children be too lax with propriety."

She turned to Lady Abigail, "It wasn't that he didn't mind, he just didn't see the harm. Things are different now. We must respect his wishes."

"Of course, Your Grace," Isabella said to comfort the worried look on Lady Wintercrest's brow. "I would never have assumed otherwise."

"I know, my dear," Lady Wintercrest said, reaching across the tea table and patting Isabella's hand lovingly.

Isabella sat alone in her room to eat her dinner before taking Jacqueline down to her grandfather. She wondered what Lady Wintercrest had meant by harm. She had started to speak of Lord James and then stopped. Was it after finding out he had fathered a child by a commoner that the duke had insisted on creating a more profound separation between his family and others?

Mrs. Peterson had been hired on after the arrival of Jacqueline. Other than the duke himself, she seemed the sole enforcer of stations. In fact, neither Lady Abigail nor Lord Bellfourd seemed like it was commonplace. Isabella imagined it was a drastic change to have their father suddenly make demands on them that were never made before.

Her heart sank deeper as she thought of the duke. If Jacqueline was 'the harm' that the Duchess spoke of, no wonder His Grace kept a distance from the child. He had called her here to find closure and instead saw her as a stain on his son's memory.

Isabella determined, at that moment, that she would do everything in her power to help the duke find a place in his heart for the little girl. She would show him that this small child was capable of so much more than he thought. Isabella would prove to him that Jacqueline could be raised a proper young lady and, in doing so, hopefully, find her a place as part of the Duke of Wintercrest's family.

12

"*I* have some fun news for you," Lady Abigail said as she walked up to Isabella.

It was now just two days before Jacqueline's birthday and Isabella was frantically doing her best to finish the lace cuffs on her small dress.

Isabella had found a seat out in the garden to do her work today as it was one of those rare days of sun. She even went as far as to remove her bonnet, like Lady Abigail so often did when she was outside.

Lady Abigail came to sit next to Isabella on the stone bench with a few letters waving in her hand.

"I have a letter from Christian," Lady Abigail continued.

Over the last few months that they had spent under the same roof, Lady Abigail and Isabella had become close friends. As long as they were out of the eyes of the duke, they were able to chat and visit just as Isabella had once done with Louisa.

"Mmm," Isabella responded, looking fixedly at a particularly tricky stitch.

"He says that on the night he wrote this letter," she flipped the page back to look at the date, "four days ago, he went to a lavish ball held by the Earl of Cunningham."

Isabella knew the name well. She had gone to school with Lady Lydia Prescott, daughter of the Earl of Cunningham. Isabella didn't regularly have trouble getting along with people, but Lady Lydia was particularly unfriendly toward her.

As best as she could guess, Lady Lydia had been a favorite of Mrs. Mason until Isabella had arrived. She never liked when Isabella was presented before prospective parents to recite her French. Isabella didn't have any sour feelings toward Lady Lydia in return, but made sure to avoid her so as not to develop any.

"While he was there he made the acquaintance of your dear friend, Lady Louisa."

This got Isabella's attention. She put her embroidery down and turned to Lady Abigail.

"You see, I told him about her. Well, what you told me of her, anyway."

Isabella smiled. Lady Abigail was always one to pass along any story, no matter how trivial.

"He said that he danced with her twice and found

her to be a very welcome dance partner. He sang wonderful praises of her and also her older brother, Viscount Dunthorpe," Lady Abigail added looking back at her letter. "I suppose you must have also met the Viscount?"

"Who? Oh, Colton. Yes," Isabella said, not recognizing his proper title at first. "He is just barely a year above Louisa. I am sure your brother and Colton really got along, too. Colton is such a jokester," she said with a whimsical tone.

Though Colton was a good brother, and very close to his sister, he had enjoyed playing pranks on them as children when Isabella stayed with Louisa on holiday breaks from school.

"Do you miss London, then?" Lady Abigail asked softly, placing a hand on top of Isabella's.

She knew that Lady Abigail was speaking of the people she left behind more than the place itself.

"I do miss Louisa, her whole family really. They were always so kind to me. Often, Father was away on extended voyages and the Lady Gilchrist was kind enough to invite me to family dinners."

"It must have been so lonely to have your father always away."

"Not really," Isabella answered. In all honesty, she never knew any other way, and so couldn't be sad for it. "I was at Mrs. Mason's school from eleven to seventeen. I had plenty of companions there and enough work to keep me busy."

"And later, when you were done with your schooling?"

"I had Louisa. We met at school, you see. And, as I said, her family often invited me to join them for dinner and parties."

"I love the stories you tell Jackie about your father. It must have been wonderful when he did come home and spun such amazing tales for you. They remind me so much of Christian," Lady Abigail said with melancholy.

"You must be very close to Lord Bellfourd to miss him so."

"We were, growing up, despite our age difference. Christian, Mother, and I were like three peas in a pod. I didn't really know James that well; he was almost fifteen years older than myself. He was grown and gone by the time I was really old enough to remember much."

"Gone?"

"Oh, you know, he would stay at the house in London or go to France. He had a very adventurous spirit in that way. Not like Christian adventurous. It was more like he wanted to sample all that life had to offer."

"I remember when Christian left for the navy," Lady Abigail continued, "I was so sad and lonely. I know it wasn't for the best reason, but I was happy when he was able to come home. He would always write me letters of his time out at sea, but I suspected he kept much of the harsher realities of that life away from me. I worried about him so much."

"I've heard Lord Bellfourd tell a story or two to Jackie about his time in the navy," Isabella said. "Do you think he misses it much?"

"I am not sure if it is so much missing being in the navy, though certainly, he did enjoy it, but more the freedom he was allowed."

"What do you mean? I would guess any form of the military to be very strict?"

"That's true. Christian wrote me a few times in the beginning that he would be treated severely if his buttons were not shined properly and the like," Lady Abigail said with a little laugh. "It was more the freedom of not having father's constant attention."

"I sometimes think that is why James stayed away so much. Father is a hard person to truly please. He put a lot of pressure on James, as the eldest son. Christian and I were free to do whatever we wanted. Father never bothered with either of us."

"I have noticed that His Grace can be a little severe on his family," Isabella said, as delicately as possible.

She was thinking of Jackie and wondering if that precious little girl would ever meet her grandfather's standards.

"He is so stuffy," Lady Abigail let out in a huff. "When

we were little, Mother was always a good barrier between him and us. He has gotten so much worse now."

"He doesn't care much for Jackie," Isabella said cautiously.

Lady Abigail gave a little shrug of defeat. "He doesn't like the 'impropriety of her existence,'" she said, deepening her voice to sound like her father. "I think he fears getting to know her. Then, he would love her as the rest of us do. It would prove his silly standards wrong."

"I am sure it was tough for His Grace, for all of you, to lose a member of your family so suddenly. Perhaps he just needs time to mourn, in his own way, and then he will come around." Isabella said this, hoping it to be true, else all her work to endear the child to him was for naught.

"I think Father's mourning over James stopped the day he got the letter. He was so upset that James had done something so shameful. He put so much pressure on James to always do what was proper, to live the scrutinized life of a duke, even as a child. Father felt betrayed when he learned of Jackie."

"Surely he shouldn't put that blame on Jackie, though," Isabella replied, doing her best to understand the Duke of Wintercrest.

"I couldn't agree with you more. Sadly, she is the one left to shoulder that weight, and so she must, in my father's eyes."

"I am certain there must be a way to soften his heart,"

Isabella said, revealing her desires in the name of her pupil.

"I wish you the best of luck in that regard," Lady Abigail retorted, not entirely sure that such a feat would ever be possible.

Isabella re-entered the manor via the service entrance just before sunset. She planned to stay in her room and complete the last of the sewing before her dinner was brought up.

Isabella was surprised to see small huddles of servants talking amongst themselves in the dining hall. She found Betsy out of the crowd and made her way over.

"Oh, Miss Watts, ye'll never believe what just happened," Betsy said, just above a whisper. "It's somethin' dreadful."

"What happened?" Isabella asked as she entered the small circle of maids talking.

She knew most of them, or at least had said greetings in passing.

"His Grace was on 'is way dun the stairs when he had a spell and took a terrible tumble."

"Is he alright?" Isabella asked with genuine concern.

"His Grace's groomsman was not too far away," another maid finished the story, "and came running to help. He is propped up in the large drawing room close to the fire. The doctor was sent for."

"Well, he has been very ill," another maid added, this

one named Sally, Isabella thought. "I can't imagine this will help His Grace improve."

"You saw 'im just last night, did ye not Miss Watts?" Betsy asked.

All eyes fell on her.

"Yes, I took Jacqueline to the drawing room. He was struggling with a cough these last few weeks, as you said, Sally, but he was really looking very healthy last night. I do hope that this new event won't set him back."

"I am not exactly sure why so many of you are standing around gossiping," a loud voice boomed into the dining room.

Immediately, the small groups of servants turned and went quickly back to work. Isabella didn't have to turn to know the voice came from Mrs. Peterson. Sadly, Isabella made the mistake of turning and looking at her anyway. Mrs. Peterson narrowed her eyes at Isabella, seeing that she was part of the gossipers.

"I am very disappointed to see you here, Miss Watts. Someone with your upbringing should have had the common sense not to take part in idle chatter."

"It wasn't idle chatter. I just came indoors when the sun got too dim to see by. I asked Betsy what the matter was, and she politely informed me. We were just discussing how concerned we are for the duke," Isabella retorted with her chin held high.

"Call it what you like," Mrs. Peterson spoke with an

exasperated tone. "I will ask you to retire to your room now for your supper. Perhaps a little cream on your cheeks too," she added just to embarrass Isabella in front of the other servants. "You seem to have caught quite a bit of sun today."

Without another word, she turned on her heels and left the room. Isabella instinctively moved her hands to her cheeks. They did feel a little warm but not at all burned like the housekeeper had made it seem.

"Dinna fash," Betsy said, waving the rotten woman off, "ye look fine. Just a lil rose, is all. I dare say it's good to get a lil sun when ye can in these parts."

"I only took my bonnet off for a short while," Isabella said, then suddenly realized she had left it outside on the stone bench. "Oh, I think I forgot it."

"Well, go and get it then," Betsy said as Isabella hesitated to go back through the service entrance. "I'm the one bringing your supper tray tonight; I'll make sure to wait till ye come back in."

"Thank you, Betsy," Isabella said, taking her hand in gratitude before turning to leave the common place.

Isabella hadn't gone outside past dusk since the first night she arrived at Wintercrest Manor. She knew the way to the little garden and bench well, but things did seem a bit more ominous now with the thick darkness covering the grounds.

Isabella walked quickly, only hearing the sound of her

own muslin skirt swishing against her legs. She was practically at a run, so off-put by the darkness.

Isabella turned the sharp corner leading into the small garden alcove, and stopped dead in her tracks. Standing at her bench was the figure of a very large man. She could see nothing of him other than the outline of his body. In his hand was her bonnet.

She hesitated a moment. She had only two bonnets, the one in the stranger's hand, and a nicer one to wear on Sunday. Was she willing to make her presence known to this stranger in a darkened corner of the estate for a simple head covering?

Turning and leaving as silently as possible seemed like a better choice. She hoped it was nothing more than a gardener and she would be able to come back in the morning to retrieve the article, but not wanting to take any chances that it was otherwise.

Before she could take more than two backward steps in retreat, the figure turned and faced her.

13

"Please forgive me, but I believe that is mine," Isabella spoke softly, trying to hide the quiver of fear in her voice.

"Is that you, Miss Watts?" a gentlemen's voice called back.

Isabella relaxed, realizing that the voice belonged to Lord Bellfourd.

"Lord Bellfourd," she said, taking a step forward to retrieve the hat from his outstretched hand, "you gave me such a fright."

"Are you afraid of the dark, Miss Watts?"

Isabella could only make out his outline in this dim light. She didn't need to see, however, to picture the teasing smile he had playing across his lips.

"I am not," Isabella said, faking offense. "However, I

can't say I wasn't startled to come upon a stranger in the dark."

"Well, I suggest not walking the grounds at night," Lord Bellfourd retorted.

"I could say the same for you." Isabella paused for a beat and then changed to a serious tone, "I didn't know you were expected back from London so soon."

"I wasn't. In fact, no one knows I have arrived. I came to surprise Jackie for her birthday."

"How very kind of you. Oh, Jackie will love it!" Isabella said with glee.

"Would you sit with me for a moment?" Lord Bellfourd asked, taking a seat on the stone bench. "I know the sun has fallen, but I don't think it is too chilly. I'm not ready to go in myself just yet. I would appreciate the company."

Isabella wrapped her thin shawl around her arms a little tighter. Though it was much colder than she was used to in the summer, it wasn't particularly chilly. There wasn't a breath of air tonight, and with the sky clear of clouds, the tremendous dark expanse overhead was littered with glittering stars.

She also hesitated for another more obvious reason. It wasn't exactly proper for a single lady to be in the company of a gentleman without supervision. Even worse, here alone in a darkened corner of the garden.

She then remembered that she was no longer a lady. No one would care to take this purely innocent encounter for anything but what it was. The Marquess certainly knew what was proper and seemed to never care of it. She would now take his stance on the matter, free from any fear of repercussion.

Without saying a word, Isabella came to sit next to Lord Bellfourd. For a minute or two, they sat in silence, appreciating the beauty of the clear night sky.

"Will you be returning to London, then, once Jackie's birthday has passed?" Isabella finally asked.

"No," Lord Bellfourd answered decidedly. He gave a little chuckle and tugged on the hem of his traveling jacket. "I did come for Jackie, but that was just an excuse to leave."

"I don't understand what you mean?"

"I couldn't stand it," Lord Bellfourd blurted out. "The dinners, the balls, the people. It is all so...so..." He struggled to find the right words. "So like my father," he settled on.

"You don't like the society of the season?"

"I can't bear it," he said, looking down at her. "It never really bothered me much before since it didn't matter much to me. In fact," he added with a whimsical tone, "I used to make fun of my brother any time he chastened me for acting poorly. He would say 'your actions reflect on our family name.' No doubt he got that from Father."

"Now, I seem to be filling his shoes and it turns out he was right. No one cared what I did or what event I went to when I was just Lord Christian or even Captain Grant. Now, it seems every move I make is weighed and judged."

He let out a long gust of air like he was deflating. Isabella completely understood the pressure he spoke of. She could only imagine it was that much harder for a man of his rank. She had to smile a little, knowing that more than likely it was made even worse by being a single returned naval officer with a dukedom in line.

"Count yourself lucky that you got away," he added with a renewed playful tone.

"I wouldn't go quite that far," Isabella said, turning to look up at him.

Even in the dim light of the stars his red hair had a golden sheen to it. Isabella could see his brows drawn in a furrow at her response.

"It was my home- all I knew," she answered his unasked question. "I loved London and the society that came with it. For a while, I wished I never left. Certainly, there were aspects of it that were less than favorable, but that can be said of any lot in life."

"Well, I can't imagine there is anything less than favorable to be said about your new home," Lord Bellfourd chuckled, relaxing from his earlier frustration.

"Well, I do have to say my student is much better than I could have ever asked for and the household has been very kind and warm..."

"But?" Lord Bellfourd encouraged.

"But the weather is dreadful," Isabella let out with a blow of her own defeat. "No matter how warm my fire is, how thick my shawl is, I will never get used to this dreary, damp region."

Lord Bellfourd laughed heartily at her declaration.

"It's not funny," Isabella jeered. "I suspect I will be a frozen icicle by wintertime."

"Oh, that would be a terrible predicament wouldn't it?" Lord Bellfourd said, getting control of his merriment. "I am glad to hear that you are getting along well with the household, though. I did think of you from time to time while I was away," he confessed.

"You did?" Isabella responded in pure shock.

Yes, they had taken walks together with Jacqueline and spent a few evenings together when Isabella brought the child down to her grandfather, but she had never expected to be on Lord Bellfourd's mind at all. Especially not while he was away from the manor and with so much else to occupy his thoughts.

"Well, sometimes it couldn't be helped," Lord Bellfourd explained. "I met your friend Lady Louisa."

"Yes, your sister just got your letter today and told me."

"She sang your praises regularly and often told me how dreary her life was now that you were away."

"I do miss her so," Isabella said, unable to mask her sorrow in that fact.

"Why not invite her here for a visit, then?"

"Oh, I couldn't! No, that wouldn't be right at all," Isabella assured herself, as much as she wished otherwise. "I will just have to be satisfied with our letters and knowing that she is still my friend despite the circumstances."

"That is exactly why I left. I can't stand that so-called fine gentlemen and ladies would sever acquaintances when friendship is needed by someone the most. I cannot bear that kind of logic. If it isn't too forward, may I ask what brought you to Wintercrest? I understand your father passed, but, if it isn't too personal, why choose to be a governess?"

Isabella took a deep breath. Though most of the house knew that she was raised as a lady and had since fallen in status, she had yet to actually tell anyone the whole of the story, except for Louisa, of course.

"When my father passed, he had no male heir. His estates and business were turned over to his partner, Mr. Smith," Isabella did her best not to spit out the last word with venom.

"And this Mr. Smith was not able to see you comfortably?" Lord Bellfourd asked.

"Mr. Smith had some negative feelings toward me. He proposed marriage when I was but seventeen. I declined as politely as I could, but he never seemed to forgive me for wounding his pride."

"So he mistreated you in retribution?" Lord Bellfourd asked, appalled. "How could such a thing be stood for?"

"Well, he removed my father's property and belongings under the guise of paying off debt my father had incurred. But, in my opinion, he did it just to be harsh."

Isabella's hand went unconsciously to the locket around her neck. She still had moments of fear that Mr. Smith might show up at Wintercrest Manor, demanding the necklace from her.

"As selfish as it is for me say, I must confess I am glad of Mr. Smith's deplorable treatment."

Isabella turned to look at him in shock.

"It brought you here. I am eternally grateful for the light you have brought out in Jackie and the friendship you have shown to myself and my sister while I was away."

"Well," Isabella said, glad that the darkness hid her blushing, "I will admit that coming to Wintercrest Manor was a tender mercy given me in an awful situation."

"I suppose it's best we go inside now," Lord Bellfourd said reluctantly.

Isabella suddenly came to a remembrance of the events in the servants' dining hall. She stood up abruptly.

"Oh my, Lord Bellfourd, I should have told you right away. Your father took a tumble on the stairs today and the doctor was sent for."

Lord Bellfourd stood too. "Is he alright?"

"I'm not entirely sure. I only heard of the accident, myself, not too long ago and then came out to retrieve my bonnet when I realized that I had left it outside."

"Well, then let's go and see together," he said holding the crook of his arm out for Isabella to take.

Isabella didn't think he actually meant that she should go with him to see, merely that he was being a gentleman and walking her back to the house. She took his arm, grateful for the steady help as she navigated back.

One thing she had learned about Lord Bellfourd over the short time that she had known him was that he was very sure-footed. He walked confidently and even pointed to a root sticking out ready to trip her long before she, herself, could see it.

They got to the front of the house and Isabella moved to thank Lord Bellfourd and return to her bedroom. Hopefully, Betsy had just left her supper, not waiting for Isabella's return. She worried that she might have gotten Betsy in more trouble with the housekeeper, though it seemed that nothing Isabella could do was right in the eyes of Mrs. Peterson and she wondered if that courtesy was given to all the help and not just herself.

Just before splitting off, a carriage pulled up along the gravel drive and up to the front gate. Perhaps forgetting that Isabella was still on his arm, Lord Bellfourd walked quickly to meet the arrival.

14

*I*sabella did her best to keep up with the Marquess as he hurried to the side of the doctor exiting the carriage. She could hear the quick rustling of her petticoats and prayed she wouldn't trip over them.

"Dr. Thornton," Lord Bellfourd said as he reached the elderly man. He stretched into the vehicle instinctually, knowing there would be a cane there, and handed it to the gentleman.

Dr. Thornton looked up at Lord Bellfourd with squinted eyes behind his spectacles. He was quite a bit shorter than the Marquess, which was only made more apparent by his hunched stature as he leaned on his cane.

Isabella couldn't help but wonder if Dr. Thornton might need a doctor himself. He was well on in age, with a severely wrinkled face and long hook nose. His whiskers that grew long on the side of his face were white as snow and stood out wildly.

He wheezed a bit as he inspected the pair that came to meet him. Finally, he held out his hand and shook Lord Bellfourd's.

"How are you, young Lord Christian?" he asked in a breathy voice.

"I am quite well. May I also introduce you to the honorable Miss Isabella Watts."

Isabella turned and opened her mouth to Lord Bellfourd. She wanted to correct him but decided it wouldn't be polite to do so.

He looked back at her and seemed to tell her with his eyes that he didn't find her address a mistake.

"Pleasure to meet you, Miss," Dr. Thornton said as he began the slow walk toward the house. "How is His Grace doing?" he said, changing the subject.

"I'm not sure. I just arrived myself and Miss Watts informed me of the accident. I'm sure he will recover well, though, won't he?" Lord Bellfourd asked with noticed concern in his voice.

Though the duke didn't often see eye to eye with his children, there was still a significant amount of affection for their father.

"I can't say till I see His Grace. He is no spring chicken," Dr. Thornton laughed at his own joke, then covered his mouth with a handkerchief when it turned into a cough. "A great fall can be hard on older bones," he added more seriously after he caught his breath.

"You know," Dr. Thornton said in Isabella's direction as they slowly made their way into the manor and down the long foyer, "I was here the day Lord Christian was born. I have seen him through many colds and even a broken arm, if I remember correctly," he added, reaching back in his mind.

"Yes," Lord Bellfourd said confirming his tale. "I fell out of an apple tree," he explained to Isabella.

She looked up at him with a smile. She liked that she could see the twinkle in his azure eye as he spoke. She realized how much she had missed looking up at him, seeing the light in his teasing smile and hearing his smooth voice, since he had been away.

"Yes, you were quite the wild little chap, if I remember correctly," Dr. Thornton said with the friendliness of a family doctor. "Your sister, or even your brother, God rest him, never caused so much trouble, if I remember right."

"I suppose that is why I took to the sea so well," Lord Bellfourd responded.

"Yes, I suspect the danger and adventure of a naval carrier suited you well," Dr. Thornton agreed.

Isabella couldn't help but hear the sadness in Lord Bellfourd's words. Between that and what he had confided in her tonight, she suspected that he missed his old life greatly. Perhaps that was why he felt such a kinship with her. They were both living a life contrary to what they wished, doing instead what had been chosen for them.

They arrived at the drawing-room door. Isabella hesitated and let her arm slip. Before coming all the way out of Lord Bellfourd's crook, he reached across and patted her hand with his, keeping it in place.

Isabella looked up at him with questioning eyes.

"I would like you to stay, if you please. I know it would be a great comfort to Abigail. She has written that you are such a dear friend to her. I am sure she could use some support."

"Of course," Isabella said, relaxing her hand again into his arm.

"Thank you," he said softly, smiling down at her.

Isabella couldn't help the blush that rushed to her cheek. Lord Bellfourd was charming, even at such a sad time. Isabella couldn't help but feel her heart flutter as he looked at her so sincerely.

"Christian!" Abigail said, getting up from her spot on the sofa and coming over to him.

Lord Bellfourd took his sister into a warm embrace and Isabella respectfully stood to the side.

"What on earth are you doing here?" she asked.

"Well, I had planned on surprising Jackie for her birthday. Miss Watts found me out while I was sneaking around the gardens. I think I gave her quite a scare," he said, adding a wink in Isabella's direction.

Lady Wintercrest came and hugged her son, "Providence, no doubt, sent you this way."

"Miss Watt told me of Father's accident. Is he alright?" Lord Bellfourd said, searching the room for him.

"It's hard to say for certain," Lady Wintercrest said with a glisten in her eyes. "He was so uncomfortable sitting in the chair here, but I feared he might hurt himself worse if he went up to his chamber. Mr. Larson had his bed brought down to the study and, just a few moments ago, helped him to lie down."

Lord Bellfourd took his mother's hands in reassurance. "He will be alright. I will take Dr. Thornton to him now. You and Abigail wait here."

Lord Bellfourd left with the doctor to see to his father. Lady Wintercrest dabbed at her eye with a white lace handkerchief.

"Thank you, Isabella," Lady Abigail said, taking her hand, "for informing my brother." She lowered her voice. "I don't know that Mother would have fared well taking the doctor to inspect him."

"Of course," Isabella squeezed Abigail's hand in reassurance. "Anything I can do to help, please let me know, and I would be happy to do it."

"Perhaps, if you don't mind, would you sit with us till Christian and Dr. Thornton return?"

"Certainly," Isabella said taking a seat with Lady Abigail on the sofa.

A few minutes passed, the three ladies sitting and waiting, before the door opened. Their three heads turned quickly to see who it was. It was only a maid bringing in a pot of tea. She set it down on the small table and left quietly.

"Lady Wintercrest, may I pour the tea for you?" Isabella asked.

"Yes, please. Thank you, Miss Watts. I fear my hands are shaking too much now to do it myself. He was just so pale, and in so much pain," she added, barely above a whisper.

Isabella's heart went out to Lady Wintercrest. Though there was a vast difference in age, and most likely an arrangement to their union, the duchess genuinely cared for the well-being of her husband.

Isabella poured out the tea and served it to the two ladies.

Upon finishing, she said, "If you would like, Your Grace, I could play a little on the pianoforte for you. It might help calm your nerves."

"Thank you, Miss Watts, I would appreciate that."

Isabella made her way to the pianoforte. She had gotten in quite a bit of practice over the last few months. Often, after Jacqueline presented her accomplishments to her grandfather, she was left to visit with the ladies and Isabella would play softly on the piano.

She shuffled through the music, coming to a calming piece by Handel. She felt the tension of the room soften as she made her way through the music. She was grateful that she could be of some help to them while they waited on news.

Finally, after just over an hour, Lord Bellfourd re-entered the room. He was alone. Lady Wintercrest stood at his entrance and Isabella stopped her playing.

He came and sat in the vacant chair by the fire. He was visibly worn from his travel, followed by a long evening tending to his father's bedside.

He took his mother's hand, "Dr. Thornton thinks he might have fractured his hip. He also noticed that father's side was very tender and breathing a little strained. It could just be some bruising compiled with his recent illness."

"But it could be something worse," Lady Abigail said, reading what Lord Bellfourd was inferring but not speaking.

Lord Bellfourd gave a solemn nod. "He may have also fractured a rib."

The duchess raised her handkerchief to her mouth to stifle a sorrowful gasp.

"Dr. Thornton has bound it up tightly, set his fractured hip as best he could, given him something for the pain, and instructed him to get strict rest for at least the next six to eight weeks. Hopefully, it is just bruised and will heal quickly. If it is fractured, it might have punctured his lung, which could be causing the difficulty breathing."

"What is there to do?" his mother asked.

"The best thing to do is just to let him rest as comfortably as possible. I have already seen the doctor to a room for the night. I didn't think it was right for him to travel home so late."

Isabella looked at the clock on the mantle. She hadn't realized how much time had passed but it was getting close to eleven.

"Dr. Thornton will check on Father again before he leaves in the morning and will return as often as needed. The best we can do is pray that he recovers quickly," Lord Bellfourd added to both his mother and sister.

Lady Wintercrest nodded solemnly and caressed her son's cheek in a motherly fashion.

Upon standing, she said, "I think I will go and bid your father goodnight and get some sleep myself. You should do the same, Christian; you look dreadfully tired."

"I'll come with you, Mother," Abigail said, standing to join her mother's side.

"Thank you, Miss Watts," Lady Wintercrest said before leaving the room, "your music was just what I needed to get me through the night."

"You're welcome," Isabella said with a curtsy. "If there is anything else I can do, Your Grace, I would be happy to help."

Lady Wintercrest nodded and gave a weak smile before leaving the room.

Isabella made ready to leave, herself. She turned to Lord Bellfourd to say goodnight. Instead of staying by the fire he stood and came over to her.

"I will see you to your room, then," he said reaching out his arm again for her to take.

"It's not necessary," Isabella said.

"I insist. I feel bad that I kept you here so late. The least I can do is see you safely to your door. You never know where dark, strange figures might be lurking," he teased.

15

*L*ord Bellfourd grabbed the candelabra that was situated on the piano and led Isabella out of the drawing room. They walked through the foyer and up the massive stairs in silence. After getting halfway down the walkway, Lord Bellfourd started to look around, confused.

"Are we coming to your lodging shortly or should we stop and camp for the night," he said in a joking tone.

"If you would just leave me there at the bottom of the stairs, I am certain I can make the remaining journey on my own."

"Stairs?" he asked in surprise. "Why on earth are you put so far away from the rest of the household?"

"I don't mind it and enjoy the walk," Isabella said repetitively. "I only feel bad for poor Betsy who must travel so far each day to deposit my breakfast and supper. I told Mrs. Peterson, I would be happy to eat in the servant hall to save the trouble, but she wouldn't hear of it."

"That does seem quite tedious and unnecessary to have a maid make the trek several times a day. I see Mrs. Peterson's point, however. So, instead, from now on, you must take your morning and evening meals with us."

"I couldn't. Your father wouldn't have it. It would be too inappropriate."

"If you haven't learned yet, I don't care much for silly societal rules, especially ones that force a lady to dine alone every day. As for my father, he is not in a state to have an opinion, and I will happily take charge of this particular obligation for him."

"Well, if you think it won't cause harm," Isabella faltered in her resolve, "I am most grateful for your kindness, Lord Bellfourd." She did rather hope to save Betsy from the nasty trip several times a day.

"Good, and maybe, since you now are in my confidence, you might consider just calling me Christian and permit me to call you Isabella, as I notice my sister does?"

"Absolutely not!" Isabella said, stopping at the bottom of the attic stairs. "I will happily let you call me whatever you wish, but I simply refuse to do the same. Whether you like it or not, you have a title now and the responsibility that goes along with it," Isabella said in an instructive tone.

"It is ridiculous. We are all human beings, walking the same path that leads to the same end."

"Be that as it may, it is who you are," Isabella insisted.

Lord Bellfourd seemed to weigh this in his mind. It was something that he would continue to struggle with, Isabella thought, until he accepted his new lot in life.

"I shall take your words under advisement, but still encourage otherwise, if only in privacy."

"When would that ever be?" Isabella asked with a laugh. The thought of the Marquess of Bellfourd in a private setting with the governess was a preposterous one.

Lord Bellfourd made a show of holding up his candelabra in the dark to look for others. He smiled back down at her, with a teasing twinkle in his eyes. No words needed to be said; she had caught his meaning.

He bowed in gentlemanly fashion to Isabella. "Goodnight, Isabella," he said, still holding that twinkle, with the golden rays of light reflecting from his tightly pulled back hair.

"Goodnight, Lord Bellfourd," Isabella gave him a similar curtsy but made a point to say his name slowly.

He popped a candle out of its place in the candelabra and handed it over to Isabella.

"For the walk up," he said, before turning and making his way back down the long walkway and to the opposite side of the manor.

The next morning, as Isabella awoke and dressed, she

wondered if she should go down to the breakfast room. Her answer came when Betsy arrived with the basin of hot water.

"Lord Bellfourd gave this to his groomsman this mornin' for me to pass along," she said, handing over a small note.

Miss Watts,

I hope you will find the courage to join Her Grace, Lady Abigail, and myself in the breakfast room this morning.

Regards,

Lord Bellfourd.

"What's it say?" Betsy asked as she practiced yet another hairstyle on Isabella.

"It says I have been invited down to breakfast with the family. I don't know that I should go," she added quickly.

"O' course, ye hav'ta go. I'll make your hair verra fine today, as well, and ye'll enter a proper looking lady."

"But that's just it- I'm not."

"Yes, ye are," Betsy encouraged.

"Not anymore. And I fear that doing such things will only make things harder in the long run. Jacqueline won't need a governess forever. When the time comes for me to leave, I don't want to have unrealistic expectations of my life."

"I see yer point. Best just write a note back. Tell His Lordship that, though he is incredibly kind to you and you are good friends with Lady Abigail, you just couldn't bear to sit for a meal in his company and would much rather eat up here alone."

Isabella scrunched her nose up at Betsy, hearing her words dripping with sarcasm.

Betsy rested her hand on Isabella's shoulder and spoke with wisdom beyond her years, "There's not any wrong in taking a good friendship that is offered. Life can turn and be verra hard at times. Take the good when it comes."

Isabella took Betsy's hand and squeezed it gently. With a glisten to her eyes, she thanked Betsy for her words of encouragement.

Isabella hesitated before the breakfast room doors. She lifted her hand to knock, then lowered it again.

"Is there something you need, Miss Watts?" Mrs. Peterson said, appearing from nowhere.

"No, I..." Isabella faltered.

"Miss Watts, I'm so glad you got my note," a voice called from behind her.

Isabella turned to see Lord Bellfourd sauntering down the hall. He looked much more refreshed than the night before.

He opened the breakfast room door and motioned for Isabella to go on before him. She hesitated for a moment, torn between the friendly gesture in front and the venomous daggers from behind.

Finally, she bid Lord Bellfourd a good morning and

made her way in. She heard him give a cheerful salutation to Mrs. Peterson before entering the room himself.

Lord Bellfourd had a very smug look on his face as he kissed his mother on the cheek before helping Isabella into her chair.

"Mother, I hope you don't mind. I invited Miss Watts to dine with us."

"I don't mind at all," Lady Wintercrest said with a polite smile in Isabella's direction. "You look very pretty today," she added for good measure.

"Thank you, Your Grace. May I ask how His Grace is doing this morning?"

"I saw him just before coming to breakfast," Lady Wintercrest answered. "The doctor saw him early this morning before departing. He was in a grumpy mood over the early hour. Of course, the doctor has others to tend to and couldn't stay long. I took his cantankerous disposition as a good sign he was feeling better," she added with hope in her eyes.

"That is wonderful to hear," Lady Abigail said as she, too, entered the room. She said her good mornings around the table and took her seat.

"Tell us, Christian," Lady Wintercrest said, halfway through the meal, "how was your time in London?"

"It was fine," Lord Bellfourd said, doing his best to hide his distaste for the season.

"Just before leaving," he continued, "I went to a ball hosted by the Earl and Countess of Cunningham."

"Oh yes, Lady Mary Cunningham! How is my dear friend?" Lady Wintercrest asked conversationally.

Isabella did her best not to show any recognition of the name.

"I only spoke with her for a brief moment. She was very sad that you were not able to make it to London. She suggested coming to visit you at the end of the season."

"That would be so wonderful," Lady Wintercrest said clapping her hands together.

"Well," Lord Bellfourd added cautiously, "I believe it might have something to do with her daughter Lady Lydia Prescott visiting along with her."

"That's right. Mary's daughter is only three or four years younger than yourself. It would be a wonderful idea to have them both visit."

"Wonderful for who?" Lady Abigail asked with a giggle. "I can't believe, dear brother, you were in town for scarcely half a season, and already you find yourself someone's beau."

Isabella kept her eyes on her breakfast plate and nibbled at her toast. She didn't know why but raging jealousy ran through her veins at the mere thought of Lord Bellfourd courting Lady Lydia. Most likely it was because she had such high regards for Lord Bellfourd.

"I am not anyone's beau. This is my point, exactly," he

said turning to his mother again, "I wouldn't want to encourage a wrong opinion."

"Oh, nonsense," Lady Wintercrest waved him off with a new light of excitement in her eyes. "She is a friend, visiting with her daughter. It would be ridiculous to rumor otherwise."

"What about Father's condition. He won't be fully healed in time. It might not be prudent to have guests."

"You told me the doctor said six to eight weeks before he was whole again. She would not be here until well past that. Even still if His Grace is not well, he will understand my need for a visit with a dear old friend of mine."

Lord Bellfourd looked unsure of his mother's motives. More than likely, the duchess was planning to spend the remainder of the summer plotting with her friend to play matchmaker.

"I will write to Lady Cunningham this afternoon and inform her that she is most welcome to come stay with us."

16

*T*he night of Jacqueline's birthday was a wonderful celebration. Happily, both Isabella and Mrs. Murray had joined the family and the birthday girl for a beautiful celebratory meal.

The duke was still unwell and in a lot of pain. Therefore, he was not able to join in on the festivities.

After dinner, the whole party retired to the drawing room for presents and, more importantly, Jacqueline's performance at the pianoforte for the family.

"A new dress for my doll," Jacqueline exclaimed as she took out Isabella's modest gift. "Merci, Mademoiselle Watts," she said, hugging her governess.

"That turned out so lovely," Lady Wintercrest said, "you really have a talent for embroidery."

"Thank you, Your Grace," Isabella responded shyly.

Spending the last two days with the family for meals had created a more comfortable atmosphere for Isabella in the home.

"Well, are you going to play for me now, Jackie?" Lord Bellfourd asked as he tickled his niece.

Jacqueline giggled, then got up to take her governess' hand. The walked over and sat down at the piano together, as they had so often in the school room over the past few months.

Isabella began by playing a sweet melodic undertone. Waiting for her time to enter, Jacqueline plunked away at her memorized keys in the right order to make the tune of Twinkle, Twinkle Little Star.

Once the song was done, the room burst into applause. Jacqueline got up and curtsied just as Isabella had taught her to do.

Isabella noticed Mrs. Murray in the corner dabbing at a stray tear.

"Awe, Nursie," Lady Abigail said affectionately. "Are you getting all soppy eyed on us?"

"Ach, no. It's just a fine thing to have a wee lass so willing to take music lessons. Much more enjoyable than say, cleaning marmalade off the pianoforte," she added with a teasing tone.

"It was only the one time," Lady Abigail replied. "I don't think my governess was anywhere near as wonderful as Isabella. I am sure I would have been proficient at it, if I had such a magnificent tutor."

The night ended with a plate of petit fours and tea before everyone retired to their respective rooms. Isabella happily held onto Jacqueline's hand as she skipped her way up the massive stairs to her room, with Mrs. Murray on her other side.

Over the last few months, Isabella had watched Jacqueline blossom from a quiet child to a joyful little girl. Isabella hoped that her presence had helped Jackie feel more comfortable in making Wintercrest Manor her home.

After depositing the little girl to bed with her nurse, Isabella retired to her own room. She had received a letter just that morning from Louisa and was excited to sit down and read it before bed.

My dear Izzy,

I hope that my letter finds you well.

The season is in full swing now, and I can scarcely find time to have a quiet evening at home. Typically, this would be an exciting time.

I fear that without you here, I perceive things to be rather dull. I am often dreading our various dinner engagements and dances, knowing that I will not have you there to make it all the more enjoyable.

I did have a pleasing chance encounter that I thought I might share with you. It was at an event held by the Earl of Cunningham. I am sure you know why I was most especially dreading this engagement.

Mother insisted that Colton and I attend. So, with great reluctance, I went. It was there that two marvelous happenstances occurred.

The first, I was introduced to The Marquess of Bellfourd. He was kind enough to recognize my name in meeting, and asked if I was the friend you spoke to his sister about. Once I confirmed it was correct, I spent a greater part of the night in conversation with the gentleman.

It was a pleasant time, spent reminiscing about some of my fondest memories with you. Lord Bellfourd even danced with me- twice! I do think, for the most part, it was to keep himself otherwise engaged.

I am sure you can only imagine the scene that followed the heir of a dukedom with no current attachments.

I must admit that one of the interested parties was none other than Lady Lydia. This is what brings me to my second occurrence. While Lord Bellfourd was yet talking to my brother, Lady Lydia came to join in the small party we had formed.

I am sure I don't have to remind you how awful she was to me as a child at Mrs. Mason's school. I still don't think I could ever forgive her for dipping my hair in ink during our lessons. Life was undoubtedly horrid with Lady Lydia before you joined our school.

Well, Colton was well aware of who Lady Lydia was, and how she had tormented me as a child, and when she came to join our group, he went out of his way to not include her in the conversation.

Apparently, this didn't deter her, as she seemed to have some connection to Lord Bellfourd's family.

Lord Bellfourd and Colton were discussing the Marquess' time as a captain in the Royal Navy. I am sure you can guess that Colton was enthralled by his tales, wishing that he, too, could have a taste of adventure. Lady Lydia took the opportunity to comment to Lord Bellfourd on his "bravery, when surely other men would shrink at such dangerous settings."

Now, you know I am not one to often speak up and say what I think, as you are so frequently courageous enough to do, but Colton, on the other hand, never shies away from a situation.

My dear brother looked Lady Lydia right in the eyes and said, "I dare say a sign of true character and bravery is when one stands up to their persecutors and refuses to let their taunting dishearten and run them away from the battle."

Of course, Lord Bellfourd did not entirely grasp his meaning, but both Lady Lydia and I did. She rose up quite shamefully and excused herself from our company.

I know that my brother can be a very trying tease at times, but I don't think I could have ever been prouder to call him my sibling than at that moment.

I hope that, in some way, it made Lady Lydia think on the harsh way she treated not only me, but so many others as a child. I fear, though, that a lady of her personality will always find the need to bring others down to make herself feel all the better.

I do hope that you are still getting on well in your new home.

You must write back to me soon and tell me all about your pupil's reaction to her birthday gift. You were always an excellent hand at embroidery and I am sure that it was a beautiful treasure to behold.

I hope that someday our paths do cross again but until then, you shall remain my dearest long-distance friend.

Louisa

Isabella smiled down at her friend's words as she read them over a second time. She missed Louisa terribly. It wasn't until she saw the smudge of ink on the third read through that she realized she was crying.

If she thought long and hard about it, there wasn't much she could say with certainty that she missed about her life back in London. Louisa was one of the few people her heart dearly ached to see again.

Isabella drifted off to sleep that night with a single thought in her head. Perhaps, one day, she would be reunited with her sincerest, most faithful friend.

17

*D*ear Louisa,

   The last few months passed by in a blur of activity. With autumn arriving, I have begun to feel what authentic cold weather is like up north.

   I am spending much of the day occupied with Jackie and her studies. Jackie is incredibly smart and has already learned to read the Lord's Prayer and several other Bible passages on her own. We have also worked to improve Jacqueline's handwriting in both English and French so that she might start to write to her mother on her own.

   With the return of Lord Bellfourd for the remainder of the summer, we have had many glorious afternoons outside, exploring the vast estate Wintercrest has to offer in his company.

   For Jackie's seventh birthday, the Marquess bestowed upon her a very fine pony of her own. Because of this, at least two or three days a week, Jackie and I spend our afternoons out riding.

I offered to stay behind while Lord Bellfourd took his niece on these equestrian trips, but he insisted I join them. I must admit that I did not realize how much I had missed riding. It reminds me so much of our many trips riding through the parks in the warmth of a London summer.

Though the Duke of Wintercrest has recovered from his fall, he is sadly still not in the best of health. He remains in his study, in bed, for most of the day. He still struggles to take in air and says there is an awful pain in his side when he stands. The doctor has been by many times to attend to his patient, but I fear there is not much else that can be done for the duke.

Because of his condition, he refuses to see Jackie at all. Instead, I stand before him twice a week and explain to him all that Jackie has learned thus far. I do my very best to show her in the most glorious light, in hopes that the duke will find favor with her but so far, it is to no avail.

With the duke still so ill, Lord Bellfourd has taken on the responsibilities of the house. I can see that it is a great weight on his shoulders and one he still struggles to accept. I do my best to show him, every day, that the improvements he has made to the estate and the household make Wintercrest all the more enjoyable to live in.

One such change was the move of my quarters from the attic to the room adjoining the school room and apartments that Jackie uses. I did enjoy my little attic room and port window, but cannot complain, for it is a much shorter distance to travel to my pupil.

I am also happy to find that the accommodations in my new room are much better furnished for the post of governess. I have a small bookshelf, which I happily use for the novels I brought with me. I also have a lovely fireplace with a comfortable chair beside it, where I can read and embroider in the evening. There is also a small writing desk that I am now using as I write my letters to you.

I am also happy to say that the proximity has been a lessened burden on Betsy, who had the terrible task of walking all the way to the far end of the house to bring me supplies each morning.

Betsy has become such a kind friend to me. Each morning, as she deposits my basin of hot water, she also takes a moment to practice her skills in plaiting hair. She hopes to be a lady's maid someday, and I dare say she will be, with such a gentle touch and fantastic talent.

Although these last months have been filled with joy, something is weighing me down in the back of my mind.

As I told you in my last letter, Lord Bellfourd has invited me to take breakfast with the family and occasional family dinners.

It was at this that I learned how close of a relation the Earl and Lady Cunningham have with my present company. In fact, Lady Wintercrest is such dear friends with Lady Cunningham that she has recently invited her, as well as Lady Lydia, to come stay at the manor after their time in town.

I am sure you can guess the main reason for such encouragement to bring Lady Lydia here. I am not only dreading the arrival of the lady but the possibility of Lord Bellfourd attaching himself to her.

Lord Bellfourd is such a warm and kind gentleman, I can't even imagine him finding interest in a woman with such a high nose in the air.

I know that my feelings toward Lady Lydia have been tainted by past experiences. I tell myself every day, as we draw closer to her arrival, that I must not judge the lady by our childhood, but cannot help but do so.

I genuinely hope that she is a changed woman and much more agreeable company. I do, however, find solace in the fact that if she is not, I will often be able to retire to my own privacy and not have to spend much time socializing with her.

I suppose that is one of the many excellent benefits I have in my new station.

Warmest Regards,

Izzy

18

*a*fter leaving her letter to be posted, Isabella made her way up to Jacqueline for her morning lessons. She was very excited about the upcoming plans she had for Jackie's education.

They would spend the morning reading *On the Approach of Autumn* and other poems by Amelia Opie, a favorite of Isabella's. Then Isabella planned to take Jackie out after lunch for an afternoon of exploring the changing foliage of fall.

Aside from collecting colorful leaves and warm color flowers to decorate the school room, Isabella hoped also to catch a few caterpillars. She was excited to make a project of them for the duration of the winter and following spring months.

Isabella remembered doing such a project herself as a

young girl. Each week she would take care of and carefully watch the fattening caterpillar till it retired to its magical cocoon. Isabella recalled the charm of watching the insect expand from its home the following spring, a beautiful new creature.

Isabella was excited to share such a memorable experience with her pupil. It was not only an informative lesson in natural science, but also an easy comparison to the process of oneself developing into a beautiful, graceful young lady.

After a cozy morning reading by the fire and a light luncheon, Isabella followed the excited Jackie as they made their way out past the central gardens of the estate. Isabella came armed with a large basket, prepared for collecting treasures, and a jar home for caterpillars.

Isabella tightened the thick woolen shawl that Mrs. Murray had knitted for her closer to her bodice. She was so grateful for Mrs. Murray's motherly tendencies and was confident that she would have frozen without them this winter.

The sky was turning from its usual, everyday grey to a much more sinister hew of green. Because of this, Isabella decided they should not stray too far past the safety of the manor in the event of rain.

They walked joyfully along the wooden paths extending outward from the manicured gardens in a happy step. From time to time, Jackie would stop to point out an orange-hued leaf that had fallen to the ground or a wild-flower still finding bloom in the late season. All were collected and tucked safely in Isabella's basket.

They finally arrived at the small meadow that Jackie enjoyed so much. It was wide and open with deciduous trees framing its outline. Just before entering the field, Isabella caught a movement and stopped Jackie from going any further.

"Look," Isabella whispered, coming down to Jackie's level.

Jackie focused her eyes on the meadow in front of her. Then she gasped in delight as she saw two white ears poking up from the tall grass.

"Miss Watts, is it a white rabbit?"

Both girls crouched quietly at the edge of the meadow while they watched the top of the white rabbit hop from place to place. Every so often, he would stop and lift himself on his hind legs to sniff the air for danger.

"It must be," Isabella said very softly. "Look how he hops around."

"Do you think I can follow him?"

"Marvelous idea. Though, you must let me come with you," Isabella said, setting her basket to the side.

"We must move slowly and quietly. If we frighten him, he will run in a flurry and he may lose his path home."

Jackie nodded in understanding. They moved very

slowly and cautiously as they followed the snow-white bunny to his home.

Isabella didn't pay much mind to how deep the two had crept into the woods, nor did she remember her own admonition to watch the sky for rain.

Finally, the rabbit stopped just before a burrow at the root of a tree. Isabella and Jackie hid behind a large pine and watched. The rabbit stood up, sniffing the air one last time to check for danger before quickly darting into his home.

"Let's go, too," Jackie said with innocence.

Before Isabella could respond, a giant droplet of water made its way through the trees and landed right on top of Isabella's bonnet. She looked up, remembering the darkening sky. Another fat drop of water fell right on her forehead between the dark curls that framed her face.

"Oh dear, I wasn't paying attention. Jackie, we must hurry home before we get soaked."

"We haven't collected our caterpillars yet," Jackie said to the sky.

It seemed to Isabella that Jacqueline was telling the sky to hold off on its autumn downpour. Unfortunately, it didn't listen.

Isabella and Jackie ran from tree to tree seeking some shelter from the torrential downpour of rain. By the time they got back to the meadow, they were both soaked to the bone.

Isabella wrapped her own woolen shawl around Jacqueline's pelisse hoping to keep as much cold and moisture off of her as possible. Running as fast as she could in her soaked petticoats, Isabella scooped up the basket of treasures and empty jar and made her way, Jackie in hand, back up to the manor house.

By the time they made it to the service entrance at the side of the house, Isabella could scarcely see in front of her, so thick were the sheets of rain coming down.

She hurried Jackie inside to the protection of the house. She found Mrs. Murray waiting for them in the dining hall.

"Oh, I was worried something fierce over you two lasses," she said coming to them and peeling off Jacqueline's sopping shawl hat and jacket.

"The rain just came so suddenly," Isabella said through chattering teeth.

"Well, we best get the wee lass upstairs. I'll have a nice hot bath made for her."

Isabella nodded in agreement, but before she could make a move, Mrs. Peterson entered the room.

"Miss Watts, I would like a word with you, if you please," she said curtly.

"Can it not wait till they've had a chance to get some fresh, dry clothes on?" Mrs. Murray replied, having no fear of the housekeeper like all the other servants.

"It's alright," Isabella assured the nurse. "I will be but a moment and join you both upstairs."

Without a further word, Mrs. Peterson turned on her heels in her usual fashion, expecting Isabella follow. She did as was expected and accompanied the housekeeper to her small office.

Isabella stood for a moment before the harsh wooden desk in the small office. There was no sound save the rustling of Mrs. Peterson's keys and the dripping of Isabella's skirts.

Mrs. Peterson had originally been as equally unkind and unfeeling toward Isabella as she was to the rest of the servants. That had changed, as of late. Since the change of her living quarters and the daily invitations to dine with the family, Mrs. Peterson had taken on a particular dislike for Isabella.

She was now continually interjecting herself, not only into every movement that Isabella made, but also into Jacqueline's education. Isabella was an affront to the propriety Mrs. Peterson made it her mission to uphold in the Wintercrest household.

"I don't like to discuss matters with His Grace concerning the running of his staff unless absolutely necessary," Mrs. Peterson began, her cool brown eyes looking hard on Isabella. "I feel I have no choice after today."

"No choice about what?" Isabella asked, confused.

"You took young Miss Jacqueline out in abysmal weather, brought her back chilled to the bone, and quite possibly caused her to catch her death. I cannot sit by silently when such frivolous liberties are taken with a young child's health."

"You speak as if I purposefully took her out into the rain," Isabella retorted, shocked at what she was hearing. "We go out every afternoon, as His Grace has instructed us to do. Naturally, I meant to keep today's exercise short, but we unfortunately still got caught in the rain. I hurried her home as quickly as was possible."

"I don't care to hear your excuses," Mrs. Peterson waved off. "I am in charge of seeing this house run smoothly and I cannot do so if I am constantly watching over you and the decisions you make. I am sorry to say that I will be recommending that His Grace remove you from employment."

"Remove me from employment?" Isabella stammered, shocked at the accusations and threats thrown at her.

Isabella knew keenly that this action had nothing to do with her ability to teach, or even care for, Jacqueline. It had everything to do with her friendship with Lord Bellfourd and Lady Abigail. Mrs. Peterson was looking for any reason to remove her and find what she deemed a more suitable replacement.

"You would honestly go to the Duke of Wintercrest, while he is still very much frail, and burden him with such a trivial event. It was nothing more than an accident. I never meant to keep Jacqueline out in poor weather. The duke, himself, was the one who instructed me to take

Jacqueline on daily walks. I can't imagine he would dismiss me because one such event had a poor ending."

Mrs. Peterson seemed to think this over. Was it really worthwhile to disturb His Grace, when he was already so frail of body, with the worrisome obligation of replacing a governess?

"I suppose you are right," Mrs. Peterson said, standing and placing her hands in front of her. "I will take it up with Lord Bellfourd instead. Please stay in your room for the remainder of the evening until I send for you."

Mrs. Peterson waved her hand by way of excusing Isabella from the room. Isabella was stunned into silence, something she would admit almost never happened to her. She opened and closed her mouth a few times before turning on her heels and storming out of the room.

19

*I*sabella stayed close to her fire in her room that evening. She had changed into her dressing gown allowing her stockings and shift to dry by the heat of the fire. Isabella was worried about Jaqueline since she hadn't been allowed to see the child before being banished to her room for the night.

If only Isabella hadn't pointed out that small rabbit, Mrs. Peterson would have no reason to encourage the Marquess to terminate her service at Wintercrest. She wrung her hands again.

What was she to do? Though Lord Bellfourd was not entirely fond of Mrs. Peterson, he would certainly take her word that Isabella had been irresponsible in the care of his niece. Lord Bellfourd dearly doted on his niece and would do anything if he thought it was for her health and wellbeing.

Was she to be thrown out on the streets this very night? Would she at least be given time to secure employment elsewhere? Even if she was, how was she ever to find another station. She doubted that she would get a recommendation. It seemed impossible that she would ever gain another placement in such conditions.

There was a soft knock at Isabella's door and she quickly ran to answer it. Unfortunately, it was only Sally with her dinner tray.

"Thank you, Sally," Isabella said as she set the tray on the small table by the window, much like the one in her former room.

"I suppose everyone downstairs knows about..." Isabella said, unable to find the right words.

She wished it was Betsy who had brought her tray. With Betsy, she could be more open. Even ask her what a person was meant to do in such an instance. She had only gotten the employment via her family lawyer. How was she to seek a new situation without his help?

"Yes, Miss. I'm sorry to say news travels very fast downstairs," Sally said with pure sincerity.

"Do you suppose Mrs. Peterson will really do it? That is, recommend to Lord Bellfourd that I be removed?"

Sally's eyes hit the floor and that was answer enough. Perhaps the deed was already done, and Mrs. Peterson was simply satisfying herself with making Isabella wait in the unknown.

With glistening eyes, Sally excused herself from the room, unable to answer.

Isabella sat down in her chair, and looked at the meal before her. She could barely touch her boiled potatoes as she listened to the seconds tick by.

Finally, she came to the realization of what must be done. She would use the small funds she had at her disposal and return to London. There she would do the unthinkable and give herself to the mercy of Mr. Smith.

She was overwhelmed by a wave of sorrow and fear. Her heart ached to leave what had become her home and quivered at the thought of Mr. Smith.

She saw no other way around it. Tears slipped silently down her cheeks as she looked out the window and held on to her locket. Would he be even more cruel to her because she had taken the trinket with her? Perhaps he would even have her thrown in jail.

A knock at the door woke her again from her fears. She quickly wiped her eyes before opening it.

Mrs. Peterson stood solemnly before her. Isabella opened the door fully to let the housekeeper in. Mrs. Peterson did not move from her spot, however.

"Lord Bellfourd will see you in the library," was all she said before turning and walking down the hall.

It was such a short, rude statement that Isabella didn't

know what to make of it. She had assumed Mrs. Peterson would enter smugly and tell her to pack her bags. It was apparently up to Lord Bellfourd, himself, to see her properly terminated.

Isabella quickly slipped into her still-damp shift and cotton stockings. She decided to put on her best ember-velvet evening dress. If she was going to be removed, she would do it in the finest way possible.

She did her best to fix the sodden black curls that lay flat against her face and rub the swollen tears from her green eyes. Taking a deep breath, she held her head up high, squared her shoulders, and left the room.

Isabella stood before the library door. She took a steadying breath before knocking.

"Come in," Lord Bellfourd called from within.

Isabella entered the room and shut the door behind her. She found Lord Bellfourd sitting behind the desk that was once in the study next door. The library was fashioned into a temporary study for Lord Bellfourd since his father was still recuperating and unable to leave the office.

He was looking down at some work on his desk. Isabella couldn't bear to meet his gaze and instead looked at the hands folded in front of her, as she stood before the Marquess.

She let her eyes travel around the room just once. She was surprised to be alone with the Marquess. She had almost expected to see Mrs. Peterson standing behind him at his right with a big, fat, smug grin across her long face.

She had spent many times alone with the duke discussing the educational progress of her pupil and never once thought a second about it. Being alone in this candle lit room with the Marquess made her feel a little less like an employee speaking with her employer.

She was almost positive that despite any teasing he may have made in the past, in that moment, Isabella was no longer a friend but an employee. Not just that, but a servant who hadn't performed her duties up to standard.

"Isabella, whatever is the matter?" Lord Bellfourd said, looking upon her fallen countenance.

He got up from his seat and came around to her side. The culmination of fear and guilt overflowed within her and Isabella started to cry softly.

He gently led her to a pair of chairs in front of the fire. Kneeling in front of her, he gave her a soft white handker-chief. "Please tell me what has you so upset, so that I may fix it," he said, looking at her with concern.

Isabella met his soft blue gaze with her own fearful green eyes. "I am so sorry, Lord Bellfourd. I didn't mean to cause any harm to Jackie. We simply lost track of time. I understand if you are going to dismiss me, but please let me at least see Jackie one last time, to say goodbye."

"Dismiss you? Why on earth would I do such a thing? Jackie has learned so much; she loves you dearly."

"Mrs. Peterson informed me that she would be recommending that you terminate my employment."

"She may recommend as she likes," Lord Bellfourd said with a smile, "She is not lord of this manor." He reached out his hand and touched her chin just briefly. Isabella lifted her gaze to meet his. "Your departure from this house will never be my doing. I promise you that," he said full of emotion.

He let his hand fall before smiling softly at her. He stood and walked over to a small cabinet with some glass decanters on top.

"Here, have some sherry," he said, handing her a small glass. "It will settle your nerves."

Isabella took it gratefully and sipped slowly as Lord Bellfourd took a seat in the adjacent chair.

"If you don't mind me asking, Lord Bellfourd, why is it that you asked me here, if it was not to excuse me."

"After Mrs. Peterson informed me that you and Jackie had been caught in this terrible weather, I went to Jackie's nursery to check on her. Mrs. Murray told me she had a nice warm bath and had only gotten halfway through her dinner before falling asleep. She was exhausted, but I assure you she is very well," he added, to calm Isabella's concerned brow over the child.

"I asked Mrs. Murray if you were well yourself. Since you had not been back to the nursery after coming out of the rain, she wasn't entirely sure. I simply asked Mrs.

Peterson to bring you to me so that I might inquire for myself on your condition."

"I wanted to go to Jackie," Isabella explained, "but Mrs. Peterson confined me to my room."

Lord Bellfourd's rust-colored brows furrowed in frustration and he slammed his cup down on the table next to him.

"That is preposterous! You are never to be confined anywhere, or kept from Jackie. I will speak to Mrs. Peterson at once."

"Please don't, Lord Bellfourd. I fear she already dislikes me so much. I don't want to make things worse."

"I don't want you to feel uncomfortable here, Isabella, so if you wish me not to speak with her, I won't. I do ask that if there are any more problems, you come straight to me. Promise you will?" he asked with a tone of concern.

Isabella hesitated. Overstepping the authority of the housekeeper couldn't be the right thing to do.

"You are not just the governess here," he added, reading Isabella's thoughts. "You are a dear friend to my sister and you have been a great support to me during my father's illness. The entire family sees you as a true friend and a great blessing. I want you to feel comfortable to come to me with any problems that arise."

Isabella struggled to keep her emotions in check. Coming to Wintercrest Manor had been a more significant blessing to her than it ever could be to them.

"I promise, Christian," Isabella said softly.

At hearing his name softly escape Isabella's lips, Lord Bellfourd's eyes lit up with pleasure. "Wonderful," he said showing her his full handsome smile.

He paused for a moment, then looked at her with his cat eyes, "Would you mind terribly..." he started. He rubbed his chin seeming to think of how to ask his question. "You see, Mother and Abigail have already retired for the night, but I still have a great deal of work ahead of me. If it wouldn't be too much of an inconvenience, would you stay here with me for a while and keep me company?"

Isabella blushed at his question. Her stomach spun with butterflies at the prospect of staying here, as an intimate friend, while he continued his work.

"Of course, if you are too tired yourself, I understand," he added, when she didn't answer right away.

"No. I mean, yes." She gave a soft laugh at her silly nervousness. "What I mean to say, Lord..."

Lord Bellfourd raise a brow at her.

"I mean, Christian, is I would be happy to keep you company. I have some embroidery in the drawing room I can work on.

She liked the feeling of speaking his name almost as much as seeing the joy it gave him.

"I will send someone to fetch it for you, then," he answered with a satisfied grin playing on his square jaw.

Isabella sat quietly in the chair by the fire. For the most

part, they worked in silence. The only sound in the room was the crackling of the fire and scratching of Lord Bellfourd's quill. From time to time, Lord Bellfourd would walk over from his desk and place another log on the fire.

It was a comfortable silence between them as they went about their own work in each other's company. Occasionally, when Lord Bellfourd went to stoke the fire they would take a moment or two to talk.

Soon, the hour grew late. Isabella hadn't realized how tiresome her stressful night had actually been, till she settled down next to the warm glow of the fire. Without knowing it, she dozed off to sleep in the library chair late in the evening.

Lord Bellfourd saw her sleeping state, and not wanting to wake her, took the jacket he was wearing and gently draped it over her resting body. He looked down at her as she lay asleep with the glow of the fire dancing lightly across her soft dark lashes. He had never felt such a gripping pain in all his life as he did in that moment when he saw Isabella's tear soaked cheeks. He also had never felt as much pleasure as the moment he heard his name slip from Isabella's lips.

He went back to his desk to quietly finish his work as he contemplated his feelings toward the young lady sitting next to him. Surely, the last year had been a great hardship for her and she was in a delicate state. She seemed so sincere in her friendship with his family and, more especially, his niece, but he wondered how she honestly felt about him.

He shook his head with a silent laugh. He couldn't develop feelings for the governess. Such a thing would simply be too much for his father.

He didn't particularly agree with the standards held by the Duke of Wintercrest, nor had they ever exactly been on good terms with each other, but he couldn't bring himself to think such thoughts that might upset his father and therefore worsen his fragile health.

20

*I*sabella woke in the morning with her neck sore and confused as to where she was. She felt a light shaking and realized she wasn't alone. She sat up quickly, confused by the jacket laying over her.

"Lord Bellfourd," she stammered looking at the tall figure standing over her. "I'm so sorry, did I fall asleep? Wait, is it morning?" She looked around the room, noticing it was much lighter.

"Yes," Lord Bellfourd said with a chuckle. "I'm sorry to say I kept you up far too late last night. You fell asleep and I couldn't bring myself to wake you."

"So, we stayed here all night?" Isabella asked, dancing between confusion and horror.

"No. I had a very restful night in my own bed. You, however, did sleep here all night. It is still early though. I thought I should come wake you before the servants found you. I figured there had been enough talk about you last night."

"Yes," Isabella said, standing up.

She did her best to brush the wrinkles out of her delicate velvet dress and feel that her hair wasn't too much of a terrible mess.

"I'm sorry. I must be a dreadful sight," Isabella said.

"Not at all," Lord Bellfourd said with a soft smile.

It made Isabella blush. She handed back his coat from the previous night without looking up at him again. He had no need for it. He had already changed into a vibrant green morning jacket and a soft blue waistcoat that brought out the color of his eyes.

"Well, I had best be off, then," he said taking a step back from Isabella. "I will see you at breakfast, though?" he half stated, half asked.

"Yes, of course, Lord...I mean, Christian," she corrected herself, much to his satisfaction.

Isabella hurried up the stairs of the west wing and into her room. She found a basin of hot water already waiting for her. She prayed that it had been Betsy who deposited it.

Betsy wouldn't mention Isabella's unused bed without asking her about it first. Any of the other maids, however, and she was likely already circulating gossip in the dining hall.

After changing into a fresh cotton dress in a soft pink

with a blue waist ribbon, she did her best to re-do her hair before making her way out of the room again.

Isabella stopped in to see Jackie who was having her morning meal with Mrs. Murray.

"Oh, Miss Watts, wasn't yesterday so exciting!" Jackie said, upon seeing her teacher.

"Exciting is not the word I would use," Isabella said in return.

"May we get our caterpillars today, since we could not get one yesterday?" Jackie asked in her sweet fashion.

"Are you feeling well enough to venture out again?" Isabella looked her pupil over. She was wearing a navy-blue cotton dress with matching spencer jacket, all decorated with small, blue velvet bows around the trimming. Mrs. Murray had fashioned Jackie's golden locks into a long loose look with two matching, blue ribbon bows to adorn it.

She didn't seem to be feeling ill or looking pale to Isabella, but she wasn't going to take chances.

"I am very well, thank you," Jackie responded politely, like rote memorization.

"Well, if you promise you are feeling well, and there is absolutely no chance of rain, then I see no reason why we can't go and collect some specimens," Isabella said with a light tease.

After promising to return after breakfast, Isabella made

her way down to the morning room. She was, however, stopped short in the hall by Mrs. Peterson.

She stood there, as if she had been waiting for this moment to come.

"It is only a matter of time before His Grace is well again," she stated simply.

Isabella was fully aware of her meaning. As soon as the Duke of Wintercrest was well enough to move about, the estate duties would fall back to him. All Mrs. Peterson would need was one more reason to dismiss Isabella, and the duke would be much more easily swayed than Lord Bellfourd.

"I pray every day that His Grace will recover quickly," Isabella responded, indifferent to the woman's threats.

Isabella held on to the comfort of Lord Bellfourd's words from the night before. He would never allow her to be removed from the estate. Surely, his word would have more sway with his father than that of the housekeeper.

Isabella didn't wait for a response from Mrs. Peterson but, instead, walked past her without a second glance. Her heart was racing, and she struggled not to ball her fists. It was horrid of that woman to harass her so.

Though Isabella did pray every day for the duke to return to health, she couldn't help but think of the day that Lord Bellfourd would be solely in charge. On that day, she was sure Mrs. Peterson would find herself without employment. Isabella hoped that she would still be around to see that day come to fruition.

"Good morning Your Grace, Lady Abigail," Isabella said, coming into the breakfast room.

She let the whole encounter with Mrs. Peterson wash away from her memory.

"Sarah, my lady's maid, told me this morning that Jacqueline and yourself got caught in the downpour yesterday afternoon," Lady Wintercrest said in conversation. "I do hope you both didn't get too wet. It is a terrible time of the year to be exposed to sickness."

"We did get caught, quite unexpectedly. I am happy to say that I visited Jackie just this morning and she was in good health and spirits."

"Yes, I expect she found it to be a fun adventure," Lady Abigail added.

"Indeed, she did," Isabella agreed.

"Rainstorms can be hard to spot in these parts," Lady Wintercrest continued. "I, myself, got caught in a few when I first came to Wintercrest. Sometimes a good soaking is beneficial for the skin," she added with an encouraging smile.

Lord Bellfourd entered the room and, greeting all present with a good morning, took his place at the table.

"Christian, I am so glad you are here. I was worried we wouldn't see you this morning after you had such a late night in the library."

For an instant, Lord Bellfourd flashed his crystal eyes in Isabella's direction, but she didn't look back. He was satisfied with the little rose coloring that brushed against her cheeks at the mention of the late night.

"Yes, I had a lot of work to get through, Mother."

"Well, I hope the worst of it is done. I have just received very exciting news in the morning post. It seems that Lady Cunningham, as well as her daughter Lady Lydia, have accepted my invitation. They will be joining us here no later than the end of this week."

"That's wonderful for you, Mother. I am glad to hear that you will get some time to visit with such a dear friend of yours."

"Well, it is not just good news for me, but for you as well," Lady Wintercrest encouraged.

"Oh yes, dear brother," Lady Abigail giggled, in teasing fashion. "This is your opportunity to secure a most desirable match."

Lord Bellfourd gave his sister a pointed look that showed he didn't like her joke. "I don't think Lady Lydia will find Wintercrest to her liking," he said, obviously referring to himself and not to the estate.

"Well, of course, she would. Why shouldn't she? Wintercrest is a wonderful place that any young lady would be honored to call home," the Duchess replied, clearly understanding the undertone message her son was getting across. "That said, I do expect you to be at your very best," Her Grace added as an afterthought.

"Of course, Mother. I had told the cook to roast a whole animal in front of the house, as the natives in the West Indies do, but since I am to be on my best behavior I will cancel the meal," Lord Bellfourd retorted with a tease.

21

Though the morning was just as grey as the day before, by the afternoon there were short breaks in the thin clouds, allowing for moments of sunshine. Isabella determined that the weather was safe enough to go outside and collect their science project.

For the second time in two days, they walked along the wooden path to their favorite meadow. Only this time, both girls promised not to go chasing any white rabbits.

Isabella brought an old quilt with her and laid it down on the long, soft grass, heavy with the end of summer. She sat contentedly while Jackie went about the meadow recollecting autumn treasures to add to Isabella's basket.

"I found one," Jackie called out to Isabella.

Isabella got up from her seated place with the jar in hand and made her way over to Jackie.

"Oh, look at that one," Isabella exclaimed, leaning down to get a better look at the plump green caterpillar munching away happily on a cloudberry bush.

"Do you think he will spin me some silk?" Jackie asked her teacher.

"I'm afraid not," Isabella said getting her jar ready for its new inhabitant.

"But he is so fat, he must have extra he can spin for me," Jackie said with a sad tone.

"I am sorry to tell you that it isn't the size of the caterpillar that determines if it spins silk but the variety. Only silk worms spin silk cocoons."

"May we catch one of those too, then?" she asked in innocence.

"Unfortunately, they do not live freely in this part of the world. If you would like, however, I will tell you a story my father told me. It is about the time he sailed on a boat full of silkworms as a lad."

After scooping her plump new friend into his home, Jackie followed her teacher over to the blanket to hear the tale.

"You remember I told you how silkworms escaped China," Isabella said in a dramatic tone.

Jackie nodded her head in excitement, "Two monks went to China and hid them in their walking stick to take back to their home."

"Do you remember where their home was?"

"Byzantine Empire," she replied smartly.

"Very good, Jackie," Isabella praised.

"Well, of course, that was hundreds of years ago. So, by the time my father was a lad, the silkworm had traveled all the way to France, and even to a few producers here in England.

"This was the cause of my father's voyage. He was assigned to a small merchant ship that was to sail to India to acquire the best silkworms possible for an aspiring nobleman.

"He said that when they got to India, he saw colors his eyes had never beheld. Women were draped in silks of bright green and orange, with gold bangles tinkling as they walked. He smelled spices that had never reached his nose before. He was very reluctant to leave when the time came to set sail again. He was just fifteen years old, entranced by the beauty of the exotic land, and felt no holds to return to his homeland."

"What of his family?" Jackie asked.

"Well, my father's parents both died when he was a very small boy. He was raised by an older brother. He had to get a job and provide for himself at a very young age which is why he took to the sea.

"So, very reluctantly, he had to go back to his ship because he had contracted with the captain to stay aboard for four more years.

"But as he walked the lower decks of the ship he was amazed to see what lay before him."

"Were there just little worms crawling everywhere?" Jackie asked with a giggle.

"He expected as much, but it was not so. You see, he told me that silkworms were very particular creatures and liked things just so. The only way one could move them was while they were still in their eggs."

"So, when he came down to the storage deck of the ship, expecting creepy crawling worms," she said tickling Jackie with a piece of long grass, "instead he saw boxes and boxes lined with small shelves with little white eggs safely nuzzled in straight little rows.

"Along with the worms were large mulberry bushes. You see, not only are silkworms very particular about the temperature they live in but they only have a taste for one type of plant."

"They are awfully picky little things," Jackie proclaimed, scrunching her button nose. "Just like Grandpère."

"Oh, I know your grandfather can be very severe at times," Isabella said, comforting the child, "but he does what, in his mind, is best."

"Also," Isabella said, as a side thought, "think of His Grace like the silkworms. Yes, they are very particular creatures but, because of it, something beautiful results. His family is the beautiful result of your grandfather's life work.

You are part of that family," Isabella encouraged. "You are the great beauty that came from one particular silkworm's life of toil."

Jacqueline seemed to think over her governess' story. "Nursie said your father was Baron Leinister. How could that be if he was a poor sailor?"

"He inherited the title from his older brother who died very young. He had received it, in his turn, from an uncle that had no children of his own. My father was a much older man by that time and had already started his own business of merchant ships."

Jacqueline seemed to think this over in her mind. Isabella was sure that the peerage was a hard concept for a young child to grasp, but necessary for her circumstance, none the less.

"Does that make you a lady, then?" she finally asked, thoughtfully.

"No," Isabella said with a soft laugh. "It did, however, provide me with an exquisite education, for which I am most grateful. Without it, I don't believe I would have been permitted to be your instructor. That would have been a terrible turn of events."

"I'm glad to have you, too," Jackie said, wrapping her short arms around Isabella's waist.

Isabella happily held the hand of her little pupil as they skipped their way back into the house. They walked the gravel path that led to the main entrance of the house and the most comfortable access that led back to the school room.

Upon entering the house, Isabella was surprised to see that they were not alone in the foyer. Standing before her was the newly arrived Lady Cunningham and her daughter, Lydia.

"Pardon me," Isabella said, intruding on the greeting.

"Oh please, come in, Miss Watts," Her Grace called happily. "Please present my granddaughter to my dear friend."

Isabella walked Jacqueline up to the new guest and she curtsied politely.

"Lady Cunningham, may I present Miss Jacqueline De'belmount and her governess, the honorable Miss Watts," Lord Bellfourd politely announced.

"And this is Lady Lydia Prescott."

"We have met before." Lady Lydia did not return the girls' curtsies.

Lord Bellfourd looked to Isabella with a questioning brow.

"Yes, it's true," Isabella answered his unasked question. "Lady Lydia and I attended the same school in our youth."

"Did you really?" Lady Cunningham said. "What a wonderful happenstance. And you are the child's governess?"

"Yes, Lady Cunningham."

"Well, you are fortunate, indeed, to have her, then,"

Lady Cunningham said turning to Her Grace. "Mrs. Mason's School for Exceptional Young Ladies is the finest in all of London."

"Oh my!" Lady Lydia exclaimed suddenly, taking a step back. "I believe something in your basket just moved!"

Jacqueline reached into the basket and pulled out the jar. Holding it up for all to see, she happily declared, "His name is Henry. We were out for our afternoon walk and collected some beautiful autumn leaves to decorate the school room and Henry, for a nature study."

"My dear Miss Watts," Lady Lydia said with a demeaning tone, "Did you not learn that nature is meant for outdoors? I fear we may all be crawling in insects soon by the look of that basket," she added to the rest of the party with a laugh.

"I'm fairly certain that education in the natural world is important for all children," Lady Abigail retorted, clearly not liking what Lady Lydia had said. "What better way than to bring it in out of the cold and study it?"

"I do have to say," Her Grace added, attempting to smooth over the conversation, "that little Jacqueline has blossomed with the help of her governess. We have been very fortunate to have her with us.

"In fact, Miss Watts," she continued coming to an idea, "would you please bring Jacqueline down to the drawing room after dinner. I would love for Lady Cunningham to see her piano accomplishments."

"I would be happy to, Your Grace,"

As Isabella curtsied and turned to take Jackie upstairs, she could still hear Lady Lydia's voice as they walked to the drawing room.

"I am certainly glad I am not a governess. I couldn't imagine spending my days outside, digging around in the dirt, all in the name of education. What a cumbersome life that must be."

22

*I*sabella readied herself for the evening as best she could. She chose, instead of changing into one of her evening gowns, to wear a simple brown skirt with a white button top and matching brown spencer jacket.

She could only assume, had she gone down in her usual evening attire, as all the other women would, she would be chastened by Lady Lydia for going above her station.

Honestly, she knew Lydia would go out of her way to make her life miserable no matter what course she took.

Isabella was deeply concerned over Lydia's presence. Of course, Lady Abigail had been right to jest that the visitation was for matchmaking purposes. Had Lady Wintercrest picked anyone in the world besides Lady Lydia, Isabella would have grinned and borne it.

Even with her growing attachment to Lord Bellfourd, she would have been willing to stifle her feelings, if she knew that he would be happy with a proper lady. Lady Lydia, on the other hand, was nothing but a pompous brat who spent her childhood vexing Isabella, and many others, every chance she could.

Isabella took a calming breath, smoothing her skirt one final time, before leaving her room to pick up her ward. She was surprised to find Mrs. Peterson present in the room.

"Mrs. Peterson? Is there something I can do for you? I was just about to take Miss Jacqueline down to the family."

"I am well aware of your purpose here tonight," Mrs. Peterson said tartly. She had been especially short with Isabella since trying to have her removed. "I am here to escort you both to the drawing room."

"We are perfectly capable of finding it on our own," Isabella retorted, motioning for Jackie to come to her side. "I thank you for your kind offer, but we are quite able on our own."

Jackie gave a quick hug to her nurse. Mrs. Murray was perched in her regular chair next to the nursery's small stove fire, knitting.

"I am well aware of your familiarities with the drawing room," Mrs. Peterson said with an obvious undertone of disapproval. "It is proper, however, for me to see you in and make sure Her Grace is ready to receive you with a footman's introduction before you go barging in."

Isabella did her best not to stick out her tongue at this horrible woman. Sadly, politeness got the best of her, and she merely nodded her head in acceptance.

They walked down the stairwell in silence, Jackie's little hand inside Isabella's.

"Why is this horrible lady coming with us?" Jacqueline asked just above a whisper, in French.

"It is not polite to call someone horrible," Isabella said out of the corner of her small mouth.

"She cannot understand me," Jackie retorted in pure innocence. Her big blue eyes were looking up at Isabella, unable to comprehend why a change was coming from their usual routine.

"It matters not if the person in question can understand, it is still not polite," Isabella replied with a gentle smile to her pupil.

"Is Grandpère better, then?" Jackie continued.

Isabella could see that, below the gold ringlets, Jackie's mind was turning to create an answer to her own question.

"I am sorry to say that he is still not recovered. If you remember, Her Grace had guests arrive today. I suspect we must be on our best behavior due to this fact, even the housekeeper."

"Miss Watts," Mrs. Peterson said in an irritated tone as

they came to stand before the drawing room doors. "I would remind you that you are not to encourage the child to speak French."

"Of course, Mrs. Peterson," Isabella said, doing her best not to grit her teeth.

"Please wait here while I make sure they are available for your intrusion. Quietly, please!" she added before walking into the room, herself.

Intrusion? Isabella was doing her best to control her temper and the words that seemed to fly out of her mouth at such instances.

"Villain," Jackie said under her breath when Mrs. Peterson had gone.

"Oui," Isabella agreed.

Both girls couldn't help but giggle. It was at that moment, when both the tender Jackie and her governess were thus engaged with hands over mouths to stop their girlish laughter, that Lord Bellfourd came up behind them.

"And what mischief might you two be up to tonight?" he asked as he strolled up, hands in the pockets of his evening jacket.

Isabella turned, flushing red with embarrassment. Her flushed cheeks soon calmed when she came to meet the look of playful delight in the Marquess's blue eyes.

"I told Miss Watts that..."

Isabella shushed the girl before she could continue.

She got down to Jackie's level, "Some things must be left between just us girls," she explained.

Lord Bellfourd raised a rusty brow in question to Isabella's action. "Are you encouraging my niece to keep secrets from me," he asked in a teasing tone.

"Absolutely," Isabella retorted with her own playful gleam in her green eyes.

"All girls must have some secrets. It is often how we make our lasting friendships."

"Well, I suppose I cannot deny you that," he said in agreement.

He took a step closer, bowing his head, as he so often did when he came into proximity to someone so much shorter than himself.

"I must ask you to share one small secret with me, however," he said in a confident tone. "Why are you standing outside the drawing room?"

"One could ask the same of you?" Isabella said, jutting out her small chin just slightly.

"Well, I had no intentions to skulk in the hallway. I am just on my way from my father's side and off to hear the wonderful playing of my little Jackie." He swiped at Jackie's cheek with a playful pinch.

"How is His Grace doing?" Isabella asked with genuine concern in her voice. She had not seen him for the last few weeks, so ill was his constitution.

"I'm afraid no better and he seems only to get worse. The doctor stepped by yesterday and fears that the damage done to his lungs, either from sickness or the fall, is irreversible."

"I pray for him every night," Isabella said, instinctually raising her hand up and resting it on his arm in comfort.

"I know that Jackie does, as well, with Mrs. Murray. We all pray that he will return to health."

Lord Bellfourd removed his hand from his pocket and took Isabella's with a thankful squeeze.

"I appreciate that very much, Isabella."

Isabella hesitated to remove her hand from his touch. Though his hands were rougher than that of a typical gentleman, no doubt due to his life at sea, it was warm and comforting.

Lord Bellfourd smiled softly, just a twitch at the side of his mouth really, before opening it to speak. However, before the words escaped, the drawing room doors were flung open.

Much to the surprise of all the eyes in the drawing room, there stood Isabella and Lord Bellfourd hand in hand, with the cherubim child smiling up at both of them.

Instead of letting go quickly like Isabella wanted to do, Lord Bellfourd instead moved Isabella's hand into the crook of his other arm. He leaned down and offered his, now free, hand to the service of escorting Jackie as well.

Jackie giggled, hopped to her uncle's side, and stood tall as she walked in like a real lady.

"I was just coming from my father's side when I happened upon these two fine ladies," Lord Bellfourd said smoothly.

He certainly had the charm to play off any potentially embarrassing situation, Isabella thought.

"Come here, Jacqueline," Lady Wintercrest called, noticing the entrance of her granddaughter.

She had been in deep conversation with Lady Cunningham, and they two were perhaps the only ones who hadn't seen the shocking proximity of the Marquess and governess.

"Oui, Madame," Jackie said releasing her hold on her uncle and skipping over to her grandmother's side.

Isabella couldn't help but smile as she watched Jackie's beautiful gold curls bounce against the fire glow as she happily obliged.

"I was just telling Lady Cunningham that you sing so beautifully. Would you sing that nursery song your mother use to sing to you?"

"Yes Grandmère," Jackie said dutifully.

"Oh, how splendid," Lady Cunningham said, clapping her gloved hands softly. "I can already tell by your voice that you must be an outstanding singer."

"Now, just stand there, so we may all hear you," Her

Grace said, pointing to the middle of the room. Her face was glowing with pride.

"Lord Bellfourd, do come sit down," Lady Lydia cooed. "I would hate for you to be so far and not hear this little treat."

Lord Bellfourd started to move closer in the room, Isabella on his arm, when she slipped her hand out. He raised a questioning look back at her.

"I should like to take my seat back here, if you please, Lord Bellfourd," Isabella said politely.

"Come now," Lady Lydia called. "You don't want to miss it."

Lord Bellfourd gave a soft nod of his head to Isabella in farewell before coming to stand next to his seated mother.

Isabella enjoyed the sound of Jackie's soft rendition of Au Clair de la Lune. She did have a beautiful singing voice. So, in the darkened far corner of the drawing room, Isabella sat with her eyes closed as she absorbed the lovely words.

Isabella opened them, surprised to find the Marquess watching her. He didn't look away when their eyes met. He towered high over his mother, with one hand resting on the high back of the chair, watching Isabella most intently.

Isabella blushed and looked away, thankful for the shadow of her seated position. Lord Bellfourd, too, let go of her gaze and turned to look on Jackie just as she finished.

All in the room clapped most heartily. Lady Abigail

invited Jackie to sit at her side once the song was done and the room went back to quiet conversations.

"Lord Bellfourd," Lady Lydia cooed yet again. "Please do tell me how His Grace is doing? My mother and I have both been so worried about his health."

"I am afraid very poorly, Lady Lydia."

Lady Wintercrest reached up and took her son's hand instinctually. They had already lost James, the thought of losing the duke in such quick succession seemed more than any one family could bear.

"How unfortunate," Lady Lydia said with what seemed like very little honesty in Isabella's opinion.

"Perhaps a carriage ride around the estate might help him. I have heard quite often that fresh air can do wonders for healing," she continued.

"Sadly, I don't think my father can leave his current room, much less take a trip outside."

"What a shame. I was hoping to take a ride and see the splendid grounds. Mother spoke of them so much on our trip up here, from the last time she visited."

Isabella did her best not to openly wrinkle her nose at what she was hearing. Lady Lydia was unmistakably using the poor health of the duke to secure an intimate ride with Lord Bellfourd.

Lord Bellfourd hesitated a moment. Indeed, at that moment, there was the proper thing to be said. In fact, it was expected by Lady Lydia.

"I have a wonderful idea," Lady Wintercrest chimed in before anything could be decided in Lord Bellfourd's mind. "Christian, why don't you show Lady Lydia around tomorrow afternoon?"

"Of course, Mother," Lord Bellfourd said to appease that wistful hope hanging in his mother's soft eyes.

The night continued much the same. Isabella sat in her corner, Jackie played games with her aunt, and the duchess and her friend remained deep in conversation. This left the Marquess to make conversation with Lady Lydia.

He did so politely, and with all the grace of a future duke. Isabella couldn't help but see the fallen crest of his brow or notice the sheen, so often present in his blue eyes, missing.

After Jackie gave her third yawn, Isabella was happy to insist that it was time to take her student up to bed. Jackie happily agreed, utterly exhausted from the long day.

As Isabella laid in her own bed that night, she reflected on many things. The significant change in the household with the arrival of guests was, of course, at the forefront of her mind. Also apparent was the tingling feeling she still felt at her fingertips from Lord Bellfourd's grasp.

Isabella wondered if she had only imagined him disinterested with Lady Lydia because she so detested the lady. Had she made up the reluctant manners of his speech and the bored set of his shoulders?

She also couldn't help but wonder if more repercussions would occur with Mrs. Peterson after that evening's events with Lord Bellfourd. She told herself, yet again, not to worry and that her job's security was in the hands of the Marquess, and not the housekeeper.

It was with these uneasy thoughts that she finally drifted off to sleep.

23

*D*ear Louisa,

    I am disappointed to inform you that my happy life here at Wintercrest has drastically changed in the last few days.

    As you might have expected would happen, Lady Lydia came to visit the duke's household along with her mother. Though I find her mother to be a very kind, charming lady, it is with a sad disposition that I must confirm your earlier sentiments of Lady Lydia.

    To make matters worse, she is clearly here with only one purpose in mind. That is, to win the affection of Lord Bellfourd.

    Lady Wintercrest and Lady Cunningham are all too eager to try their hand at matchmaking, as I suppose any mother would be.

    I thought that perhaps my dislike of Lady Lydia might be, at first, clouding my judgment of the lady and that perhaps I saw things not really there.

However, I was assured that this was not the case when, just yesterday, Lady Abigail came to join me in the garden in the early evening.

She told me that while Lord Bellfourd was taking Lady Lydia out for a ride in his curricle, they happened to see little Jackie and me leaving the small family graveyard outside of the estate chapel.

You see, I take Jackie there at least once a week on our afternoon walks to lay some flowers at her father's grave.

According to Lady Abigail, Lady Lydia asked Lord Bellfourd if he was aware that I was taking the child to the family's private cemetery.

When he said he was not, she went on and on for several minutes about my presumptuous behavior to do what I will with the child without the permission of the household.

Lady Abigail then confirmed to me that she too found Lady Lydia utterly ridiculous.

I do feel terrible on behalf of Lady Abigail. Surely, if the Marquess does end up attached to Lady Lydia, I would not be far from out of employment, but Lady Abigail will be out considerably worse than me.

She fears greatly that if Lord Bellfourd decides to marry Lady Lydia, she will have lost a second brother. Between this and her father's ever-worsening health, I fear she couldn't stand it.

I did my best to assure her that it was very much too soon even to consider such notions. That being said, however, I cannot help but share in her apprehensions of where this path is currently leading.

It may not even end up being the choice of the Marquess to make. With his father gravely ill and the dukedom at stake, I feel that Lord Bellfourd is being pressured to take on a wife and secure the line of succession.

Lady Lydia, though we both know has many character flaws, is the daughter of an earl and a very likely match for Lord Bellfourd.

We both know that arrangements in such situations have not to do with feelings of the heart.

I have grown to care for the whole Wintercrest household, more than I ever thought imaginable. For this reason, my heart is breaking at the thought that Lady Lydia may very likely be the new mistress of the manor.

I hope, for the sake of Jackie and Lady Abigail, and not my own, that this will not be the case.

Your friend always,

Isabella

Isabella finished her letter and, grabbing her hat and bonnet, prepared to take it into town herself.

It was a warm Saturday afternoon and Isabella rather enjoyed the idea of walking to town, something she had only done a few times since coming to Wintercrest.

"Where are ye off to?" a voice called out to Isabella as she entered the servants' dining hall.

Isabella recognized it instantly as that of Betsy. Isabella turned to find her friend sitting alone at a table finishing a very late luncheon.

"I'm going to town to drop off a letter to post. Can I get you anything while I am there?" Isabella asked her friend.

"Well, actually if you dinna mind terribly. I do have an item or two I was hopin' to get but have been avoidin' goin' myself, of late."

"You have?" Isabella said coming to sit by her friend with concern. "Has something gone wrong with your Mr. Johnson?"

"Only that he isn't *my* Mr. Johnson."

"Oh Betsy, I'm so sorry to hear that. I know you were truly taking a liking to him."

Isabella reached out and took Betsy's hand in compassion.

"Ach, nothin' to fret about, I suspect," she did her best to wave off the hurt.

"If you don't mind terribly, please tell me what happened. Perhaps I could help in some way."

"I dinna think much can be done about it. One day I was walkin' to market, and Mr. Johnson wasna waitin' as usual. I dinna think much of it till I saw him at market walking next to Sally."

"Oh, that rake!" Isabella said with venom.

"Aye, well it is what it is," Betsy resolved herself. "I haven't been able to brin' myself to go to market since that day, though."

"And you shan't ever again, if you don't want to. I will happily get any things you may need," Isabella said with the heart of a true friend looking out for the broken-hearted.

Isabella walked to town with her letter in a basket that also included a short list from Betsy. The only item that she had absolutely needed to get was some fabric. Her cousin was turning sixteen in a few weeks, and she hoped to make her a lovely dress as a gift.

Isabella only paused once on the road, as she made her way to town, to look along the fencing of a house she thought might belong to Mr. Johnson. But with none, save some chickens, out and about she could not determine much.

She stopped to post her letter first and was surprised to find that she had a message in return. It was from Mr. Jenkins, her late father's lawyer, and probably the only one who knew of her employment beyond Louisa.

Isabella tucked the letter safely into her basket and went on her way to the small mercantile shop. The dress that Betsy was planning to make for her cousin was a cream cotton in a flowing design for what she explained was a Scottish tradition on All Hallows' Eve.

She said that, though she and her family were good

Christian folk, like many of those rich in their Scottish heritage in these parts, they participated in the druid tradition of Samhain that night.

A grand bonfire would be built, small children would dress as ghosts and little people, to blend in with the ones said to be free for one night. The maidens of the village would dress in white and dance around the fire.

Though it seemed a bit wild and strange to Isabella, in all honesty, it didn't seem to differ much from its counterpart of the Mayday celebration. Thinking of Betsy there with her cousin, as they danced and warded off the evil spirits while commemorating the memory of their long-gone ancestors in the pure white gowns, Isabella decided she would try her hand at gifting one to Betsy as well.

Isabella had, after all, made the dress for little Jackie's doll. Though she had never done more than mending and embellishing garments in the past, Isabella figured it couldn't be so difficult to make one. Probably just a doll's dress only larger.

She picked out the simple cotton fabric that Betsy asked for, then, using her own wages from employment, Isabella purchased a cream-colored cotton fabric and a matching lace overlay. Isabella was determined to make sure Betsy was the most beautiful maiden at Samhain. Then Mr. Johnson would regret his decision to show his affection elsewhere.

Isabella was so excited for her scheme and surprise for

Betsy, that she scarcely noticed much as she made her way back home. It was because of this that she was taken on by a great shock when a horse seemingly appeared from nowhere right behind her.

Isabella turned, frightened, and fell to the side of the road, basket and all following her to the ground. Immediately, the Barouche with the Wintercrest emblem on the side came to a halt.

24

"*I*sabella, are you alright?" Lady Abigail's voice called out from the open carriage.

Before Isabella even got her bearings, Lord Bellfourd jumped out of the coach and rushed to Isabella's side before the driver had stopped entirely.

"Do forgive me, my lord, I did not see her as we came around the bend," the driver said, most apologetically.

"Please don't worry yourself, Samuel," Isabella said, righting her basket and making sure all was safe. "I was lost in my own thoughts. I should have been listening and gone to the side of the road on your approach."

"None the less," Samuel said, stepping down from the carriage, "I beg your forgiveness, Miss Watts."

"And I heartily accept it," Isabella said.

She meant to stand on her own, but Lord Bellfourd was

at her side and reached down to lift her up himself. He inspected her, once she was on her feet.

"Are you sure you are quite alright, Isabella?" he asked, his soft blue eyes searching her own.

"Yes, quite fine. No damage is done, My Lord," she replied, smoothing out her skirt and taking a step back. She was keenly aware of the two pairs of eyes watching from the carriage.

Lady Abigail, she had no problem with; Lady Lydia sitting next to her, however, was a different matter.

"Bring her into the carriage," Lady Abigail called. "She is much too shaken up to continue to walk."

"Oh no," Isabella protested. "I couldn't. I wouldn't want to interrupt your outing."

"You have scarcely ever been an interruption not wanted, and I can safely say that that is still the case today."

"But my hem is all dirty from walking; I will muddle the carriage."

Lord Bellfourd bent his head low just slightly, as was needed for his towering height, to see the hem of Isabella's muslin walking dress. It did have a small dusting of dirt and mud from the occasion of her walking on the road.

"Muddy hems we can manage just fine. Provided there is no jewelry dangling from it?" He reached out his arm to Isabella and bent to pick up her basket for her.

"You are a terrible scoundrel for bringing up such a

memory," Isabella replied, taking his arm and walking with him to the carriage.

In her fall, her bonnet had slipped from her head, having not pinned it in place, and her lush black hair was a stark contrast to the white sheen of her skin.

Since Lady Abigail and Lady Lydia were seated next to each other, Lord Bellfourd helped Isabella to the opposite side of the carriage, before handing up her basket to rest next to Samuel in the driver's seat. He sat next to her in the carriage and Isabella struggled to keep her breath from their proximity.

The Barouche moved onward with a call from the driver. With a slight lurch, they were off again at a comfortable trotting pace.

"You must have had a very successful trip into town, Isabella. How you didn't tip over from the weight of your basket alone is a small miracle," Lord Bellfourd teased.

"I suspect the staff has just recently been given their monthly earnings," Lady Lydia interjected. Her cool brown eyes were holding Isabella in an unfriendly manner. "I know as soon as my staff receives their earnings they go straight into town and spend it all away at once."

Isabella wanted to tell Lady Lydia that she had made a horrid assumption. In fact, she had found, in her new position, that much of the staff rarely spent so much as a pence of their earnings. Much of it went back to their families, or was saved up for the chance at a happier life.

"It isn't all mine," Isabella said instead, toward Lord Bellfourd. "I was also picking up some items for Betsy. She is making a Samhain dress for her cousin to celebrate her sixteenth birthday."

"Samhain?" Lady Lydia repeated in shock. "Is that some pagan ritual? I cannot imagine being involved in the slightest way in such a thing."

Lady Lydia opened her silk fan and waved herself, though it was not the least bit warm with the open carriage affording a soft breeze. Isabella watched Lady Lydia puff out her cheeks indignantly.

"Actually, it is quite fun," Lady Abigail said, stretching to her full height in her seat.

"Abigail? You naughty little thing," Lord Bellfourd said, reaching forward to tug playfully on Lady Abigail's dark red curl that came to the side of her bonnet. "Have you been to the festival?"

"Yes, I have," she replied, jutting her small chin out. She had a dusting of freckles on her nose, no doubt from all the times she took her bonnet off outside.

Isabella knew many women who would use concoctions to painstakingly remove such marks, but on Lady Abigail's face, it was quite fitting to her wild spirit.

If Isabella was willing to admit it to herself, she had been one of those ladies who always shielded herself with bonnets and parasols, as well as used lemon water at any sign of a blemish.

It did seem rather silly to her now. Even at her youthful age of eighteen, Lady Abigail looked to be a beautiful young lady, and what some would call blemishes were part of that beauty.

"Well you must tell us all about it, then." Lord Bellfourd encouraged his sister with a hearty smile on his square jaw.

"You see," Lady Abigail started excitedly to tell her story. "I convinced Nursie to tell me all about the festival. Of course, it wasn't that hard, you know how she loves to spin stories."

Lady Abigail turned to Lady Lydia. "Nursie was my nanny, Mrs. Murray. She is also currently Jackie's caretaker."

Lady Lydia didn't seem to like to have special explanation given to her. It made her look like an interloper on a close friendship of three.

"After she told me," Lady Abigail continued, "I just had to go and see it for myself. In all honesty, I thought she might have fibbed a bit to scare me. She spoke of little people and ghosts that walk the earth for one night a year. She said that small children were made to dress as such, for fear the little people might snatch them up otherwise."

"She told me little folk could tell who the naughty children were from the good ones and liked to take them home and turn them into little folk themselves. To be on the safe side, all parents make their kids wear woodland clothes and dirty up their faces. That way, if they were naughty, the little people would think they were already one of them."

"I imagine all children loved the opportunity to run around dirty for a day," Lord Bellfourd chimed in.

"To be sure. But, you see, I thought she was fibbing just to keep me on my best behavior. You see," Lady Abigail directed to Isabella, "this was just after the jam on the piano keys incident."

Isabella covered her mouth to stifle a giggle. She couldn't help but picture Mrs. Murray, irritated by the sticky clean up, weaving a scary, animated tale to put her ward into place.

"So, how did you make your escape?" Lord Bellfourd asked, enthralled by the tale.

"Well, I was twelve at the time and you had just left for the Navy," Lady Abigail continued. "I made my escape in my white nightgown, dressing gown, and slippers. I removed the rags from my hair but did not know how to put it up myself, so it lay limply all around me. My face I scrubbed with the ash from the fireplace, just for good measure. I scarcely know how I was able to sneak out of the house unnoticed, except for the fact that most of the staff must have already left for the festivities themselves."

"Oh, Lady Abigail," Lady Lydia said in astonishment. "I do hope you weren't seen. I can't imagine what being found in a dressing gown in the middle of a pagan ritual would do to a lady's reputation."

"Actually, I was found out," Lady Abigail said with an edge of spit.

Both ladies gasped, though for very different reasons.

"I ran all the way through the dark to just outside of town. I could see the glow of the bonfire at the back edge of a tenant field. As I got closer, I found myself walking with many others, making their way to the same place. It didn't seem to me that anyone recognized me for who I was, or so I thought in my childish mind."

"How could they not," Lord Bellfourd stated, "with your fine dressing gown, and deep red hair?"

"Of course, now I can see that is true. But at the time, in my youthful confidence, I thought myself a very good trickster with my smudged face."

"Oh, it was so magnificent," Lady Abigail continued, caught up in her own memory. "There were long tables decorated with cornucopias and delicious treats. There was a great big fire where children danced and played, and even a small group of musicians."

"Standing in a straight line, just to the side of the fire, was a row of young maidens all dressed in white with crowns of harvest flowers. Upon their arrival, the merriment stopped, the kids stood back, and the women themselves encircled the fire. The musicians played a soft tune that grew in power. The ladies all danced, an ancient movement of flowing white fabric, along with the song. Oh, it was simply magical," Lady Abigail said with a romantic sigh.

Lady Lydia just sat there, too shocked by the telling to speak. From time to time, she turned her brown eyes to Lord Bellfourd, certain he too must be disgusted by this tale.

"When the dance was done, I found Nursie at my side, hands folded in front of her. I suspected, for a long time after that, that she might be a fairy herself for how quietly she always seemed to appear."

"All she said was, 'come along home now, lass,' and we both walked the road back home. She washed my face with cold water and tucked me back into my bed. We never spoke of that night after that," Lady Abigail ended with a sheen of happy childhood memory to her soft blue eyes.

"What an adventurous childhood you must have had," Lady Lydia said, doing her best to find a way to compliment a tale she deeply disproved of.

The small party was just beginning to pull onto the long drive that lead up to Wintercrest Manor.

"Do you have fabric in that larger basket to make your own Samhain dress?" Lord Bellfourd said teasingly as he turned to inspect the basket sitting by Samuel again.

"Yes, I dare say that you would be quite in your place at such an event," Lady Lydia said coolly.

"No," Isabella said, doing her best to ignore Lady Lydia's remarks. "I am hoping, however, to make one for

Betsy. She has been so kind to me these past months. Though I am not sure I am up to the task."

"I am certain you will be," Lady Abigail praised. "The little dress you made for Jackie's doll was pretty enough to be worn by the queen herself."

"Well, if that is the case, I shall practice my manners for when Her Royal Highness Betsy is given her new gown," Lord Bellfourd teased again, letting his happy conscience shine down on Isabella.

They pulled up to the house and Lord Bellfourd exited and turned to help each lady down.

"I thank you for the ride," Isabella said, bidding the party goodbye.

Lord Bellfourd reached up and grabbed the basket to hand back to its owner.

"I dare say- are there also some treacle tarts I see poking out? You must have a sweet tooth then?" Lord Bellfourd added, handing back the basket.

"They, and some lemon drops, are treats for Mrs. Murray and Jackie."

"I have always been under the impression that too many sweets for children breed bad behavior," Lady Lydia said, intruding on the conversation.

"Well, if that is the case," Lord Bellfourd said, turning back to Lady Lydia, who promptly placed her hand in the uninviting arm of the Marquess, "then Jackie is the most rotten child of all, since I often sneak her bonbons and peppermint sticks."

He tipped his beaver fur hat, that matched the dark brown of his morning coat perfectly, before bidding Isabella goodbye.

"Please do give her an extra lemon drop for me," he added with a wink in farewell.

Lady Abigail came to stand by Isabella. "If you don't mind terribly, perhaps I could join you and possibly help as you begin to make your new gown?"

It was clear that she had all she could stand of Lady Lydia for the day.

"Thank you; I would be grateful for the company."

The two ladies set off together for the side service entrance arm in arm, while Lord Bellfourd lead Lady Lydia to tea in the drawing room through the main door.

"Is it wise to let your sister spend so much time in the company of Miss Watts?" Lady Lydia asked of Lord Bellfourd as they entered the manor.

"She is not just the governess; she has also been a great friend to Abigail these past few months when she was unable to go to town for the season."

"Yes, but she is a servant. How can you expect your sister to find a proper match if she is lowering herself to such standard?"

"She may be an employee of this manor," Lord Bellfourd said with stern finality, "but she is also a good friend to all of the household, and I would hope you remember that in future."

Though Lady Lydia did not, in any way, like the answer that Lord Bellfourd returned to her, she did enjoy the idea of a future at Wintercrest Manor.

25

*D*ear Miss Isabella Watts,

    I am hoping that my letter finds you in good health. I am writing to inform you that your first quarter of income was delivered to me, per the agreement made with Mr. Smith. I will be sending it to you post haste along with this letter.

    I hope that you have settled in well in your new position as governess of Wintercrest Manor.

    I do have one other matter that I would like to bring to your attention. Since your departure and the subsequent liquidation of your father's assets, Mr. Smith has been most adamant in learning your whereabouts.

    Because of his coarse nature, he has been to see me at least six times since your departure about this matter. I have chosen to keep your location from him. Though he may be a gentleman, I fear he may not have gentlemanly thoughts in mind on account of your situation.

Though he was not happy that I would not divulge your employment to him, I thought he had decided to finally give up on this venture and move on with his life.

I was sadly mistaken. I found, just last Tuesday, an advertisement in The Morning Chronicle for information pertaining to your location, which even alluded that you are wanted in questioning of a criminal nature.

I have enclosed a clipping of said article with this letter. Though I still don't think it is wise to make known your location to Mr. Smith, I fear something must be done to appease the man. I fear he will otherwise never stop his pursuit of you, Miss Watts.

I wait for your reply as to what you would like me to do in such matters.

Your humble servant,

Mr. Jenkins

Isabella looked into the large envelope the letter had arrived in. Inside was a small sum of money, which she promptly hid inside a false book on her bookshelf, and the newspaper clipping.

Attention!

One Miss Isabella Watts is wanted in the question of items missing from the possession of a Mr. Smith of J. Watts Shipping

*& Trade Co. If any information can be given on the above-stated
female's location, please contact Mr. Smith at his place of business for a small compensation.*

Isabella gripped her necklace in horror. He had gone so
far as to call her an outright thief in The Morning Chronicle. All of this because she refused to give up her very own
locket to his greedy paws.

Her heart beat fast and her palms were clammy at the
thought. Would anyone in the area receive The Morning
Chronicle? It was a London paper, widely distributed in
town, but she wasn't sure that its popularity would travel so
far up north.

The only person who she thought might have such a
thing delivered was the duke himself, probably the last
person in the world Isabella would want to read such a
thing.

She grew even more nervous as she thought back to all
the breakfasts she shared with the family. Often, the post
and various newspapers would be delivered to Lord Bellfourd at this time for him to look over.

She hastily looked back at the date of the letter. The
papers Lord Bellfourd received would be a few days behind
what was posted in London due to travel. Perhaps if she
had time, she could intercept the offending paper before it
reached his hands.

It had been only three days since the letter was posted

to her. More than likely, she would have to act quickly if she was going to prevent anyone in the house from coming upon the article.

She hoped that if she sent Mr. Smith the charm with no postscript, he would leave the whole matter be. She cherished her locket dearly, but keeping it was not worth giving up her new home.

Sadly, she knew in her heart, it was not the locket that Mr. Smith truly wanted but her demise. No matter what she did to appease him, he would always find another way to come at her and disgrace her further.

She sank down onto her bed, full of hopelessness. She thought back to the words she heard the Marquess had spoken to Lady Lydia just that afternoon.

He had said she was a friend to all the household. Would he consider her as such if he knew the devious thing she had done before arriving?

Collapsing entirely onto her mattress, she let her tears run down her cheeks. Despite the knowledge that giving Mr. Smith the locket wouldn't do much to help her situation, she knew she must do it anyway. Though she knew he would do everything in his power to disgrace and belittle her at every turn, she would not let her attachment to a charm open the way for Mr. Smith to come into her life yet again.

Two days later, when Isabella was able to find some free

time, she walked back the way to town, this time with a much more sullen countenance and a noticeable weight removed from around her neck, to deliver a parcel to the postmaster.

She also sent a letter to Mr. Jenkins, thanking him for his continued friendship as well as the information pertaining to Mr. Smith. She informed him that she had done everything in her power to recompense the wrong Mr. Smith believed she had caused him. Isabella prayed that this would finally be the end of the matter.

Unfortunately, she was sadly mistaken when she returned home that evening. One of the lady's maids was sent to her room with a note from Lady Lydia. It stated that Lady Lydia requested her presence for a short private conversation and Isabella was to meet her in the garden at her earliest convenience.

With fall starting to creep in, Isabella grabbed her warmest shawl and made her way out again at once to see what Lady Lydia could want.

Ironically, Isabella found Lady Lydia sitting on Isabella's favorite stone bench with a book in hand. As dusk was beginning to fall, she couldn't imagine that Lady Lydia was actually reading by the quickly dimming light.

"Oh, good. I was worried you weren't going to get my letter. Come and have a seat by me, dear," she said closing her book and patting the cold stone next to her.

Lady Lydia was being awfully kind and even bordered on cheerfulness. It was not a good start, in Isabella's mind.

"Isn't it a funny thing that us two girls from London's finest ladies' school end up here together so far north?"

"I suppose so," Isabella said, coolly trying to measure where the conversation was going.

"Clearly, you must know what my mother and I have intended for this visit. In fact, I might be so bold to say Her Grace, herself, wishes it to be so," Lady Lydia said with a proud air.

"So, it must be quite obvious that I have a concern for the wellbeing of Wintercrest, including who Lord Bellfourd and Lady Abigail associate themselves with."

Isabella swallowed hard. She still could not determine what game Lady Lydia was playing.

"Imagine my surprise, when, just this morning, I noticed this on the back of The Morning Chronicle which Lord Bellfourd had in his hand."

She opened the book to her page, and Isabella saw that she had not been reading the literature but rather a copy of Mr. Smith's inquiry.

"I wanted to bring it to Lady Wintercrest attention immediately, fearing that a criminal might have infiltrated their household. In the end, however, I thought I might lay the case before you to see if some sort of recompense could be made."

Isabella narrowed her green eyes at the horrid lady. She

planned to use her new knowledge as a means of black-mail. It certainly wasn't below the typical scheming that Isabella had seen from her, during their years at Mrs. Mason's School for Exceptional Young Ladies.

She knew fully well that Lady Lydia would use any means necessary to get the results she desired. Right now, that desire was focused on becoming the future Duchess of Wintercrest.

"I have returned the item in question just today. I don't see how you can use such things to your advantage."

"Oh, on the contrary, I see it very well. It matters not if you attempted to resolve your criminal act. It was done all the same. Can you honestly say that the duke would still want you in his house if this was brought to his attention?"

Isabella thought this over. She wasn't sure if the duke would see things Lady Lydia's way or not. Either way, his state had only worsened, she had been told, and she wouldn't dream of bringing anything to his attention that might weaken him in any way. For the health of her employer, she would submit to Lady Lydia's will. She may not have particularly gotten along with the duke, but he was a good, honest man that didn't need any more hard-ship on his plate right now.

"What do you want of me, Lydia?" Isabella said exas-peratedly.

Lady Lydia formed her slightly rounded face into a satisfied grin. She knew she had Isabella right where she wanted her. Dare she say, a childhood dream finally come true.

"I have a short list of demands, if you would like to continue your employment here at Wintercrest Manor," Lady Lydia said in a joyfully baneful way.

26

*I*sabella made her way, quite sadly, to her room. According to the agreement with Lady Lydia, she was to have no interaction with the rest of the household. She was to refuse any invitations from Lord Bellfourd, Lady Abigail, or even Lady Wintercrest.

She was to make any time with the household, as governess to Jacqueline, as brief as possible and then quickly make both their exits.

Aside from her short mornings with Betsy, and afternoon lunch with Mrs. Murray, her sole companion was Jackie. Of course, she couldn't share her sorrow with the child. Poor Jackie had already noticed enough the fall in her countenance and had asked if there was something the matter. Isabella, of course, would not get the child involved in such matters.

She spent all her afternoons and evenings in her room, as instructed by Lady Lydia, so as not to interlope on anyone in the garden.

She settled herself to take the time to work on Betsy's dress. With Lady Abigail's help that first day, she was able to measure and cut out pieces to the proper size as best she could. Her nights of solitude gave her ample time to work the tedious hand sewing of creating the garment.

Isabella missed the company of Lady Abigail and her youthful energy when she talked. She even missed the occasional teasing that came with conversations with the Marquess. Part of her wished she had never gotten to be such good friends with the Wintercrest family. Now in the absence of their companionship, she felt so much emptiness.

There was nothing to be done about it. The duke's health continued to worsen and Lady Lydia was all too happy to carry the offensive newspaper clipping with her wherever she might go.

In any instance when Lady Abigail or Lord Bellfourd would try to include Isabella, Lady Lydia would take it out most carefully to flaunt before Isabella's eyes.

Between the wicked ways of Lady Lydia and the constant fear that Mr. Smith might happen on her, Isabella felt she was becoming a shell of herself.

Soon the time of All Hallows' Eve was upon them and

Isabella was happy that she had at least finished Betsy's dress in time.

She asked Betsy to meet her in her room just after supper for a surprise.

"Oh, my! Why, this can't be meant for me?" Betsy exclaimed, pulling back the brown paper Isabella had wrapped the garment in.

"Of course it's for you, you silly." Isabella felt the warm glow of happiness reach her cheeks for the first time in a very long while.

"'Tis so fine. I could never wear such a thing," Betsy protested softly, touching the lace overlay of the ivory dress.

"You certainly shall. I will help you put it on and together we will create the finest hair. Mr. Johnson will think twice about looking past you after tonight. I will make you the belle of the festival."

She hugged Isabella in a tight embrace. Both girls had tears brimming in their eyes.

An hour later, Betsy was dressed and looked absolutely stunning. Her soft brown hair was pinned up in a sweeping chignon with some of Isabella's white ribbon decorating it. Small ringlets surrounded her face and two large ones sat perfectly on her left shoulder.

Isabella added a thick satin white ribbon around the high waist to the ivory lace gown.

"I look just lovely," Betsy said, standing before the round mirror in Isabella's room.

"Oh, Isabella, ye must come with me," she said, turning and taking Isabella by the hand. "We shall go together and ye shall have a grand time. Forget yer woes for a time."

"I wish I could," Isabella said, letting her brow fall again in sorrow. "I walk such a dangerous path as it is, I couldn't risk it."

Betsy had been the only one to whom Isabella had shared the truth of Lady Lydia's devious ways. She trusted Betsy and knew she wouldn't judge her harshly for taking the locket.

"How would the lady ever ken ye went? She certainly won't be there, just us local folk. Aye, the other servants will recognize ye, but they will say naught about it."

"What about Mrs. Peterson? She, too, would be happy for any reason to get me in trouble."

"Ach, Mrs. Peterson? At Samhain? I would no sooner expect to see the likes of her than to see the Devil 'imself!'"

"I suppose it would be fun to go. I must confess, I am a little curious after Lady Abigail's tale of her adventure. If you don't think any wrong will come of my being there?"

"It's like Mrs. Murray told ye, 'Whit's fur ye'll no go past ye.'"

"What's ever meant to be will happen," Isabella repeated, remembering when Mrs. Murray had spoken the words to her.

Though she was sure Mrs. Murray had taken her unhappy state to be because of Lady Lydia's ever-growing attention from the Marquess. Though it was a small part of it, it wasn't the root of her current problem.

"Yer meant to be here. This is yer home now, yer no a chancer for havin' just a wee bit o'fun."

"Alright, if you think it will be safe," Isabella finally conceded.

"Right then! Let's get ye all bonnied up as well," Betsy said, walking over to Isabella's closet of dresses.

Thirty minutes later, they were out of the room and on the road to the festivities. Isabella had changed into a simple, cream-colored morning dress with small green vines decorating the front.

Isabella wore an extra thick petticoat and brought with her a woolen forest green shawl that Mrs. Murray had made to stave off winter's chill.

Isabella couldn't help the skip to her step as they neared the glow of a fire just past a freshly cut field.

They walked around the piles of barley, stacked like little-pointed huts as they dried, and back to where the music and light both increased.

Isabella was amazed at what lay before her. She had been to a few public hall dances and expected it to be much of the same. Perhaps slightly livelier than a private event, but none the less, not much different.

She was mistaken. The crowd around the three bonfires was so full of chatter it was almost hard to hear. The children were running around, soot-faced and in ragged clothes. Most of the little girls had their hair down and flowing in the wind with garlands of pinecones and flowers adorning them.

She made out the outline of a small band just to the side of the main fire pit. It was by far the largest and even from a distance, she could feel the heat of it.

She could just make out the sound of a lively jig over all the chatter. There were even a couple or two already dancing beside the fire.

It looked to Isabella like most of the servants and all the town was there for the evening's festivities.

There were two long tables dripping in delicacies and roasted meats. Large cornucopias decorated the center-piece, every so often bursting with apples and even an orange or two. She wondered how that had been managed.

"I must leave ye now," Betsy said to her friend. "'Tis almost time for the dance. Will ye be alright, then?"

"Yes, of course. Go on. I can't wait to watch you."

Isabella watched her friend make her way through the crowds and to a group of young ladies waiting just on the other side, all dressed in white.

Isabella walked along the edge of the crowd, stopping only once to help a small child sneak a tart from the table, so that she could continue to have a good view of her friend.

"I suppose I wasn't the only one to be curious about Abigail's story," a rich voice said next to her.

Isabella looked up, very surprised to see Lord Bellfourd standing there. He was dressed rather relaxed in high boots, pantaloons, his cotton shirt, and long riding jacket. Isabella couldn't help but notice that his cravat was simply tied in a napoleon knot, something he did himself, no doubt, upon exiting the manor.

His shadow was very angular as he looked over at Isabella, which only enhanced the wicked gleam he so liked to sport on his square jaw when he was unconventional.

"I did not think..." Isabella hesitated, rising with panic. What would Lady Lydia do if she found out that Isabella was there, and standing next to the Marquess, no less? "I was hoping not to be noticed tonight," she finally settled on.

"Mums the word, I swear it," Lord Bellfourd said, winking down at Isabella. "Though I scarcely see how you could go unrecognized. I could spot your dark hair and amber eyes in the fire glow from all the way across the festivities," he teased.

"Betsy invited me to watch the dance. I couldn't help but be intrigued by it."

"I said hello to her in passing, too. She does look wonderful in that garment you made for her. You are very talented."

"Thank you, Lord Bellfourd, but I can't take all the

credit. Mrs. Murray did have to help me a bit with finishing it."

"Mmm," he said, now turning to Isabella and furrowing his brow, "Lord Bellfourd is it? I must tell you," he said with that sly grin, "I too, am incognito. Therefore, you have no choice but to remove my title from your utterance."

"Well, since you agreed to keep my secret, I suppose I will have no choice but to also keep yours in return."

"That's very kind of you, your ladyship," he said with a teasing bow to Isabella.

His eyes stopped at the neckline of her dress, however.

"If you don't mind me asking terribly, where is your locket? It seemed so treasured by you and always adorned your neck, but it has been missing as of late?"

"Oh, yes. That. Well..." Isabella stammered for an explanation but was luckily halted by the hushing of the crowds.

All attention and focus went to the line of fair maidens dressed in white as they made their way around the central circle. It was almost a mesmerizing trance to watch as they danced and swayed with turnip lanterns hanging from a ribbon in each girl's hand. It was both ominous and beautiful all at same time as they swayed and twirled around the bonfire.

Betsy stood out, not just for her exquisite dress but the light that shone from her as she moved about the pit.

Isabella couldn't help but scan the crowd for the Mr.

Johnson she had never met. She hoped her eyes would fall upon a young man crestfallen with regret and then she would know for certain this was the man who had lost the greatest prize.

She had no such luck, however. Most of the faces were happy and just as mesmerized as her own. She even caught a few small girls dancing and twirling around just outside the circle of maidens. Their sways were filled with the anticipation of someday being the maidens themselves.

After the dancing was done, everyone lifted roars of cheers. The band started again and this time, many couples came to dance around the fires.

Betsy came skipping over to Isabella with a slightly younger girl in tow. The family resemblance was easy to see between them, even in the dim light of the fire.

"Isabella, I must introduce ye to my kin, Fiona."

"It is so good to meet the one I have heard so much of. You both danced beautifully."

"Thank ye," they both said in unison.

It was then that Betsy noticed the Marquess at Isabella's side.

"Beg yer pardon, yer Lordship," she said with a curtsy. "May I introduce my cousin Fiona to ye."

"It is a pleasure to make your acquaintance, Miss Fiona," Lord Bellfourd said with a dashing bow. "If you would please excuse me, however, I feel I am in need of some of those delicious tarts over there."

"Try the apple pasties," Fiona interjected. "My mum made those ones."

"Then I shall be sure to grab one and doubt I will be disappointed," he bowed once more.

Before turning to leave, however, he held out his arm to Isabella, "Would you care to join me?"

Isabella blushed a bit, hearing the girls at her side giggle as she placed her hand in the crook of his arm, and followed him over to the table of goodies.

27

The evening continued for Isabella in a memorable sort of way. She stayed at the Marquess' side for most of the night and even danced to a few folk songs that she knew from public balls.

Though the attendees knew clearly that it was the Marquess at the festivities, they treated him as one of their own. It was the greatest gift bestowed upon the Lord of Bellfourd to once again feel at home as he had in his naval times.

Finally, as the night began to wind on, Isabella thought it is best that she return home and retire for the night. After all, she still had a full day of lessons with Jackie on the morrow.

"I will walk with you home, then," Lord Bellfourd said. "Let me just stop at Mr. Johnson's barn to collect my horse."

"Mr. Johnson?" Isabella exclaimed.

"Yes," Lord Bellfourd said, a little confused by her excitement. "He is the tenant that works the land we are on."

"Oh, to be true," Isabella clapped her hands gayly, perhaps a little too much so after the sweet fermented cider she had earlier. "That would be the elder Mr. Johnson and he has a son about Betsy's age."

"Well, I would say that Alden is a bit older than Betsy, but yes."

"Oh Christian," Isabella said taking his hands. "That is so wonderful."

"It is," he said with a little laugh, enjoying Isabella's giddy behavior. "Why is that you have taken a liking to the chap."

"No, don't be silly," Isabella said hooking her arm in his and encouraging him to take her with him to the barn. "Betsy has been sweet on him for some time. He was sweet on her too, but then for some reason, set his eyes on another."

"I wanted to make the dress for Betsy so that she could show that scoundrel, Mr. Alden Johnson, that he had made a grave mistake."

Lord Bellfourd took possession of his chestnut steed from a much younger boy who was dozing away in a soft pile of hay in the barn. Isabella couldn't help but smile as she watched Lord Bellfourd place a shiny new copper in his hand.

They walked on in silence down the road for a short while.

"Is that the only reason you made Betsy look so nice tonight?" Lord Bellfourd finally asked.

"What do you mean?" Isabella inquired from the other side of the horse that walked between them.

"I just mean, you dressed her all up as a fine lady. Perhaps you hoped that Mr. Alden would do more than regret his change in affection."

"If by that you mean, see the true value in Betsy and fall hopelessly in love with her? I suppose, yes. I am a romantic at heart, after all."

"You are?" Lord Bellfourd said, but seemed to think this over. "You know it doesn't matter," he finally said.

"What doesn't matter?"

"What she wears, how she looks. If he truly loved her, he would see beyond the physical and love the girl inside. Outward situations matter little compared to the condition of the heart."

Isabella felt the conversation turn to something with a much deeper meaning.

"That is quite a nice thought, Christian, but there is always more than just that simple statement to consider."

"And what would that be?"

"Well, the feelings of family members, for one," Isabella blurted out with obviousness.

"It is a silly thing if you ask me, to stake one's own life's happiness on the sensitivities of others. Certainly, that is no way to live."

"You are saying you don't think we should feel any attachment to our family. That each person, upon the age of adulthood, should turn from those who loved and raised him and care not for how his affections might affect them."

"I don't suppose I would put it quite that dramatically," he said with a smug grin catching Isabella between the horse in the soft moonlit night. "But no, I don't think a person should base his own happiness on what others, even his family, might want of him.

"Do you suppose," he continued, "if your father knew of Mr. Smith's proposal to you, he would have wanted you to take up such an arrangement?"

Isabella thought this over. Truthfully, her father, though loving and giving of every want, rarely spoke an opinion on the matter of marriage. She wasn't sure if her father would have been for such matters so as to benefit his company, or against it, in support of her refusal.

"I honestly don't know."

"Alright, but let's just say, for argument's sake, that he wanted you to marry his business partner and, in fact, whole-heartedly endorsed it. Would you have married him then?"

"No!" Isabella blurted out without thought, as she often did when overcome with emotion.

"Precisely. Certainly family's, and even societies', thoughts and opinions matter, but in the end, we each live our own lives. We should all be allowed to choose who we will spend the rest of our lives with, no matter her status."

Isabella felt Lord Bellfourd's eyes on her and she couldn't bear to look at him, for fear of giving away her own feelings.

"Well then," she said, lightening the mood, "I shall congratulate Betsy heartily on the morrow for stealing away the Marquess of Bellfourd's heart."

Lord Bellfourd gave into unrestrained laughter at Isabella's proclamations, much to her satisfaction.

They walked the remainder of the journey in contented silence. Isabella walked with him to deposit the horse in his own stall, and then, together, they walked into the main foyer of the manor. Parting at the opposite stairwells, Lord Bellfourd bowed politely and bid Isabella goodnight.

Isabella could scarcely sleep despite the late hour. If the festivities were not enough to keep her alert, the cryptic words spoken before parting the company of Lord Bellfourd certainly were.

She had long since admitted to herself that she felt an attachment to the Marquess. Never in all her life would she expect him to do the same. Such a thing surely couldn't be allowed.

She replayed the night's events over and over in her head as she lay awake under her quilts. Constantly, she second-guessed if she saw more than there was. But then, Lord Bellfourd's words came back to her:

'We all should be allowed to choose who we will spend the rest of our lives with, no matter HER status.'

Had he meant Isabella when he uttered that phrase? Isabella certainly wanted to let herself hope so, but also feared to allow such excitement to grow inside her.

She stayed awake pondering these things till she could see the dim early light of the day breaking. Despite her need to ready herself for the day's tasks, Isabella finally drifted off to sleep, with thoughts of Lord Bellfourd on her mind and in her heart.

"Isabella? Isabella? Are you not well?" broke through the haze of what seemed like only a few seconds later.

It was Lady Abigail sitting at the side of Isabella's bed, her youthful face drawn with worry.

"Why? What's going on?" Isabella said, surprised at how hoarse and dry her throat felt.

"Betsy came to get me. She said she came this morning with breakfast, but you were not awake. When Mrs. Murray informed her that you had not left your room to attend Jackie she thought you must be unwell. She came to me straight away. Are you ill?"

It was clear that Lady Abigail asked in true concern.

"No," Isabella said softly, still attempting to get her bearings on the preceding night and following morning.

"My goodness, what time is it?" Isabella said, shooting up in her bed, now coming to her senses.

She instantly regretted such movement as her head began to swirl most painfully.

"You are ill," Lady Abigail instead. "I should have the doctor fetched for."

"No, please don't. I will be alright shortly," Isabella said, eyes closed as she rubbed her temples. She was willing the massive pain to leave her body. "It must have been that cider. I had far too much of it."

Lady Abigail squealed with glee and made a little bounce on the bed. It produced another moan of discomfort from Isabella.

"Oh, sorry, dear, but does that mean that you went to All Hallows' Eve last night?" Lady Abigail could barely contain her excitement.

"Yes. After I gave Betsy her dress, she insisted I come along."

"Oh, did she look fine in her new dress? You must tell me every moment of it."

"Of course, but first I must see to Jackie," Isabella said, struggling to rise again.

"Absolutely not!" Lady Abigail said with a firm hand pushing Isabella back down. "You are not well enough.

Mrs. Murray will happily look after Jackie for the day, and Christian and I will take turns entertaining her."

Lady Abigail stood and propped up the pillows behind Isabella in a motherly fashion.

"You stay right here and rest. I will have Betsy send up some cold water and broth. You don't move a muscle out of that bed until your head is much better."

Isabella smiled weakly at her dear friend.

"And perhaps when you are feeling up to it, you will share with me every moment of your night."

"I promise," Isabella responded happily.

She wondered, however, before she drifted back to sleep if she should tell Lady Abigail every moment. For instance, the fact that she spent almost the whole of the night with her brother.

28

*D*ear Louisa,

    I must tell you, foremost, that of all the fermented fruit drinks, cider is my very least favorite. I had some of the poisonous elixir whilst sneaking off to a local town festival called Samhain yesterday evening.

    I have since been confined to my bed with a most painful ache in my head. I am just now writing to you because I can stand no longer to lay still in my bed covers. I do apologize, however, if my writing is not its best in this letter due to the health of the scribe.

    I, however, must fight through the unwell feelings and quickly write all I can remember to you before it is lost to me. I can honestly say that last night was one of the best of my life on a variety of levels.

    To start, Samhain is a night of festivities when all spirits, both good and bad, are said to walk the earth and druids connect with those lost to thank them for a bountiful harvest. Of course, now it is more of a cultural tradition than of a religious nature.

Though some may look down upon such activities, I find that taking a moment to show gratitude and remember those gone is a very wonderful idea.

Normally, such things would be frowned upon to attend, though I should mention the idea only came to me when Lady Abigail herself claimed to sneak to such an event in her youth. I am happy to say, however, that one of the perks of my now lowered position in life is that I am afforded many more freedoms, without judgment of my actions.

I went with Betsy. She, as well as a few other maids, all dressed in white and danced around the fire in a most magical turn. Though I was at first reluctant to go, Betsy convinced me otherwise. I am eternally grateful for her encouraging friendship.

It was much to my great surprise, upon arriving at the festivities, that I found that I was not the only one to have my interest sparked my Lady Abigail's tales. The Marquess of Bellfourd, himself, found me amongst the crowds and came to my side.

At first, I felt very embarrassed, perhaps even a little worried. I was not certain that the duke and duchess would be happy to hear of their governess participating in pagan traditions. And certainly, if for any reason Lady Lydia was to find out, the remainder of her time at Wintercrest Manor would be even more unbearable than it has thus far been.

I already expounded to you the conversation we had in the garden and the offending article that she has chosen to hold over my head.

As the night proceeded, Lord Bellfourd chose to stay by my side. It was most refreshing to have his companionship again without the added party of Lady Lydia.

After the druid maidens performed their dance, the area was opened to all couples as a lively band played. I would say it was much the same as a public dance hall from that time on.

Lord Bellfourd joined right into the party as if he was one of them. He took Betsy on a turn around the bonfires, and then also her younger cousin Fiona.

I also couldn't help but be caught up in the festivities. I first danced with Samuel, the coachman, and Mr. Hillary, the postmaster. As I am sure this will come to a great surprise to you, I was even asked to dance by Mr. Larson, the head butler.

I must confess my mouth most surely dropped to the ground when he came to ask me. Though I knew he had a mild Scottish accent and therefore most likely came from farther up north as so many of the servants do, I would never have considered him the type to frequent uproarious events.

There he was, however, and actually, a very jolly dancer. We danced two jigs together before I had to stop and catch my breath.

I originally worried that an outdoor festivity would be too

cold to stand, but with all the movement and warmth of the fire, one could not even tell we were outside.

While I took a moment to catch my breath, I drank the delicious but beguiling cider and watched Betsy, His Lordship, and other familiar faces dance around.

I so wish I could take that image in my mind and make it into a portrait. I am certain, if it was done, the world around could see the image of joy and happiness encompassed into one.

I cannot help but to smile now as I remember and write these words to you.

The look on Lord Bellfourd's face as he danced around the fire's glow was one that I had never fully seen on him before. It was, however, one I saw quite often on my father as he spoke to me of his next adventure. It was pure happiness, without restraint. I could see clearly why he had so many reservations about coming back to his home, after being free out on the ocean.

Perhaps it is also the same reason that my own father never gave up the adventure of a voyage. It created a light and freedom for a man who couldn't find it otherwise.

After catching me watching him, Lord Bellfourd promptly came to my side and insisted I dance with him.

I suppose the only thing better than seeing a moment worthy of a portrait is becoming a part of it.

Soon the night grew late, however, and I felt that I was in great need of the warmth and calm of my bed. The night of merriment had led to many more cups of cider, and I was already feeling the effects of it.

It was on that walk back to the manor, with Lord Bellfourd to accompany me, that he said the most interesting things. I am not sure if I can trust my memory of the event, but it seemed to me that he might have alluded to sharing some of the feelings that I have already shared with you, that I have for him.

As I said, however, I cannot be entirely sure that I heard him right, or only heard what I hoped he would say.

All I can say with complete certainty is that I have grown far too close to Lord Bellfourd, his family, and the whole of Wintercrest. I fear they have all found a place in my heart that can never be removed or altered.

Your Dearest Friend,

Isabella

29

*I*sabella's unwell feeling did pass within the day and, that evening, she told Lady Abigail all in the confines of her bedroom. Well, all but the one phrase spoken by Lord Bellfourd that would not seem to leave her.

The following week went on much the same. The only difference was that the article that Lady Lydia continued to hold over her carried no weight any more.

Not only had she found more courage in Lord Bellfourd's words, but she was also elated to hear that Lady Cunningham would be ending her visit earlier than expected. Instead of staying into and through the winter, she planned to leave over the next few weeks due to the fact that the Duke's health hadn't improved.

With Lady Lydia gone, Isabella would no longer have

that dark cloud hanging over her and things could go back to the way they once were.

It seemed to Isabella like things were beginning to fall into place in the most wonderful ways.

That joy was not exclusive to Isabella, though. It was only a few days after Samhain that Betsy came bounding into Isabella's room, breakfast tray in hand, with the brightest smile Isabella had ever seen.

"You look very high in spirits today," Isabella said in greeting to her friend.

"Oh, and I am," Betsy said setting down the tray and coming to sit upon Isabella's bed, as they so often did while they exchanged information.

Isabella came to sit next to her, excited to hear what could have possibly brightened Betsy's countenance so.

"I have spoken with Mr. Johnson again," Betsy started.

Isabella shrieked with delight and clapped her hands excitedly.

"Oh, you must tell me everything," Isabella encouraged. "I was so disappointed that I never met him the other night. Lord Bellfourd told me later that we were on his father's farm."

"In a lot o'ways I owe it to ye for it all," Betsy started. "I knew well who's farm was to host and had no plans to attend myself. When I saw that beautiful dress ye made me, I just had to go."

"And he saw you, the fine lady, and was mesmerized at once," Isabella encouraged with girlish excitement.

"I suppose so. He came up to me after the druid dance and tried to speak wi'me."

"Tried?"

"Aye, I'd have nothin' o' it. He had ignored me all those weeks, so I was determined to do the same to him."

"Then, the next day, I was going to town to fetch some herbs. Ye wasn't the only one to have too much o' the cider," she said with a weak smile. "It gave me the collywobbles fierce and I needed some peppermint tea to calm myself."

"Oh, Betsy, I'm so sorry. Here I was lying in bed, while you too were feeling ill. You should have told me and I would have found a way to hide you in my bed covers so you too could get some rest."

"Dinna fash," she said with a wave of her hands. "You didn't know it was so strong and at least had an excuse for bein' worse the day after. I've been drinkin' that stuff since I was a wee lass. I knew what too much would do to me, but did it anyway."

"But you will never guess who came running out of his barn as I passed by his fence."

"I would have to say one Alden Johnson."

"Yer right! He came runnin' out the barn and asked if he could walk me to town. I told him he was free to walk to town anytime he wanted, didn't mean I had to speak with him none. It was right braw," she ended with satisfaction.

"Well, he did walk with me. He didn't wait for me to let him, just spilled it all out. Said he was told that I had taken a shinin' to o'nother. Said it near broke his heart."

"And he was so broken hearted he started to spend time with Sally instead," Isabella replied skeptically.

"Well, I said the very same thing to him. Apparently, Sally is his cousin," she added with a giggle.

"No," Isabella gasped.

"Aye. I was so mad at the both of 'em I never spoke with Sally again from that day on. Come to find out their mothers are sisters and them two grew up good friends. When he was down in the basket, she was his shoulder to cry on."

"Oh, how comical. It sounds like it was right out of a Shakespearean play."

"Well, it's all on account of ye and the fine dress ye made. Without it, I'd never gone. Now, Mr. Johnson says he doesn't want to risk me getting away again."

"Oh, how glorious! Of course, I'll miss you dreadfully when you go, but I'm so happy for you."

"I suspect it won't be 'till next spring that we are married, so ye don't have to worry that I'll be running off right away."

"A spring wedding. That will be so beautiful."

"I plan to wear the dress ye gave me. I don't expect much fancy, but I hope it will be bonnie enough, though."

"You will look just like an angel coming into that

church, spring flowers around your veil. That Mr. Johnson is a lucky man."

Both girls continued to giggle, forgetting all about breakfast and the day they had ahead of them.

Betsy was just leaving Isabella's room, remembering herself, as Mrs. Peterson came marching down the hall.

"I don't know what you two think you are about, but in this house, I expect promptness without dawdling!"

Mrs. Peterson glared at each one fiercely. Her bun pulled so tight against her head that Isabella was almost certain it gave her whole face the look of stretched leather.

"Wur tearin' the tartan and got a little lost for time is all," Betsy explained. "We meant no harm by it."

"Whether you meant to harm or not, you are late. You should be halfway through cleaning your rooms by now. And you, Miss Watts," Mrs. Peterson turned in Isabella's direction. "You have already delayed your pupil one day. Is it really necessary to keep Miss Jacqueline's education waiting yet again?"

"We are sorry, Mrs. Peterson. As Betsy said, there was no malicious intent behind it. Betsy had some good news to share, is all," Isabella said, looking to her friend with a smile.

"Good news shall be had on your own time," Mrs. Peterson spat back bluntly before turning on her heels.

Both ladies were left in the hall listening to the jingle of Mrs. Peterson's keys as she walked away.

"Oh my, even the iron at her skirt side seems angry with us today," Isabella commented.

It sent the girls into another fit of giggles, which they quickly stifled and went on their way about their business.

Isabella spent the remainder of her day in the company of her pupil, closed up in the school room. The weather outside was right "dreich," in Mrs. Murray's words.

Isabella could guess the meaning was something like drab and full of rain. It never seemed to break for the whole of the day. Between that and the much colder wind, Isabella could see no way for her to take Jackie outside.

By the end of afternoon tea, Jacqueline was itching for any new change of venue. It was hard for Isabella to take her much around the house for fear of interrupting the household and their guests.

Lady Lydia detested Jacqueline almost as much as she disliked Isabella. For that reason, as part of Isabella's compliance conditions, she was not to distract the household any longer with such things as jars of bugs.

With the main portion of the manor unavailable to them, Isabella was struggling to come up with a change of scenery to appease her wards restlessness.

"I have an idea," Isabella finally said when Jackie moaned at the thought of taking out her slate and chalk yet again for her arithmetic.

"I would like to take you to a place where you will see a very practical use for the fraction we are learning. We will have to do it very quietly, however. Mrs. Peterson would not be pleased at all."

The idea of leaving the schoolroom and defying Mrs. Peterson, all in one moment, was almost more than the child could bear.

"Alright, let us first change you into an older frock. It may get a tad bit messy, and I would hate to ruin such a fine rose-colored dress."

Jacqueline excitedly changed her dress, with Isabella's help, and together they quietly walked down the long walkway that led to the end of the west wing.

It had been so long since Isabella had made this journey last, but she remembered it well. There, at the end, were stairs leading up as well as stairs leading down. They led all the way to the servants' floor and were, Isabella hoped, far enough removed as to not be noticed by Mrs. Peterson.

They stepped very slowly and cautiously, much like Peter Rabbit sneaking away from Mr. McGregor. Often, they would step on a creaking board with their silken slippers and Jackie would have to cover her mouth to stifle a giggle.

Twice, they ducked around a corner as they made their way through the servants' quarters so as not to be seen. Finally, they arrived at Isabella's plan destination, the kitchen.

The room was full of bustle as kitchen maids scurried

about, stirring pots and kneading doughs. Jacqueline stood amazed at all the excitement right below her own feet that she had not been privy to.

"And what might you two be doing in here?" a merry voice called from across the room.

It was Mrs. Frederickson, the household cook. Though she was tall and gangly, she was also as jolly as St. Nick himself. Isabella had sat with her on a few occasions in the dining hall for a late-night snack.

Mrs. Frederickson had even told her wondrous tales of when Lord Bellfourd was just a lad and had snuck into the kitchen, just as he mentioned on their first meeting. She laughed heartily as she explained that Lord Bellfourd had thought himself a real Robin Hood, dashing about the kitchen and stealing the sweets. He never considered that they all saw him and knew very well what he was doing.

"Well, Mrs. Frederickson," Isabella said, making her way across the kitchen with Jackie in tow. "Jackie, here, is having a hard time grasping her fractions. I was told that you were making some Shrewsbury cakes and thought maybe we could help?"

"How would sweet biscuits teach me my fractions?" Jacqueline asked.

"Well," Mrs. Frederickson said, putting a finger to the side of her narrow nose, "if you have to ask, then I suppose you do need a lesson in fractions. Come with me, little miss," she waved her hand for the two to follow her. "I will show you all my secrets to make the best Shrewsbury's that melt right in your mouth."

A half-hour later, the dough was mixed and both Isabella and Jacqueline were wholly covered in flour.

"Now, you see," Mrs. Frederickson continued in her lesson, strangely without a crumb or dusting of flour on her own apron. "We must take this dough and make twenty-four small biscuits out of it. They must all be equal in size, as well," Mrs. Frederickson cautioned.

"Now you try it first, Miss Jacqueline," she encouraged.

For a few moments, Jackie pulled out bits of dough, rolling them into balls and lining them up. As she went, some were big, others too small. Soon, she ran out of dough before completing the task. She sighed in disappointment.

"It was a very noble effort," Mrs. Frederickson encouraged. "But I have a better plan. Gather the dough all back up into one."

Jackie did as she was bid.

"Now, we are going to roll it out into a large square," Mrs. Frederickson said doing the work with the skill of a professional.

"You could try it your way, of picking and guessing if it's enough, or we could divide the dough out evenly."

Mrs. Frederickson returned with a knife and cut the dough equally in half.

"You see this way, every time we cut it, all the pieces get equally smaller until we have the number we want."

Later that evening, just before supper, Jacqueline presented a plate of perfectly equal Shrewsbury cakes to Mrs. Murray for tasting.

"I dinna ken what looks better to eat, the biscuit or you," Mrs. Murray said, brushing some flour from Jackie's cheek with her handkerchief.

"The biscuits, Nursie, you must try the biscuits!" Jackie replied, bursting with excitement.

30

Isabella was utterly enjoying her time with her ward and could not even imagine a time without her. With the onset of fall and change into winter, the days got shorter and darker. It confined the pupil to the schoolroom more, but Isabella was finding more and more ways to excite the child. With this came more regular visits to Mrs. Frederickson for lessons in the kitchen.

Isabella also afforded herself more liberties, taking her ward to the main part of the house to pick out more books or show her embroidery samples in the drawing room. Isabella had no more fear of Lady Lydia's threats.

Lady Lydia must have also sensed the change in Isabella's demeanor because she no longer found opportunities to flash the clipping at her during their few encounters.

Instead, Lady Lydia put all her efforts into receiving

some affection from Lord Bellfourd before her departure. She played the piano, sang songs, and even started to dote on Jacqueline, in the hope of winning over the Marquess' heart.

Jackie didn't hold Lady Lydia in very high regard. Up until this point of their visit, all Lady Lydia seemed to do was complain about the child's presence. Now that she was desperate to secure affection, she completely turned a new leaf and treated Jacqueline like she was a precious child to her.

She had a way of speaking to Jackie, in a very high voice, and in the tone that one might use for an infant, that was quite vexing to the ears.

Isabella did her best to encourage Jackie to endure it as politely as possible. She also had to remind Jackie that speaking her mind in French, as she often did in the presence of Mrs. Peterson, would not be a good idea as Lady Lydia was fluent in the language.

Though Isabella had developed maternal instincts toward Jackie, she had to admit she much preferred the new treatment from Lady Lydia than what she had shown in the past.

Despite what she hoped Lord Bellfourd had meant on their walk from town, Lady Lydia was still a genuine possibility for his wife. If nothing else, Isabella felt security in knowing that if their marriage happened, Lydia would have to be kind to the child.

Isabella couldn't help but also be satisfied in the fact that Lady Lydia had apparently given up all attempts to soil her reputation.

The real reason for Lady Lydia's easing of her threats, however, came a few days before Lady Cunningham and her daughter were set to return to their own estate. It came in the form of a letter with no return address.

Isabella puzzled over the handwriting, which she did not recognize, as she made her way back up to her room.

Isabella,

You think there is any place in His Majesties Empire that you could run, and I not find you?

I have found you. You will regret the day that you denied me.

It was not signed, but it didn't have to be. Isabella's blood ran cold. Mr. Smith knew where she was. What lengths would he go to ensure her destruction?

Before she could dip into sorrow, she instead flashed with rage. There was only one reason that she would receive such a horrid threat and have lessened pressure from Lady Lydia.

She marched downstairs without a thought, letter in hand. She found Her Grace, Lady Abigail, Lady Cunningham, and the awful Lady Lydia all seated in the small drawing room taking their afternoon tea.

"Please forgive my intrusion," Isabella said, doing her

best to hide her rage behind a smile. "I was wondering if I could steal a moment with Lady Lydia."

All eyes looked on in confusion. It wasn't a secret to any in that room that Lady Lydia disliked Isabella. In fact, she had been very vocal of that fact over the course of her visit.

"I have a letter," Isabella held up for all to see, "from Mrs. Mason."

Isabella steadied her breath, doing her best to tell the fib.

"I have been writing to her regularly. When I told her Lady Lydia was here, she added a nice message for her at the end of the letter."

"Oh, how very thoughtful of Mrs. Mason," Lady Cunningham said none the wiser to the real content of the parchment.

Lady Lydia had no choice but to excuse herself from the room and follow Isabella into the privacy of the morning room.

"How dare you," Isabella started, not caring about the repercussions of rude behavior anymore. "You wrote to Mr. Smith. You gave him the address of my employment."

Isabella threw the threatening letter on the table in front of Lady Lydia. For such a hostile situation, Lady Lydia stood perfectly calm, arms folded in front of her mint morning dress, a slight smile on her thin lips.

"Of course I wrote to him." Lady Lydia finally said. "Did you actually suppose that I would allow you to work here, to poison Lord Bellfourd against me, and take away everything I rightfully deserved yet again?"

"We are not children anymore, Lydia," Isabella said exasperatedly. She struggled to keep her voice low. "I took nothing from you then, and I will take nothing from you now."

"You have cost me my position," Isabella went on, willing Lady Lydia to understand the seriousness of her act. "He will, no doubt, write to the duke. When Lord Bellfourd reads that letter in his stead..."

"You will be unemployed. Yes, I am well aware of what I did," she responded coolly as if the conversation was now boring her.

"This is my livelihood. Without this position, or at the very least, a reference, I will have no hope of securing another. I have no other means to support myself."

"How very unfortunate for you. Perhaps, instead of spending your earnings on frivolous dresses and sweets, you should have considered that the time would come when all your evil doings caught up with you."

"Evil doings? You have no idea what that man asked of me." Isabella took a steadying breath. "I admit it was wrong to take the locket when he owned all my father had, but it was just a necklace. It was of no worth to him except for the mere fact that it mattered to me."

Isabella held the empty place on her collarbone where the treasure once lay.

"As I said, most unfortunate for you. Now if you don't mind, I will return to my happy company. I do not feel comfortable being tangled in yet another one of your lies."

She picked the short letter up and looked it over. She frowned, before letting the letter fall back to the table. "Mrs. Mason, indeed." She turned and left the room before another utterance could be mustered.

Isabella paced the floor a few times, willing herself to calm down before she did something absolutely radical.

She thought of something her father had told her as a child, 'though your hair be as cool as night with no moonlight, your head can be as hot as the sun itself.'

She stood still, closing her eyes, and breathed deeply. There was nothing to do about it now. If Mr. Smith chose to write to her employer, Lord Bellfourd would be the one to receive it.

She had already told Lord Bellfourd some of the issues attached to the man, so she had to hope he would at least give her time to explain. He would understand. All would be right in the end.

Unfortunately, things do not always go to plan, as was the case for Isabella. Before the week's end, she received three more threatening letters from Mr. Smith. Each one became angrier and coarser than the last.

The land froze much earlier than expected, and Lady Cunningham was forced to extend her stay several weeks past her expected departure due to the dangerous roads.

Isabella would have to remain in the presence of Lady Lydia for a longer period of time. Even worse, Isabella feared that with the early turning from autumn to winter, she would be forced to endure the whole holiday season in Lady Lydia's presence.

As Isabella dreaded every letter now delivered to her and placed in the servant dining hall basket, Lady Lydia waited with bated breath for a letter to arrive addressed to the duke.

She was certain now that she had secured all that was rightly hers. She wouldn't allow Isabella outshine her again.

Dear Isabella,

I must admit that I am very concerned for you after your last letter. Of course, we both knew the deceit that lay hidden within Lady Lydia, but this is a most unbecoming course, even for her.

As for the letters you have told me about from Mr. Smith, I am very worried for your safety. It sounds like he may truly wish you harm.

I know you must find the protection of your distance in your favor, but what if it is not? Certainly, Mr. Smith has the means to travel. What if he was to come to Wintercrest?

I know that you are concerned that Lord Bellfourd might think less of your character if you discuss the whole matter with him, but as your friend, I must encourage you to do so, despite your fears.

From the short time that I was acquainted with him, as well as what you have told me during our correspondence, I believe he is a very understanding gentleman. He will see your side of the situation, and could perhaps aid you.

I know that you talk as if the letters and threats do not affect you, but I know your tender heart. To be subject to such horrid things, falsely accused, to endure such bereavement would be hard on anyone.

I beg you to relieve yourself of the burden you have carried alone. Seek comfort in the friendship of those around you. Hold tight till Lady Lydia is removed from your presence. Most of all know that I think of you and pray for your wellbeing each night.

Wishing you safety and love,

Louisa

31

*I*sabella considered her friend's advice. Certainly, if this situation had occurred at Rosewater House, she would have gone straight to Louisa for help. Though she found sense in what Louisa suggested, she also couldn't overcome her fear of lessening her character in any of the household members' eyes.

And still, if she went to the Marquess now, Lady Lydia was bound to find out about it. She would only use it to fuel malice and dislike from the duchess and maybe even Lady Abigail.

Isabella couldn't risk that chance. She cared too dearly for both ladies to lose their friendship. Once Lady Lydia was away from Wintercrest Manor, she would go to Lord Bellfourd and lay all her past events and their reciprocations at his feet for judgment.

All thoughts of herself and her own problems melted away as the duke's health declined drastically with the onset of winter weather. It was a mere two weeks after Isabella received her first threatening letter that the doctor came to visit one last time.

Though the doctor had attempted every treatment in his power, he feared that the sickness along with a possible punctured lung had been too much for the duke to recover from. He very apologetically told the family that the duke would most likely not last the night. The family gathered in the library that evening, just a doorway apart from their patriarch.

The room was clothed in dark veils and silent sorrows unspoken. Isabella was present at the side of Jackie. Each member of the family was waiting for a chance to say their final goodbye.

The duke struggled to breathe, could eat almost nothing, and could scarcely utter a few words. None the less, he desired to give his family members final words of wisdom.

Lady Wintercrest stayed by her husband's side through it all, gently holding his weak hand. All other family members and guests waited in the drawing room to be called in one by one.

First was Lady Abigail. She spent half an hour with her father before returning to the library very upset. Lady Cunningham, in her motherly wisdom, held Lady Abigail in her arms and let her cry.

Lord Bellfourd was next. Isabella felt sure that he would return from the room not the sorrowed, confused heir with no desire for his title, but the man she knew he could be.

He spent several hours at his father's side before returning to the library. The whole party waited in silence, though little Jackie had fallen asleep in her governess' lap from the lateness of the hour. Lord Bellfourd came from the room, his eyes swollen and red, and made his way straight to Isabella.

He reached down and lifted Jacqueline into his arms. She barely woke at the touch. He easily hoisted the limp body onto his shoulder and reached down with his hand to take Isabella's.

She took it immediately, without thought, and stood at his side, not sure what he wanted of her.

"He is nearing the end now," Lord Bellfourd said. "I want him to say goodbye to Jacqueline."

He walked the two girls into the room, looking over his shoulder only once to make sure that Lady Abigail was also following. She had already risen and come to his side.

Isabella noticed the specific words he used. Lord Bellfourd wanted the duke to say goodbye. Presumably, that meant the duke had no desire to see his only grandchild, even on death's door.

"May I be of assistance?" Lady Lydia said, standing.

"No, thank you, Father would like to be surrounded by

just family," Lord Bellfourd responded before taking the groggy Jackie in his arms and the two ladies trailing behind him.

Isabella did her best to ignore Lady Lydia's eyes falling on her with evil intent. She was almost certain that repercussions would come from this moment, but cared naught for it.

When they came into the room, it was hard to see. Only the glow of the fire lit the room. Lady Wintercrest sat in a chair, handkerchief continuously dabbing at stray tears.

The duchess was exhausted from the hours at her husband's side. Strands of her hair had fallen all directions, some glinting silver in the firelight. Though she was aged and with grown children, she still felt much too young to be widowed.

The duke was seated in his bed with several pillows. Even in the few, short weeks since Isabella had seen him last, he had aged and wasted away drastically. It looked as if the cushions around him were more to keep him in place, than to merely prop him to a seated position. Isabella feared that at any moment his frail body might topple over.

Each breath was a struggle for him to take. Even from across the room, Isabella could hear the gurgling sound of liquid as he struggled to pull in more air. His face was drawn in deep creases. The once somber wrinkles of his face now hung without the flesh beneath. Even his face looked as though it was struggling to keep upright.

Jackie finally sat up in her uncle's arms, rubbing her eyes. Isabella reached out and took the child into her own arms. Lord Bellfourd and Lady Abigail stood on the opposite side of the bed from their mother. Isabella stood back with Jackie in her arms and gave the family their privacy.

The duke could do nothing but move his eyes and watch his family gather around him. Worse, Isabella could see his mind working and, no doubt, the desires of his heart struggled to be free. It was more than he was able to handle in his weakened state. It left him nothing to do but look on as his family cried before him.

Lord Bellfourd turned and searched the room for Isabella and Jackie. "Come here," he called softly. "Bring Jackie before him."

Isabella did as she was bid and brought the child forward. Lord Bellfourd stood to the side, giving up his spot at his father's right hand to be replaced by his niece.

Isabella stood behind her ward, ready to assist in any way possible. She could only imagine how confusing and frightening this night must have been to such a young child. Jacqueline gripped both of her governess' hands firmly, a little taken aback by the state of her grandfather.

Isabella knelt down, still holding firmly to each of Jackie's hands and whispered in her ear in French, "It's all right, little one. Tell your grandfather how much you love him."

Big droplets of tears welled in Jacqueline's eyes. She didn't understand much of what death meant, but she did know it was a sort of going away, and a very sad departure at that.

"I said the Lord's Prayer just for you, Grandpère," Jacqueline said, just above a whisper.

Though he was much too weak to move or speak, the duke's eyes lowered to the face of his granddaughter. His lips, slightly tinged blue, turned up into a wavering smile and a single tear rolled down his cheek.

He struggled to move his one free hand. The Marquess reached forward, helping his father to place his hand into Jacqueline's.

Isabella did her best to choke back her own tears. Even if this unity of grandfather and child was of the Marquess' making, the duke was glad of it. Through the glow of the fire, Isabella could easily see the love and words never spoken in the gleam of the duke's eyes.

"Why is he so cold?" she whispered to her governess in French.

"Perhaps he needs you to warm them," Isabella whispered back, not wanting to tell the child the true reason why.

"I will warm your hand for you Grandpère," Jacqueline said, rubbing her two small hands over the larger, colder one.

The whole family watched as the two small palms, still slightly plump from infancy, gently rubbed the long, wrinkled fingers already beginning to grey.

"Jackie," Lady Wintercrest's voice came out hoarsely from the other side of the bed. "Sing for your grandfather, so that he may fall asleep peacefully." She did her best to smile at the child, despite her tears.

It was clear to all in the room that the end was coming. The duke's body could last no longer with the frailty of his lungs. Isabella feared greatly a dramatic parting that might be scarring to the child. She hoped that with the sense of love and release of pain over his oldest son, Lord James, the duke would be able to pass into the next life in peace.

"Oui, Grandmère," she said.

She watched her grandfather's hand between her own continuing to softly rub her warmth into him, while she sang her lullaby.

"Underneath the moonlight
My good friend Pierrot
Please lend me a pen
So I may write a note
My small candle's dying
There is no more light
Open up your door, please
Pity me this night."

As Jacqueline continued her song, the duke's eyes closed softly, and with the escape of one last tear, his breath quieted and he drifted off peacefully.

Isabella didn't need to hear the choked sob from Lady Wintercrest, holding his other hand, to know his time had passed. She waited till the child finished before scooping her back into her arms.

"Is Grandpère asleep now?" Jacqueline asked her governess.

"Yes, you did very well my little cherub. Let us find your own bed now."

She paused to hold the hand of Lady Abigail for just a second before quietly exiting the room.

32

*T*he weeks after the duke's death passed in a quiet blur. Lady Cunningham, in the end, determined to stay the year through to help her friend through her grief. Isabella understood Lady Cunningham wanting to be next to a close friend in her time of need, but couldn't help but regret that the joyous holiday season would now be spent in the presence of Lady Lydia.

Lady Wintercrest was grief-stricken by the passing of her husband. Though Isabella had never thought their marriage one of romance, it was clear that Lady Wintercrest did have deep admiration for her husband and would miss his companionship dearly.

Shortly after his passing, the duke was laid to rest in the family graveyard next to his son, Lord James. It was at this time that Lord Bellfourd was now required to take on the land, title, and seat of his father.

He did hesitate at first, often not leaving his room all the day long, so deep was he weighed down by the prospect before him.

Though he knew, with the passing of his older brother, this day would come eventually, he hadn't expected it to be so soon. Even as the late duke's health continued to deteriorate, Lord Bellfourd was certain he would right himself in the end.

Now, Captain Christian Grant was the Duke of Wintercrest. It was a weight and responsibly that he didn't feel ready for or suited to, but it was his, none the less, and so he took it upon himself.

Unfortunately, even with the sullen state of the house, life seemed to continue elsewhere. This regrettably included continued correspondence from Mr. Smith. Isabella, though she certainly didn't enjoy her letters, was settled to the fact that he was, at least, only writing to her and had, as of yet, not sent any word to the household.

"What are you ladies doing today?" a male voice came through the school room door just after the passing of the holiday season.

The newly instated Duke of Wintercrest by the House of Lords had not been to visit his niece much over the last few months. Isabella's face lit up with joy to see him there now and notice some of the old light in his eyes.

"We were examining our caterpillars to see if they wiggled. Nursie said she saw them dance, but I don't believe her," Jackie said, coming to stand before her uncle.

"Do you think, perhaps, that you could watch your little friend while I speak with Miss Watts?"

"Alright, I'll let you have her if you must," the child said, coming into her own childlike personality, "but you must promise to give her back."

"Upon my honor," the Duke of Wintercrest said, hand over heart. "If you don't mind too much that is, Miss Watts?"

"Of course not," Isabella stood up from her crouched seat next to the small jar of critters.

He held his arm out to her and she slipped in her hand happily. They walked in comfortable silence as they made their way down to the duke's office. It had been moved, once again, to its original room after the removal of bedchamber items.

The duke escorted Isabella inside and shut the double doors behind them. Instead of going over to his desk, he instead walked to the two chairs in front of a warm fire.

He more collapsed in his seat than sat. Covering his face with his hand, he exposed his true feelings that he had yet to share with anyone else.

"Oh, Christian," Isabella said taking a seat across from him. "You have looked so tired as of late. I have been so worried about you. Please, tell me what I can do to help you."

He lifted his head from his hand, ruffling his hair in the process, and relaxed into a soft smile.

"I am not sure what is to be done anymore."

"I could at least call for some tea," she suggested. "Perhaps it would calm your spirit?"

"No, thank you though."

"Perhaps just a friend to talk to, then?" Isabella asked with a hopeful tone.

"Now that, I would be happy to accept. I actually called you here because of this," he pulled a letter out from his pocket.

Isabella's heart caught in her throat. Had Mr. Smith written to the duke after all?

"It comes from a Mr. Jenkins," he said, opening it, and Isabella relaxed into the back of her chair. "He tells me that he is your father's lawyer."

"Well, he was. He is just a good friend now, I suppose."

Christian nodded in understanding.

"He explained that he was charged with sending your quarterly allowances from your father's business partner and making sure they were given to you."

"Yes, I was given a small yearly sum upon my father's death."

"He informed me that he is most concerned about your welfare because he has not been able to give these sums to you, as agreed. Apparently, Mr. Smith is refusing to pay the amount agreed. He was concerned that without it you might not be living as comfortably as you should. Were you aware of this matter?" He asked, already knowing the answer.

"Well, I was aware that I was no longer receiving money from Mr. Jenkins after the first quarterly amount. I know him to be a trustworthy man, however, and believed that he would send them along when, or I suppose if, he ever received them."

"Had I known you were in wanting…"

"I'm not. I promise you that, Christian." Isabella answered quickly. "I have more than enough for my needs."

"I suppose I just wished you would have told me when this Mr. Smith started to treat you poorly again."

Isabella half thought to tell him of the constant streams of harassment she was still receiving, but couldn't bring herself to do it. "You have been through a very rough time in your life. I didn't want to burden you with anymore."

"You seem to be the only one to feel that way at this time," the duke said with spite as he looked into the fire.

"Please, tell me. Perhaps I could help."

"I suppose that is the real reason I asked you to speak with me today. I am hoping you can help me."

"My mother," he said with a huff, "is of the opinion that, with my father passed, it is of the utmost importance that I seek a wife and secure the family name, as it were."

"It is a very practical suggestion of her," Isabella said, her heart fluttering in panic.

"I'm sure you could guess that she has a very particular lady in mind."

"I suppose she would," Isabella said, doing her best to hide her sorrow.

"I told Mother that I can't stand the thought of being married to Lady Lydia," the duke exploded, standing before the fireplace. "She is completely opposite to me in every way. In my mind, such a situation would only have a dastardly end."

"Your mother has a lot of affection for her friend Lady Cunningham, and naturally she sees the match a good opportunity for strengthening the bond between two households. Would she not understand, if you shared your feelings with her?"

"I have," he answered, staring into the fire. "Mother thinks my concern is just the reason that we would make such a good match. You see," the duke said, turning to Isabella in explanation, "she and my father were not in love. I'm not even sure how much affection ever ran between them. It was an arrangement most agreeable to both families. Just as I am counter to Lady Lydia, so my mother was the opposite of my father."

"She feels that having such a relationship can temper each other's vices and provide stability. In her mind, the whole of success in marriage isn't on matters of compatibility but on the constraints of society."

"Surely the constraints of the town do not limit you to one lady? I'm sure Lady Wintercrest will be happy for you to find affection for someone else who is in accordance."

The duke sat back down in his seat. There was something on his mind, perhaps the root of the whole conversation, that he was trying to find the right words for.

"What if I have already chosen another?" he asked, looking at her with a deep gaze. He held his hand to his chin while he studied Isabella processing the new information.

"Then I see no reason why your mother wouldn't accept your choice. She is a very reasonable woman. If you choose a lady from the proper breeding, she would be overjoyed at your decision."

"What if the woman I chose was not of a proper family? What if I knew, that though my family thought kindly of the lady in question, they might not agree with the unconventional choice I was making?"

Isabella's heart was in her throat as the duke spoke with pleading eyes. She was hoping in the depths of her soul that he was speaking of her, that the Duke of Wintercrest would defy conventions and his family's wishes, to confess his love to her.

She stopped in her thoughts, however. She could never

ask Christian to hurt his family on her account, nor should she ever wish to add to Lady Wintercrest's current sorrow.

She swallowed hard to choke down the emotion she was holding back.

"I think..." Isabella said, fighting the tears that were beginning to pool, "I think you should do what is best for your family."

He dropped his hand in shock. He couldn't believe he was hearing her right.

"You know who I speak of, do you not?" he asked.

"Yes," Isabella barely choked out with her eyes cast down at the rug.

"And you will honestly tell me that you do not feel for me as I do for you?"

"No, I will not tell you that. I won't lie to you. I care for you deeply."

"Then, why?" Christian asked bewildered.

"Because I also care deeply for your sister, your mother, your niece. I won't bring them more pain. There is enough sorrow just now."

"For just now, or for finality?" the duke questioned.

He came down on his knee in front of Isabella and took her hand in his. He looked up at her emerald eyes, not a direction he was accustomed to.

"I know the duties that are laid before me. I have settled myself to the task. I know, however, that I cannot do them without you by my side."

"You have been the friend to comfort me, to listen to me, as I struggled to come to terms with reality. You have brought light into the life of every person you have met. I know with you, I will have the courage to overcome whatever may come my way."

"Christian," Isabella said softly, taking a moment to reach up and feel the smoothness of his cheek.

The duke closed his eyes and relished her soft touch.

"I could not bear to hurt them," she repeated softly.

He opened his eyes to her, "Then we shall wait. I could wait as long as necessary, if I only knew that you too felt the same for me as I for you."

Isabella smiled down at the man kneeling before her. If he only knew how long she had held him in her heart secretly, he would laugh at asking such a question.

"I do feel the same for you," she answered softly.

He smiled up at her, elated. He leaned down and softly kissed the delicate hand he held in his. Standing, he lifted her to her feet as well.

"Then I will wait. For as long as it takes. When this time of sorrow passes, we will have our wedding day," he said, looking down at Isabella's glowing face with hope in his crystal eyes.

33

*I*sabella held the memory of Christian's hand in hers as she lay in bed. She had yet to open her eyes, but she knew that dawn was drawing near. The repetition of his words in her mind seemed to melt away all her fears.

The pile of letters she kept hidden in the bottom drawer of her dresser held no weight. It didn't scare her now. A part of her considered writing back to Mr. Smith. She wanted to tell him that she had been blessed with the affection of the duke and that he no longer had power over her. She was proud.

With Lady Lydia out of the house, and the family beginning to heal from their wounds, it was only a matter of time before all of Isabella's happiness would be complete.

She only dared share her joy with Lady Louisa through correspondence. It was too delicate a matter—too unsure of a thing, as of yet—to tell anyone else. It was a terrible burden to hide her excitement from others, especially as she had grown so close to Betsy and Lady Abigail.

With the beginning of spring, Isabella was about to complete her first year as a governess. She was happy to say that her student had changed and grown much over the last year. The most significant being, of course, her use of the English language.

Isabella particularly enjoyed this improvement because it created a deep bond between the child and her nurse. Something Isabella feared greatly was that Jacqueline would miss the maternal care that most little girls received.

With Mrs. Murray to take care of her, Isabella was assured that Jacqueline; though she, of course, could never replace her own mother, had a proper stand in. She was now able to write much on her own to her mother back in France.

Isabella was happy that even with the English Channel between them, Jacqueline was able to have a relationship with one of her parents. Of course, she had never met her father, but Isabella had made it a priority, over the last year, for the child to be aware of him, and even encouraged the household to speak of him to Jacqueline.

Isabella understood why, up until her coming, the family had rarely spoken of their deceased member. It was a painful thing, even to talk of happy memories, because it also carried unhappy reminders of departure with it.

It wasn't an easy hurdle to overcome, as Isabella had learned as a child. In fact, she supposed it was her mother's own early departure from life, and learning how to live with a grief-stricken father, that gave her the tools necessary to help the Wintercrest family overcome their own painful feelings toward sharing memories.

"Miss Watts!" Jacqueline called excitedly as Isabelle entered the school room. "It's happening! It's happening!"

"What's happening, my dear?"

"The caterpillars, they are coming out of their shells!"

Jackie was bouncing up and down with joy, her golden ringlets free-flowing around her as she tugged on her governess' arm.

"Lil lass has been a ball of excitement all morning," Mrs. Murray said, coming into the room from the nursery. "I barely got her rags out this morning. She has been nothin' but wiggles."

Mrs. Murray had a pink silk ribbon in her hand that she was still hoping to get into the child's hair. She was by no means irritated by the girl's fidgety behavior this morning. In fact, it seemed that Jackie's excitement had been caught by her nurse—she moved with lightness in her step. There was certainly more bounce in her movements than usual.

"The only way I got the lass to eat this morning was to move her little critter right to the table so she could continue to watch."

"Here, Mrs. Murray," Isabella said, reaching out for the ribbon. "I will happily place the ribbon. I suspect there will be no point in arithmetic this morning, as it seems Mother Nature has made other plans today."

Isabella took the ribbon and tied it to pull back a portion of Jackie's hair away from her face. Jackie was hopping up and down in place with her head close to the jar. Isabella suspected it was the best that could be done.

They spent the morning watching as their little friend slowly made his way out of his cocoon and stretched his wings. Jackie was so enthralled that Isabella was right to estimate that no other school work would be done that day.

When Betsy arrived at the schoolroom with the noonday meal, the newly emerged friend was just starting to flutter his wings in earnest.

"Oh, Miss Watts, can't we take him outside now?" Jackie asked, too interested to eat.

"Let us have our meal first. Then, afterward, we will take him outside and see if he is ready to use his wings."

Jackie wasn't happy about having to wait but she was an

obedient child and went to fetch her nurse for their luncheon.

Isabella wasn't entirely sure if Jackie had actually eaten anything. She spent the whole meal telling Mrs. Murray a moment by moment account of what had been happening in the jar, from the second Mrs. Murray had left the room in the morning until the second they sat for lunch.

"Miss Watts, may we take the jar outside now?" Jackie asked as plates and teacups were returned to the tray to be picked up.

"Let us look out the window first to make sure that the weather is fine enough for him. I wouldn't want to let him go if it was still chilly."

"Why not?"

"Well, he has been warm and comfortable here in your schoolroom. The fire has made it warm and cozy in here, while it was cold and snowing outside. His delicate wings cannot handle extreme cold."

Isabella walked her ward over to the large windows draped behind curtains. She pulled them back and gave a look out the window to the manicured gardens below and sky above.

There was a dark green sheen of moisture. That seemed almost always to be the case, so it wasn't much of a concern. Isabella instead studied the clouds.

She had learned once, the hard way, what happened when a storm came suddenly and wasn't going to make that mistake again if she could help it. Isabella studied the clouds carefully and determined that they were non-threatening.

"I suppose it is safe enough for us to take our afternoon exercise now," Isabella said to the squeals and delight of her student.

Isabella helped Jackie into her long coat, gloves, and fur muffler. Though it was spring now, and flowers were becoming more frequent in bloom, the wind could still have a bitter chill to it.

"I've heard something exciting has been going on in here," a deep voice called from the doorway.

Isabella turned her focus from her pupil to the gentleman taking over most of the doorway. Her face instantly lit with a smile as it so often did at his presence.

The Duke of Wintercrest ducked his head out of habit as he crossed the threshold. Though the doors in the manor were tall enough, even for his height, Isabella suspected that wasn't the case on the ship, forcing him to drop his rusty head below their lower level.

"Oh, Uncle Christian, the caterpillar is now a butterfly. We are going to go outside and let him fly," Jackie said, still full of energy.

"What a fun adventure. You must have the best governess in all the land," the duke said, crouching before his niece but winking up at Isabella.

Isabella blushed and looked away. Though they had

agreed to keep their engagement a secret, Isabella couldn't help but think that they probably weren't very good at it. Most especially Christian, who seemed to find any and every excuse to spend time with her.

"I hope you won't mind terribly if I tag along?" the duke asked, already knowing the answer.

When his niece nodded affirmatively, the duke stood to take his lady's arm. Jackie grabbed the jar from the small table where it had resided through the colder seasons, and together they went outside.

They walked in silence for a time, while Jackie found just the perfect spot to release the creature.

Though Isabella was wearing her thicker woolen shawl, she still felt the bite of the cold whenever the wind blew. She pulled herself closer to the duke for warmth. He smiled down at her as he covered her gloved hand with his leather-gloved one inside the crook of his arm.

Isabella didn't miss, however, that the smile didn't quite reach up to his blue eyes. She watched him closely as they continued to walk. She could see there was a deep weight on his shoulders.

Finally, Jackie decided on a small garden cove with early bulb blooms for the new butterfly's home. She released the lid from the jar and watched as he fluttered out. Jackie chased him around the garden as he dipped from one fresh flower to the next.

Isabella took the time, when Jackie was completely

distracted,to address her concerns with the duke's current countenance. They were walking around a small gravel path that kept the garden separate from any other.

"There is something bothering you, Your Grace." Isabella stated. "If you need someone to talk to, I would be happy to listen."

The duke smiled down at her, enjoying the fact that she knew him well enough to notice his distress.

"Well, my dear Isabella, my mother informed me this morning that she has decided to plan a very large ball."

"A ball?" Isabella asked, a little surprised herself. "I wouldn't have thought her up to such a task."

"Well, it was after receiving encouragement from Lady Cunningham that mother decided on this course of action. According to Lady Cunningham's advice, the distraction will benefit her greatly, as well as give myself the opportunity to be officially introduced as Duke of Wintercrest."

He added this ending as if he still wasn't sure how the name suited him. He had changed names, and with it, part of his identity, far too much over the last few years.

"I guess, for those reasons, it seems logical," Isabella said, still trying to understand why the duchess would want to take on such a responsibility as she still healed.

"It's all a ruse," the duke said, heated with irritation. "Lady Cunningham, and even my mother, are just looking for another way to push Lady Lydia to me."

Though Isabella was secure in her faith that the duke

had meant his words when he confessed his love, she still couldn't help but feel a pang of jealousy.

The duke stopped abruptly on the path and turned to Isabella. He reached up and cupped her face in his hands. Isabella closed her eyes and leaned into the touch. They were as completely secluded as they would ever be, and the duke wanted to take advantage of the moment.

He leaned his head down so that their foreheads touched. The duke absorbed the electricity building from their closeness. Isabella, too, felt herself melting against his touch.

"Let us announce our engagement now," he whispered softly to her.

Isabella opened her eyes and leaned her head back from him. Isabella was sure he was teasing. It was still far too close to the death of his father for such a thing. He looked down on her, full of love and honesty.

"Christian, telling your mother we are engaged won't stop the ball from happening," Isabella said, trying to lighten the mood.

The duke gave her a half smile. He wrapped one arm around her waist and held her cheek with his other.

"I don't care about the ball. I mean yes, of course I am dreading it. I hate balls," he answered her raised brow. "But, more than that, I don't want this to be a secret anymore. I want you at my side that night."

"I just think it's too soon," Isabella said. Emotion caught

in her throat as she said her true fear, "I think it would be better for you to take extra time, Your Grace." She took a step back from his embrace. The world seemed much colder.

"Extra time for what?" He asked, clearly hurt by her actions.

"Time to think things through with a clear head. Your mother isn't the only one taking on an enormous amount right now. You might see things differently in the future. I don't want you to feel bound if you change your mind."

"Change my mind?" the duke questioned in disbelief. He took another step toward her and took both her hands in his. "Isabella, I have no concern that my feelings for you will fade or clear. I would ride with you to Gretna Green if you would allow me."

Isabella looked on him, filled with her own concern. "What of your mother? I am not a proper lady."

"Had I been just Captain Grant instead of Duke of Wintercrest, would your feelings for me change?"

"Of course not," Isabella answered quickly.

"That is why I love you, why I want you to be by my side through life. I think no less of you without your father's title. My conviction will not waiver. Not today, tomorrow, or even a year from now. Though, God forbid, you make me wait so long," he added with a wicked smile.

She softened too with his encouraging words. She held his hands softly with her own. Isabella looked up at him shyly and he relaxed, knowing he had convinced her to wash away any worry.

"Uncle Christian?" a small voice called a little way up the path. "Are you in love with Miss Watts?" Jackie asked with an innocent romanticism as she observed their held hands between them. Her cheeks were rosy from the whipping wind and chasing the butterfly.

"I am afraid I am hopelessly so," His Grace said, coming down to the child's level. "But we need to keep it a secret for just a little while longer."

"Until the ball," he continued, looking back up at Isabella, "when I will announce our engagement to all."

Isabella smiled down at her future husband as he shared their secret with his niece. She nodded in agreement. She found it to be a sufficient compromise. Isabella wanted him to have time to adjust to his new way of life before adding more to it. Waiting till the ball seemed like the right choice to her.

sabella's ears perked up at the duke's words. They were all sitting around the fire in the drawing room one evening. Lady Abigail was currently teaching Jackie a children's card game, Lady Wintercrest was deep at work at a small writing desk, making a list of invitations, and the duke was reading over some mail he hadn't gotten to earlier in the day.

Isabella continued her embroidery sample but kept her ears tuned to their conversation. Her eyes only met Christian's once and he winked at her stealthily.

"I don't know if I am familiar with Lady Gilcrest. I know the name well enough, but I can't say I remember ever making acquaintance with the family. How do you know them, Christian?"

"When I was last in London, I met both Lady Louisa and Lord Colton during the Earl of Cunningham's event."

Lady Abigail paused from her game. She knew who Lady Louisa was in relation to Isabella.

"Oh yes, mother. Lady Louisa is a very dear friend of Isabella. We must invite her. I have so wanted to meet her myself."

Isabella noticed that Lady Wintercrest hesitated for just a second before agreeing and adding the name. Though she thought His Grace and herself had been very discreet, she sensed that it hadn't gone unnoticed by Lady Wintercrest.

Lady Wintercrest had certainly been kind to Isabella but there seemed to always be a hesitation in her mannerism now. Isabella wondered if she was disappointed that her and Lady Cunningham's matchmaking hadn't worked out. Isabella worried that it was something much deeper than just a failed attempt to find a match for her son.

As the night wound down, Jackie began to grow tired. Isabella expected that it was time she took her pupil up to bed. "Come, Jackie. Let us say our goodnights for the evening."

Jackie nodded her golden head in sleepy agreement before taking a turn around the room to say goodnight.

As she gave her grandmother a hug, Lady Wintercrest turned to Isabella, "I was wondering if you might come back down after you deposit Jacqueline to her nurse. There is something I have been meaning to discuss with you."

"Of course, Your Grace," Isabella said, a little bit surprised.

"Wonderful. Shall we meet in the library, then?" Lady Wintercrest continued.

"Yes, Your Grace." Isabella nodded before taking the child out of the room. She did her best to ignore the growing concern deep inside. It was not completely usual for Lady Wintercrest to want an audience with Isabella, especially a private one.

Isabella hurried to take Jackie to bed and return to the library. The wondering was enough to make her go mad. She found Lady Wintercrest seated in a chair next to a newly lit fire. Several candles had also been lit in the room to produce enough light. She was deeply engrossed, as she so often was these days, in her planning.

"Please come and have a seat," Lady Wintercrest said, setting her notes to the side. Though she was still young for a widow, the last few months had significantly aged her around her eyes.

"What is it I can help you with, Your Grace?" Isabella took a seat across from her. She couldn't help but remember the last time she had sat in these chairs. That time, it was across from Christian, who had confessed his feelings for her.

"Miss Watts, I first want to say that I have been very

happy having you here as part of our household."

Isabella was sure this wasn't a good start to things.

"You have brought so much joy to not only little Jacqueline, but to all of us. In fact, I am quite certain that without your presence, my husband would have never..." she paused as the raw emotion got the best of her for a moment. "I am certain he wouldn't have parted so peacefully. He was so hurt by what had transpired with the child's mother and James that he kept his heart very hard toward Jacqueline."

"I'm just happy that I could be a little help," Isabella said, wringing her hands in her lap.

"I have not been blind to the affection my son has for you," she stated with a soft smile on her lips. "Naturally, it would not be my first choice for my son to engage the governess. You have been more than just that and I was, at first, very willing to accept the match. I care for you dearly, Isabella, and would have been happy to call you my daughter-in-law."

Isabella was waiting for the end of her remarks which were to surely come and not be good.

"Lady Cunningham is not one to gossip, but she felt that she must bring something to my attention," Lady Wintercrest continued with considerable nervousness.

"She told me that an article was posted in London that suggested that there might have been some confusion with theft before you came to stay with us. It seems that the gentleman put in charge of your father's estates found some items missing when you left London."

"I can assure you, Lady Wintercrest, I never meant for it to happen. You see, it was a locket containing a lock of my mother's hair. Mr. Smith insisted I turn over all my possessions to him, which I did. I couldn't bring myself to give the charm. It held such a dear place in my heart."

"While I cannot say I think it is right of this Mr. Smith to require such a thing of you, it was still wrong to take the things you stole."

"I swear, Your Grace, it was just the one necklace. When I learned that Mr. Smith had put in the advertisement, I returned it to him straight away."

Lady Wintercrest pulled a letter out of her stacks of papers regretfully.

"It seems that Mr. Smith is claiming much property was taken from him," she said, looking over a letter. "Lady Cunningham only informed me because she was concerned not only for our association, but for yourself as well."

"It seems that Mr. Smith is claiming that you stole from him property amounting up to one hundred pounds."

Isabella's mouth dropped open in shock. She would have had to pick up the entirety of Rosewater and sewn it into her dress hem for that to be the case.

"He claims that he was unable to pay the debts that had been given to him on your father's passing because of this theft. Unfortunately, he testified to this matter before a judge when brought to court by those collecting the debts in question."

"I did no such thing. It is true I took the locket, but nothing more. He was given the whole of my father's estates including our London home," Isabella was doing her best to control her anger.

It seemed that Mr. Smith had no limits when it came to destroying her reputation. He had received the whole of what her father possessed, as well as complete control of the business her father built and still sought to destroy her.

"Unfortunately," Lady Wintercrest continued, "the authorities were brought in to settle the matter. According to their investigation, they cannot account for the goods inside your previous residence which now seem to be missing."

"Certainly, they could question the previous servants. I left Rosewater long before he took hold of the place and they could confirm that I left all belongings behind, except what was in my trunk."

"The servants did confirm such a fact. However, the week after you left to join us here, apparently, a solicitor claiming to work for Mr. Smith cleared out the house to sell the possessions. Mr. Smith claims that such a person wasn't employed by him, nor has he seen the possessions since. He claims it was a solicitor you had hired."

"It's not true!" Isabella said just a bit too loud. "I'm

sorry," she said regaining her composure. "What am I to do, Your Grace? It is all falsehoods. How can I possibly prove my innocence?"

"Well, I am not very versed on what to do in this kind of situation. I suppose getting a lawyer might be the initial first step."

"I know a very good one. Mr. Jenkins. He worked for my father. He will help me sort this out."

Lady Wintercrest gave a relieved sigh. "I am very happy to hear that for your sake." Her countenance fell again, "however..." Lady Wintercrest hesitated, not sure how to find the words.

Isabella swallowed hard knowing what must come next.

"However, I cannot engage myself to the duke at this time. Really, ever. My reputation is ruined. Even if I clear my name, there is no going back from what is now said of me. I cannot bring that shame on the duke, on any of you."

Isabella looked to Lady Wintercrest with tears in her eyes. The duchess was dabbing her own eyes with a silk handkerchief. "I wish it were some other way, my dear."

"But there isn't," Isabella answered with finality. Her heart turned to stone and sank deep inside her. "I will leave at once," Isabella said, standing.

Lady Wintercrest stood too. "I think it might be for the best. I fear any delay and my son would wish to get involved. It would be best to leave now before things get too far. I can have the carriage take you this night."

"Yes, of course," Isabella said, disheartened by the duchess' speed and plans already in place.

Lady Wintercrest came forward and wrapped Isabella in an embrace. She wasn't doing this out of her own desire, but for the good of her children. It would not just taint the duke but the whole family. Who would seek the hand of Lady Abigail if her sister-in-law was thought to be dishonest? And what of poor Jackie? Isabella could never do something that might later have a negative effect on the child.

Yes, Isabella would pack quickly and leave that night. She hated that even so far from London, she had still not escaped the hatred of Mr. Smith. She would not allow his evil to spread to such an innocent family, a family that had already experienced enough trouble of their own.

She returned the duchess' embrace before hurrying out of the room. Isabella did everything in her power to hold back the rush of tears threatening to fall as she quickly made her way to the west wing of the house.

Isabella quickly packed a few of her belongings. She would have to leave most of what she had behind. She cared less for the dresses and books that she had once cherished and more for the people she would have to leave.

It was more than she could bear to think of all the friends she had made and not be able to say goodbye to a single one of them.

Quickly, she got an idea. She would write a note to each

of them. She tried not to dwell on her feelings as she wrote down her love and appreciation for each member of the household who had touched her heart in the last year.

Isabella saved the letter to the duke for last. Part of her hoped that if she never got to the letter, she would never have to actually say goodbye to him. A soft knock on her door told her otherwise.

She opened it a crack to see Samuel, the coachman, standing a bit awkwardly at her door.

"Forgive the intrusion, Miss Watts. Her Grace told me you would need a ride into the village to take the early coach back to London.

"Yes, thank you, Samuel. I am just about finished here."

"I'll meet you outside, then," he added, clearly not comfortable with coming to a woman's room at night.

Isabella shut the door behind the scurrying young man and sat down at her desk to write her last, and hardest letter. Upon finishing she could barely see if it was, in fact, legible, so many tears were falling down her cheeks.

Isabella, with small bag in hand, set the letters on her pillow with Betsy's name on the top. She knew the maid would be the first to notice that she was gone in the morning and would do her the favor of distributing the rest.

She left her room and made her way out of the house as quietly as possible. Entering the Wintercrest coach, she took one more look at the manor before turning down the darkened road that lead her away.

35

*T*he next morning at breakfast, the family meal was interrupted by a very distraught maid.

"Betsy, whatever is the matter?" Lady Abigail asked, the first to notice the crying servant come in.

"I beg yer pardon on intruding," she said with a curtsy between sniffles, "but I have some letters here for ye all, Your Grace."

"Give them all to me," Lady Wintercrest said, coolly holding out her hand.

Betsy did as she was bid.

"What is this about, Mother?" the duke asked, seeing that Lady Wintercrest had knowledge of what upset the maid.

"Unfortunately, Miss Watts had to leave in a bit of haste last night," Lady Wintercrest said as softly as she could.

"Leave?" the duke practically shouted, standing. He leaned forward, both long hands on the table, "What do you mean she had to leave? What happened? Where is she?"

The Duke of Wintercrest was little concerned with masking his feelings for Isabella at such horrid news. He couldn't possibly imagine what would have made her flee the house during the night.

"She has returned to London. She will no longer be in our employment."

"What did you say to her last night? Did you make her go?" the duke accused.

"She chose to leave all on her own. It came to my attention that there were some issues regarding her character. Now, I know we all cared for her deeply. She felt the same and determined to leave. She hopes to rectify the situation and I truly hope she does."

"Is this about that awful Mr. Smith again?" the duke replied.

His mother was shocked to see he knew the name.

"I received a letter from her lawyer, not too long ago, that stated she was supposed to be receiving a small allowance from her father's business and Mr. Smith was withholding it."

"I am not going to admit that I know everything on the matter," Lady Wintercrest replied, "but it would make sense for him to remove the allowance if his allegations are true."

"And what allegation is that?"

"He claims that Miss Watts removed items from the house he inherited for the sum of a hundred pounds."

"That's preposterous. You don't actually believe this?"

"I would like to think not, but she did admit to taking at least one item. A charm, of some sort," Lady Wintercrest said trying her best to remember the night.

"A locket?" the duke asked, sitting back down in his chair. He realized that not only had he seen her wear that locket almost every day, but it had also arrived in the strangest fashion. Had Isabella sewn the necklace into her hem because she was hiding her crime?

"We all saw her wear such a thing," the duke said in disbelief that she could ever commit a criminal act. "She admitted as much to me and that she had returned it."

"As she told me last night. Mr. Smith claims there is much more, however. Neither of us agree that it could be the case, but there are past events against her."

"She did have all those books in her room," Lady Abigail chimed in, also in disbelief. "She told me she took them from her father's library before she came here. They were her favorite books and I didn't think anything of it."

"Is it wrong for her to have belongings from her home? Could you imagine being told to leave this house and take nothing with you? It is much more than any could bear. I refuse to believe these charges," the duke resolved.

"In our hearts, none of us will," Lady Wintercrest said, reaching across the table for her son. "But the fact of the matter is, she knew it would not be well for you had she stayed and your engagement been announced."

The duke's eyes widened in shock that his mother knew about their secret engagement.

"Don't be silly, Christian," Lady Abigail said, waving him off. "We all knew. You may have kept the words silent, but you couldn't hide the way you two looked at each other."

"Fine," he said, understanding that everyone knew his secret, "then you know why I will be leaving for London right away to bring her back."

"Christian," Lady Wintercrest said softly. "Think this over. She didn't want to leave any more than we wanted her too. Had she stayed, and you announced your engagement before the whole of the town, it would have had a devastating effect."

"I couldn't care a lick what the town thinks of me," he spat back, enraged.

The duke pulled his hand out of his mother's and sat back in his chair, rubbing his chin. He was still trying to process all of this. How could she have thought he would not stand by her?

"It was not just for your sake. Think of Abigail, even

Jacqueline. This would affect them too."

Lady Abigail opened her mouth to protest. She shut it promptly, however. Her mother was right. It would end any chance of Lady Abigail ever securing a marriage of her own. She sank in guilt with the realization that she was thankful that Isabella wouldn't ruin her like that.

"The world isn't always fair," Lady Wintercrest said now, to both her children. "I cannot say that I fully believe this Mr. Smith over someone I have been in association with this past year. I wish her the best, that she might be successful in clearing her name. But she has done what she can to protect those she loves and we must respect that decision."

The duke would not look his mother in the eyes. He merely shook his head, refusing to believe that he could let her do such a thing. She had no one and no means to help herself, save the lawyer. Would he still help her now that she was without the means to pay?

Lady Wintercrest slid the small parchment addressed to each of them respectfully. Lady Abigail took it and left the room without a word spoken. Christian looked down at his letter. Even in its folded and sealed state, he could see the damage of tears.

"I will give you some privacy," Lady Wintercrest said, standing. "I suspect Jackie will need some comfort of her own, which I will see to."

The duke waited till the room was fully cleared and the

doors shut before he allowed himself to pick up the parchment. He hoped that if he didn't read it, Isabella would magically appear before him and say it was all a cruel joke.

My Dearest Christian,

It is with the deepest sorrow of my heart that I am forcing myself to write to you. I know you must be outraged right now. Please know this is not Lady Wintercrest's fault.

It is better she told me of the accusations against me before it was too late for you, and for the rest of your family.

I am so sorry for the hurt and shame I have brought into your home. I wish I could say that I should have never come to Wintercrest at all. I am too selfish, however.

I will never regret the time I spent with your household, and most especially you, Christian. I only regret that your association to me may have already tainted prospects for yourself or your sister.

I will always hold you dear in my heart, but I must beg you not to do the same. Let this be but a passing moment for you. Find happiness.

With all my love,

Isabella

The duke held the note in his hand and read it again. He would have liked to crumple it into a ball. If he could have had his way, he would have charged out at that very moment on his fastest horse and not stopped till he found her.

He cared not what others would say. In fact, had she come to him, he would have married her on the spot, providing her the protection she so desperately needed.

He understood that it was for Abigail's sake that she left. He loved his sister dearly and would never want his actions to result in her detriment. But it mattered not.

He loved Isabella and he would not let her stand alone before the wolves to be devoured. Perhaps he could find a way to aid Isabella in clearing her name. Then, with that settled, he would go to her. He would not care a bit for gossip after the fact.

Once things were set right and Mr. Smith made to pay for his actions, the duke would find her. He would give her the family and the protection she deserved.

He got up out of his chair. Only the sound of his tall leather boots could be heard as he paced the breakfast room floor. He would write to her solicitor first. He would pay for the cost, no amount would be too much, to see that she was properly represented.

It would also give him a chance to keep in touch with someone connected to Isabella. The duke refused the idea to cut all ties with her. He had given Isabella his word that he would love, support, and protect her all the days of their lives.

It didn't matter if it wasn't official. It certainly didn't matter that she had released him from such commitment.

He would stick by Isabella however he could as long as he lived.

After writing first to the solicitor, to insist all billing pertaining to her case be brought to him, the duke wrote next to the Earl and Countess of Gilcrest.

The duke knew it would take at least three days for his letter to reach the recipients. Isabella having at least a half a day head on them. He prayed that, even without his recommendations and encouragements, the Earl of Gilcrest would take Isabella in.

The duke left his office upon completion of the letters and intended to see his niece. Instead of going to the nursery, though, where he could hear the voices of Mrs. Murray, Jackie, and his mother, he walked on to what was once Isabella's living space.

He was surprised to see the door partially open. He pushed it open the rest of the way to see the very same tearful maid collecting items from the shelves.

"What are you doing?" he asked startling the girl.

"Beg yer pardon, your grace. Mrs. Peterson told me to come and clean out the room."

The duke looked around him. It seemed that Isabella took scarcely more than the clothes on her back.

He thought again how absolutely ridiculous it was to claim her a thief, this poor lady who had every last item stripped from her, save a few articles of clothing and books. Then, those too, she had to leave behind.

"Leave it all," the duke said softly. "If Mrs. Peterson gives you trouble, you tell her it is my wish that this room stay intact for now."

Betsy curtsied, eyes still swollen from her crying. She stopped before she left the room and turned back to the duke.

"I dinna mean to be impertinent, Your Grace, but will you help her? She told me how awful that man was to her. She never said as much, but I suspected he continued to harass her even here."

"What makes you think that?" the duke asked.

She had never spoken to him of such harassment. He hoped that she wouldn't have felt the need to keep it from him.

"As I said, I dinna ken for sure. It was only, around the time Your Grace's father passed she started to get these letters. So many of them, sometimes three a week. They never said who they were from. Isabella always got so sullen when they came."

"Thank you, Betsy," the duke said, excusing the maid.

He scanned the room. If there were such letters, the duke could use them to prove that Mr. Smith's character, and in turn his claim, was fraudulent.

He got up and did a quick search of the writing desk. There was nothing to be found. He suspected if such letters were written, Isabella wouldn't keep them. His only hope would be that a new letter came in the next few days, before it was known that Isabella had left for London.

Without hesitation he rushed downstairs to the servants' quarters. He went first to where the mail was kept and shuffled through the post. He was disappointed to find no letters to Isabella.

"Your Grace," a solemn voice came from behind. "Can I help you find something?"

The duke turned and bore down on Mrs. Peterson. "You are not to touch a thing in Miss Watts' room, is that clear?"

"Of course, Your Grace. I assumed since she had left that we needed to clear the space for a new governess."

"There are no plans for a new governess at this time," the duke said with finality. "Also, any post addressed to Miss Watts must go directly to me. Is that clear?"

The Duke of Wintercrest stood to his full height and used the commanding voice he so often heard given by lords to their servants. He had never expected himself to do so but at that moment, his hurt and anger were leading his words.

"Yes, of course, Your Grace," Mrs. Peterson said with a humbled curtsy.

The duke returned upstairs and to his office. He had no taste for his work that day. In fact, the only thing that seemed to solely occupy his mind was the quickening of the passage of time so that Isabella could be returned safely to him.

36

*I*sabella found her second carriage ride through the country and back to London vastly longer and more sorrowful than its counterpart one year earlier.

Even entering the city she had so loved and remembered fondly had no joy for her. She exited the stagecoach and went directly to find a cab that might take her to the Earl of Gilcrest's London house.

It didn't take long for Isabella to seek out the yellow two-person cab and give the driver directions.

She only hoped that her friend and correspondent would be happy to see her. Or, at least allow her shelter for the night. Isabella was fully aware how fast news traveled in London and she was sure that by now, the details of her suspected theft were the topic of most ladies' gatherings.

Isabella did her best to calm her nerves as she stood on

the steps to the Gilcrest city abode. She luckily knew that Lady Louisa would be here. In correspondence a few weeks early Lady Louisa had informed her that they would be leaving their country seat for the season and return to London, much to her excitement.

Summoning all her courage, Isabella knocked softly on the door. She did her best to straighten the traveling skirts she had sat on for the last three days.

A butler opened the door to her, "Are you expected Madam?"

"I am afraid I am not. I am Miss Isabella Watts. If you could tell Lady Louisa that I have come to call on her, I am certain she will receive me."

"As you wish," the butler said, showing Isabella into the front room to wait.

Isabella waited no more than two minutes in the small foyer that she knew so well, before she heard the hurried steps of slippery feet.

"Oh, Isabella," Lady Louisa said, coming into the room and taking her friend into a hug. "I have been so worried about you."

"You have? You aren't surprised by my being here?" Isabella said, confused.

"No, no. Not at all." Lady Louisa took her friend's hand and brought her into the small drawing room where her mother was waiting.

Lady Gilcrest rose at the sight of Isabella and embraced her as well.

"Oh, my dear, we have all been so worried about you. I'm so glad you came to us."

"How did you possibly know of my coming?" Isabella asked.

She was indeed grateful that the household had taken her in so welcomingly. In fact, the whole carriage ride, she had replayed scenario after scenario of them turning her out right there on the front steps.

"Lady Abigail Grant sent a letter the morning after you left," Lady Louisa said, by way of explanation. "She sent her own man on horseback. He rode day and night, barely stopping, and arrived here yesterday morning."

"Come, sit and have some tea," Lady Gilcrest added to her daughter's words.

"That was very kind of Lady Abigail," Isabella said, taking a seat. "She didn't have to go through all that trouble."

"Well, I believe she was a bit worried that you may be returning to London much like Daniel going into the lions' den," Lady Louisa replied.

"I must admit," Isabella said shyly, "I was a little worried that you wouldn't receive me."

"That is a ridiculous notion," Lady Gilcrest said. "We, of course, heard the rumors and I made a point to speak up against them at every occasion."

"Yes, this Mr. Smith is a most vile man," Lady Louisa concurred. "To think he would go to such lengths to tarnish your reputation."

"I have cogitated much this fact these last three days of travel," Isabella said, feeling comfortable now in the security of friends.

"Well, dear, you just start from the beginning and we will figure this out, as we always do," Lady Louisa said, patting her friends hand.

A half-hour later, Isabella had told her friend and Lady Gilcrest the whole situation. She started with the necklace in her hem, all the way through retelling all that Lady Cunningham had written to the duchess.

"It is not very different than the telling of the matter that I have also heard," Lady Gilcrest said smoothly. She was older in age but had the grace and agility of someone much younger in years.

Both Gilcrest ladies were identical to the other, only one being older. Lady Gilcrest shared her daughter's mouse brown hair, though hers had a lot more silver in it now, and the same slender, shy, demure features to her face.

"Why do we not have the solicitor produced that removed the belongings from Rosewater? He could easily say that it was, in fact, Mr. Smith who hired him."

"I suspected that would be my first course of business. Mr. Smith did walk through Rosewater with a solicitor before my departure. I would suspect he was the man that removed the belongings. The only problem is that I don't recall his name."

"Well, this is only your first day home, so do not discourage. We will find a way to untangle this mess he made," Lady Louisa said. "Speaking of a long day of travel, you must be exhausted. Come, I will help you upstairs so that you may refresh yourself before dinner."

Isabella followed her friend upstairs to the room that they would share while visiting.

"Unfortunately, I was not able to bring much with me. I only have the dress I am wearing and a cotton morning dress," Isabella said a little embarrassed now they were alone in the room.

"Do not worry. I have more than enough for the both of us. It will be just like when we were young and shared clothes at school," Lady Louisa added with a smile.

"You have been very kind to me despite..." Isabella struggled to finish the sentence. She sat down on the soft bed.

Lady Louisa sat next to her and consoled her friend. Wrapping a warm arm around Isabella, she waited to speak till she got hold of her emotions again.

"I suppose I don't need to ask how your heart is faring?" Lady Louisa finally said.

Before Isabella could answer, there was a soft knock on the door. In came a maid with fresh, hot water for Isabella.

Both girls waited till the maid left before continuing their conversation.

"I had to leave," Isabella finally said, softly. "And to make things worse, it will never matter if I right my name. The damage is irreversible. I will always be a pariah of society. I could not bring that misfortune on the duke or Lady Abigail."

"I suppose it was Mr. Smith's intention all along," she continued. "If I would not accept him, he would find a way to make sure that no one would ever consider having me."

"I am sure the duke doesn't care about stains on reputations. Especially when he knows they are ill-founded," Lady Louisa said as she tucked back a loose dark strand that fell into Isabella's face.

"I know he doesn't care. I know he would keep his word no matter what. I couldn't let him. I care for him far too much to do such a thing to him."

Lady Louisa nodded, understanding Isabella's reasoning for severing that tie.

"I shall let you clean up and rest for a while before dinner. I know you must be exhausted. Sometimes all that is needed to find a way to right a wrong is a little sleep."

Lady Louisa left the room after expounding her words of wisdom. Isabella did enjoy the moment to refresh herself and remove the dust that seemed to cake to one's skin while traveling.

Once freshened up, she slipped into the covers.

Isabella, at first, did not think that she would sleep at all. The stress of the last few days had kept her so awake that she didn't know if she would ever truly rest again. Now that she was in the safety of friends once again and refreshed from her travels, though, Isabella slipped quickly off to sleep.

It seemed like only a few moments had passed when Lady Louisa arrived back in the room. Already, the window was growing dark with dusk.

"I waited as long as possible, but we really must dress for dinner now. If you would like, I can make excuses for you and have a tray sent up instead," Lady Louisa said, just above a whisper, as Isabella came to her senses.

"No, no. I want to come down. I must have been more exhausted than I thought. I am quite refreshed now, though, I can assure you."

Isabella got up from the bed and together, with the help of a lady's maid, both girls got ready for the evening meal. It was funny for Isabella to have someone help her dress and style her hair again. It seemed to her that it took an exorbitant amount of time rather than just dressing on her own.

She smiled to herself for the first time in three days. It did seem a silly thing that something a person was once so used to as to not live without, now, having lived without, seemed a silly thing to have at all.

Isabella came down the stairs at her friend's side. She

was trying to remember how to fit into the person she had once been. At one time, this had all seemed so normal to her, but now, without a ward to guide, it felt strange to Isabella to join the household for a meal.

Thoughts of Jackie brought a deep hurt to her heart. Though she couldn't bear the thought that she was now without the company of all of Wintercrest, little Jackie brought the worst guilt of all.

A child of only seven, she would not understand even a portion of the complexities that had led to her departure. Though Isabella had written in the letter that she would always cherish and love Jackie, she couldn't help feeling that she had abandoned her.

"Ah, Izzy, how are you, old girl?" Viscount Dunthorpe said as the two ladies entered the drawing room.

"If I am an old girl, Lord Colton, then what, pray, does that make someone three years my senior?" Isabella responded with a remembered banter.

"Dashingly handsome, I would expect," he responded, raising a dirty blonde brow.

Unlike his mother and sister, Viscount Dunthorpe Colton Frasier took his father's stronger square features and playful personality.

"Give the poor girl a chance to settle in before you go on harassing her," the Earl of Gilcrest called from his corner of the drawing room with a wink at Isabella.

He was standing deep in conversation with a gentleman

that Isabella didn't know. He was introduced to her as Colonel Macintyre. He was a portly fellow with a very distinguished mustache that seemed to mesmerize as he spoke.

"I hope you don't mind," Lord Dunthorpe said after Isabella was seated, "I have invited your friend, Mr. Jenkins, and his wife to join our small party this night."

"Oh, that is actually perfect," Isabella said excitedly.

She had planned to send a note to Mr. Jenkins and call on him tomorrow. She knew if anyone could help her out of this situation, it would be her late father's lawyer.

"I thought you might want to speak to him right away," Lord Dunthorpe said with a wink. "As soon as I heard of your arrival, I sent him an invitation."

"I appreciate it so much. Thank you," Isabella said sincerely.

She had to keep her emotions in check yet again. She had never been one for crying much, but over the last few days it had been a common occurrence. And this time, Isabella was happy to say that it was tears of gratitude for the kindness of the whole of the Frasier family.

37

The Duke of Wintercrest paced continually in his office. He had become more and more irritable of late, and the hustle around the house this morning only seemed to sour his mood further. He was the reason for all the excitement in the manor and probably should have been happy for it. However, he was most certainly not.

It had now been a fortnight since Isabella's departure and he felt that little had been done in that time.

One small accomplishment for the duke had been to convince his mother to go to London for the season and host her lavish ball there, in the town residence. She had resisted, at first, knowing full well that his reasoning was Isabella.

With a change of venue, the whole event would need to be pushed back from its pre-season timetable. It would give the duke more time, and the vicinity, to regain acquaintance with Isabella and clear her name.

Now, the house was abuzz with preparations for their departure that morning. The duke, however, refused to leave without seeing the morning post. He was expecting a significant letter that he hoped would turn everything around for him.

Over the last four weeks, the duke had been sharing correspondence with Mr. Jenkins, unknown to either his family or Isabella.

Mr. Jenkins had first hoped to produce a solicitor that had worked for Mr. Smith to destroy his allegation. Such man was nowhere to be found. Though his sudden disappearance was questionable, it wasn't enough to prove foul play.

A few days after Isabella fled, Mrs. Peterson handed the duke a letter addressed to her. He was appalled at the words written therein and couldn't believe that, for the past months, Isabella had been subjected to such vile writings.

He had immediately sent the letter on to Mr. Jenkins. It clearly proved the scoundrel harbored ill intent toward Isabella. The duke was concerned because the letter was not signed, but hoped that at least through some sort of writing comparison, Mr. Jenkins could prove the ill character of the man and his clear intent to harm Isabella.

"Your Grace, a letter has just arrived, as you hoped," Mr. Larson said, holding a parchment on a silver tray.

"Thank you," he said as he took the letter greedily.

To the Duke of Wintercrest

Your Grace,

I hope this letter finds you in good health. Am I to understand that you will shortly be joining the ranks of this most humble servant here in London?

I will be most glad for the much shorter distance our correspondence will have to travel. I can honestly say that your contributions in this delicate endeavor have made a significant difference.

I am happy to inform you that I have compared the letter that was addressed to Miss Watts, to writing I already had on hand from the offending gentlemen. I, myself, see it as a clear match.

To solidify this case, I have gotten the written word of three others to confirm that the handwritings do match. Without a name at the bottom, though, we cannot but hope that this will prove our case.

I am also glad to inform you that we have also found a second fault to Mr. Smith's claims. It has come to my attention that, just after acquiring full ownership of Baron Leinster's shipment company and all his estate with it, Mr. Smith made a large investment.

He made this investment through the mercantile company for the shipment of goods back from the recently lost colonies. He foolishly thought that he could invest in a large shipment of textiles from the country and make a market on it,whilst others were still unwilling do so in the still unfriendly political atmosphere.

In the end, the ships he sent never returned, no doubt now living their lives out in the Virginias. He lost a great deal of money, not only what he invested in the venture, but also what he had expected to gain out of it.

According to my sources, Mr. Smith had no means, within the company, to fund such an ill-planned venture. It is my calculation that he used the selling of the late Baron's goods and home to fund his expedition.

He, no doubt, thought that he would see a return in his investment before needing to use the money for its actual purpose.

With no way to pay back the debtors now calling on him, Mr. Smith turned to the claim that Miss Watts had stolen from him, rendering him unable to pay any debts.

Though he does have to prove that Miss Watts took the locket after strict instructions not to do so, I am confident that it will not be enough to prove her guilt, as Mr. Smith hopes.

I am hopeful, as I take our case before a court later this week, that in due time, justice will be served. I have little doubt that Miss Watts will be cleared of all charges in no more than a year's time.

Your Humble Servant,

Mr. Abram Jenkins

The duke sat down in his chair as he read over the letter a second time.

"A year," he breathed out loud, setting the letter on the desk.

Most certainly, the duke could wait as much time as was needed before he again engaged Isabella, but he couldn't imagine her suffering a whole year, living as she now did.

Though the duke was reassured that the Earl and Lady Gilcrest were taking good care of her, she was most certainly bound to the four walls of their house. There would be no party, no gathering that she would be accepted to. The longer this vile Mr. Smith kept his accusations up, the more irreversible the situation would become for her.

The Duke of Wintercrest would not stand by a whole year, while Isabella waited in house arrest for her name to be cleared. He wasn't sure how he would do it, but he would find a way to rectify the situation while in London himself.

He was also determined to do it before his mother's grand event, so that Isabella would be there by his side when the time finally came.

The trip to London was long and laborious for the duke, who could not seem to find any more patience for the whole situation. He sat next to his mother who was deeply enthralled in her embroidery, while his sister and niece sat across from him, biding their time with books and card games.

Lady Abigail had taken on much of Jacqueline's education in the absence of her governess. Though she was not very well trained in the art of teaching, she happily spent most of her mornings and afternoons in the schoolroom with Jackie, doing her best to pick up where Isabella had left off.

"Will I get to see Miss Watts?" Jacqueline asked, the afternoon they came into the city. "She said in her letter that she loved me dearly. Doesn't that mean she will want to see me while I am here?"

Lady Abigail looked to her mother and brother across the carriage. Though the whole of the party was aware of Miss Isabella Watts' presence in London, it was also an unspoken fact that they wouldn't be able to see her.

"I am sure that Miss Watts would want to see you. I am afraid, however, that it just might not be possible," Lady Abigail said, as delicately as possible.

She looked back to her brother who was now sternly staring out the carriage window. She watched the muscles in his jaw as he tightened them.

"Why ever not?" Jacqueline asked.

"Because," Lady Abigail said, turning back to the child, "you will be so busy with all the wonderful things to see and pretty frocks to buy, that I don't suppose you will have a moment to spare."

"I would always find a moment for Miss Watts," Jacqueline said. She knew the answer to her question wouldn't change no matter what she said. She leaned her golden head on her aunt's shoulder, "I miss her so much. It's as if I left mother all over again."

Lady Abigail placed her arm around the child and did her best to comfort her. The silence in the carriage from that moment on was deafening.

As soon as the carriage came to the townhouse, the duke went straight to his office to pen a letter. He wanted to inform Mr. Jenkins that he had arrived in London and that Mr. Jenkins should expect a call from him in the morning.

The duke stayed in his office for the remainder of the night, not even joining the family for an evening meal. He could sense Isabella's closeness and his hands turned to brush her cheek again.

He locked himself in the office for fear that if he walked out, he would continue to do so till he found himself before the residence of the Earl of Gilcrest. He knew he must wait and pace himself.

First, he would meet with Mr. Jenkins, then he would put into practice the plan he had developed on the long ride over.

It wasn't a plan to see Mr. Smith behind bars, something he would most like to do, but it was a way to end it all and again have Isabella as his future bride.

38

*I*sabella was beginning to feel her mind slipping as she turned the small garden in the back of the house for what had to be the hundredth time.

With the season starting in earnest now, Lady Gilcrest and Lady Louisa were engaged most afternoons and evenings. Though both ladies had insisted Isabella come along with them, she had firmly refused.

They were kind enough to shelter her over the past month. They didn't need the added burden on their reputation to be seen with her in front of the town.

Instead, Isabella was left at the house alone most days. She tried to stay put in the small drawing room and embroider or read, but with the glorious sun shining down almost every day, she couldn't help but want to be outside in its warmth.

She thought for a moment of when she and the duke had sat on a cold stone bench in the dark. Isabella had confessed that she could never get used to the cold weather so far up north.

When the prospect of their unity was so close, Isabella had not once considered living her whole life up at Wintercrest Manor. Now that she was returned to London, she still missed Wintercrest and its inhabitants, but she could not help but enjoy the sun.

"You wicked minx," a voice called into the garden, "out here taking turns with your bonnet in your hand." Viscount Dunthorpe said to Isabella as he made his way to her in a teasing manner. "What will the other ladies say?"

"They will not say a word of it," Isabella said, placing the confounded conformity back on her head before taking the Viscount's arm. "I am not acceptable to be in proper society. I might as well look the part."

In all honesty, Isabella had learned to despise her large brimmed bonnets, as Lady Abigail had done. But she reminded herself that London was different and the sun could be harsher.

"Don't be so down, Izzy," he said affectionately, as he took her for yet another turn. "It is right awful outside these walls. I fear the town has gotten even more gossipy since you left. It would not suit your often-loose tongue at all."

Isabella pinched his elbow in a sibling gesture. Colton had always included Isabella in his big brotherly duties.

"I have actually learned very well how to control my tongue," Isabella said, sticking her sun-warmed chin in the air.

Lord Dunthorpe looked down at her with his disbelieving brown eyes.

"It's true," she continued. "The housekeeper at Wintercrest, Mrs. Peterson, she was just about the most awful woman I have ever met. She was so cruel and short with everyone. Very often, she was abrasive with me. I did a very good job of keeping my mouth shut in those situations."

Lord Dunthorpe raised a blond brow again in disbelief.

"I did. Well, at least I did for as long as she was in earshot," Isabella added with a giggle.

"As I suspected. I suppose it is better than the governess telling off the head housekeeper. I must admit, however, I would have been sorely sad if you had said you had cured your tongue altogether. Its sharp bite has been quite entertaining for me." He thought for a moment, "Well, at least when I am not the one it is pointed at."

"It is about to be pointed at you right now if you do not stop your irritating teasing," Isabella responded, looking up at her dear friend's older brother.

"Come then, let us drink some tea. Perhaps the refreshment might protect me from your wrath or, at the very least, your pinches," he added playfully, leading her back into the house.

They went into the drawing room and each took a seat on opposite sofas. Isabella began to pour as the tea was placed before them.

"Do tell me what you have been up to over the last year. Have you finally found a young woman to tame your wild nature?"

"No," he said, leaning back in his seat and dropping an arm across the top, "I'm afraid I offend and terrify all those I encounter."

"That can't be true? You are charming."

"Yes, but then I open my mouth," Lord Dunthorpe said with a wide smile. "Most ladies don't approve of my racing or other eccentric habits."

"I suppose you would be quite a handful. Don't worry; I am sure there must be one miss up to the task of taming your wild ways."

"Yes, well, Mother and Father are quite hoping so. I think they fear that I will never marry. I suppose," he said as he wrinkled his brow in thought, "I have found plenty of misses' as you have mentioned, wanting to change me, but I would rather like one who would join me, instead."

"Well then, don't let her see you set your traps before you marry her. One look at your breakneck speed and I scarcely think she would ever get in a carriage with you again."

"You've seen me, and you still get in carriages with me."

"And I say a little prayer every time," Isabella retorted with a smile.

"I've got some news for you, Izzy," Lord Dunthorpe said after a small lull in the conversation. "I've debated telling you over these past few days, but I think I should."

"Well, what is it?"

"The Duke of Wintercrest and his family have recently taken up their London home."

Isabella did her best not to show any reaction to the news although her heart leaped instantly in her chest. "Oh," was all she could find to leave her lips.

"I found this out when we received an invitation to a ball they are having to introduce the duke officially. It is in a fortnight's time."

"I must admit, I am a little surprised they sent you that invitation. The duke thought it would be a nice treat for me to have Louisa present. I didn't think after...well, I guess it just goes to show how kind they are."

"The invitation included you, as well," he said gently. "Do you think you will go?"

"I can't imagine that I could stand to do so."

"Because of your feelings for the duke" Lord Dunthorpe said this as a fact more than a question.

"How did- did Louisa tell you?"

"No. It was just pretty easy to see that you were heart-broken. Not to mention the fact that you have talked on end about every member of that household except the duke."

Isabella looked down into her teacup, embarrassed that she had given herself away. She knew she would never overcome her feelings for the duke, but she had hoped that she was better at hiding them.

"I guess the only reason I bring all this up is that I think you should go. I know that it's not something you're going to decide on lightly, so I thought I might give you plenty of time to think it over."

"Oh, I really couldn't. Mr. Jenkins has high hopes for our case, but I can't imagine all will be solved in time. I wouldn't let your family be seen in public with me, or disgrace the Wintercrests like that."

"You will never be a disgrace to this family, so don't you ever think that," Lord Dunthorpe inserted. "As I said, I am just telling you now so that you can consider going over the next few weeks."

Isabella sat in her shared room, later that evening, reading a book. The Gilcrests were currently at a dinner that they had been invited to, so Isabella had the whole of the house to herself. A soft knock interrupted her reading.

"Beggin' your pardon, miss, but a caller's come to the door," the maid's voice said smoothly.

"A caller? At so late an hour? Please, just tell them the Gilcrests are out for the evening."

"I did so, miss. He said he has come to see you."

"Oh, alright then," Isabella said, taking a moment to fix her hair and smooth her cotton dress.

She couldn't help but get butterflies as she made her way down the stairs and into the drawing room. It had only been a few hours since Lord Dunthorpe had divulged that the Duke of Wintercrest was in London. She had thought of nothing else since that moment. As much as she had told herself that she hoped the duke would move past her, she also secretly hoped he was the one who had come to call.

However, when she entered the room, she did not see the tall, broad shoulder figure of the duke, but rather the friendly face of Mr. Jenkins. Isabella did her best to hide her disappointment both inwardly and out.

"Mr. Jenkins! How nice of you to stop by," Isabella said, sitting down.

Mr. Jenkins looked as nervous as he had that very first meeting in his office over a year ago.

"Is something wrong?" Isabella asked.

He moved in a jerking manner as he came to take a seat.

"I am sorry to call on you at such a late hour, but I figured you wouldn't want me to wait a moment before telling you."

"Yes, please do. You are scaring me a little," Isabella said as she fidgeted with her own hands in her lap.

She tried her best to seem cool and collected. Inwardly, she had been a flurry of emotions since leaving Wintercrest. She wasn't sure that she would be able to stand any more bad news if that was what Mr. Jenkins came to deliver.

"I spoke with several of my colleagues. As you know, I am preparing to take your case before a local judge and call for a public revoke of Mr. Smith's claims. I am sorry to say that, after I explained the whole of the situation to them, they did not find it very favorable to us. In fact, a fear they brought to my attention is that if we do take our current case before the courts and the judges don't side with us, Mr. Smith may take his cause with more evil intent."

"I can't possibly see how he could make things any worse than they already are." Isabella did her best to control the sorrow and rage both vying for her attention.

"Well, he could take you to debtors' court and demand the money from you. As of now, he is simply using his false claims to hold off his own debts. He may, however, take things farther. If he does so, you may find yourself in debtors' prison."

Isabella covered a gasp. She couldn't even begin to understand how her life had turned around so much since her father's death. How had she gone from a respected young woman to a possible imprisoned criminal?

"I know this all sounds very awful right now. Please, let me assure you that there is still one last hope."

"Well, by all means, tell me quickly."

"You remember that, at our first meeting upon your

return to London, I assured you that all payments would be deferred until we won our case?"

"Yes," Isabella encouraged, not seeing how this could be the start of good news.

"I actually fibbed a bit. It is not the case. In fact, the Duke of Wintercrest has asked to be sent all bills pertaining to your legal counsel and in return, asked that I keep him informed on all matters pertaining to your case."

"He did what?" Isabella stammered in disbelief.

"I have also been in conference with him much over the last few days," Mr. Jenkins continued. "He has provided me every resource at hand. I met with him just before coming here and informed him just as I have told you."

"And how is this a ray of hope for me? At the moment, I only feel shame and guilt that my past employer would take so much upon himself."

"After I informed His Grace of the current circumstances, he promptly stood and announced that he would now handle the matter himself."

"What does that mean?" Isabella asked, her emerald eyes filling with fear for his reputation.

"I cannot say with complete certainty. I would guess, however, that the duke intends to meet with Mr. Smith and settle the matter. It has been done before with gentlemen of the duke's means."

"You mean you think he will pay Mr. Smith to stop harassing me. I could never allow such a thing. There must be a way that will not involve the duke. I won't see his reputation, or his family's, for that matter, ruined over me."

"I'm very sorry, Miss Watts, but at this time, I fear that this may be the only way for you to escape such a wicked man. I don't agree with the fact that Mr. Smith will be getting what he wanted and that justice was not able to prove the right. The law is a delicate matter, and sometimes the only means of justice for wrongfully accused, such as yourself, is out of my hands."

39

The Duke of Wintercrest did his best to steady his nerves. He paced up and down the street of his townhouse for many hours before finally going inside. He couldn't believe that, after all that had been done in the protection of Isabella, that scoundrel was still going to get away with what he had done.

Had the duke been a naval man still, he would have considered settling this matter as most men did on the ship, inside a boxing ring. The duke flexed his hands again. What he wouldn't give to duel with this man.

It wasn't the way things were settled back here in town, however. The duke despised the fact that this villain would now be given everything he wanted, only to right the wrong he willfully created.

The duke didn't care much for the matter of the cost.

He would gladly pay any amount to seek justice for the woman he cared about. In fact, he liked the fact that this would give him the expedited end that he had known was necessary, before even leaving his country seat.

He hated, however, how smug he knew his unknown villain would be on the morrow, when the duke proposed any means necessary for him to retract his words.

It must have been the end that this Mr. Smith sought after all. He knew that Mr. Smith had no other means to pay over the amount owed, after such a failed venture. The moment Mr. Smith found out that Isabella was living in the duke's home, he, no doubt, produced this plan as a means to have someone else pay his own debts.

Even worse, the duke knew that once Mr. Smith saw he was getting all he wanted, it would never be enough. He had to think up some means to make sure that Mr. Smith would settle for the agreed upon amount and never come after Isabella, nay, even think her name, ever again.

The duke combed over everything he knew of the knave for the rest of the night, including most of the personal, corporate documents that he had purchased from a disgruntled employee.

It wasn't until dawn's light, that the duke finally saw the answer that had been staring at him all through the night. He smiled excitedly as he rummaged through his copy of documents, proving to himself that what he was seeing was, in fact, true.

He smiled to himself as he sat back in his chair for the first time since leaving Mr. Jenkins' office. He had the means to make sure Mr. Smith never bothered Isabella again.

The duke quickly changed into a fresh cravat and coat and made his way back down the townhouse stairs to leave at once. He knew that Mr. Smith, a man of business, would be at the docks at this early hour. The duke would not waste a minute in finally putting all back to right.

"Christian," his mother's voice called from her room before he made his way fully down the stairs.

"Are you going somewhere so early in the morning?" she asked as she wrapped a dressing gown around her.

"Yes, I have some business to attend to. It won't take more than a few hours. I should even be home in time for breakfast."

"Is this about Isabella?" his mother asked, coming to stand at the top of the stairs. "Don't think that I was blind to the real reason you insisted we all come to London. I am well aware of the various business ventures you have been making on her behalf, while we have been here in town."

"I just," Lady Wintercrest paused to make sure she got her wording right. "I just want you to pause and think about your actions first. What if this ruins Abigail's chances or maybe even Jacqueline's?"

"Do not worry on my behalf," another voice called from behind the duke's mother.

Lady Abigail also stepped from her room. She had also awoken and had been listening to the whole conversation held on the stairwell.

"I will not ask you to give up your happiness for the future chance of mine. I love you dearly, brother, and Isabella too. I will not rob you. If I cannot find a gentleman that will overlook wrongs done to my family, then I dare say I wouldn't want to have him anyway." Lady Abigail spoke with a fire that matched her red hair, currently flowing around her in a wild, early morning mess.

The duke walked back up the stairs to stand next to two of the most important women in his life.

"Mother, I do intend to right the wrong that has been done to Isabella. You are right in thinking this. I also intend to march straight over to Isabella the moment I am done with the matter. I intend to marry her."

The duke spoke the words with a tender but final tone. He wanted his mother's blessing on the matter, but also knew that he could live without it more than he could live without Isabella.

"I too, love Isabella dearly," his mother replied, "but are you sure this is the course you want to take? It will not be an easy one for either of you." She meant the words for both of her children. She looked between them, making sure they understood the gravity of the situation.

The duke kept his eyes on his sister to see that she was in complete awareness of the consequences of what she was about to accept. She looked back at him and gave a nod of approval.

The duke broke out into a warm smile and kissed his sister on the cheek.

"Save your kisses for your bride," Lady Abigail teased back, giving him a sibling shove.

"I suppose, if this is the course you wish to take, I will accept it. Your poor father would turn in his grave if he knew you intended to wed the governess. I, on the other hand," Lady Wintercrest said with a wicked grin much like the one her son often gave, "am happy that you have found someone to love truly."

The duke thanked his mother before returning down the stairs and out the door. Both ladies returned to their own rooms, though they were much too awake to go back to sleep.

The duke thought on his mother's words as he rode in his carriage to the docks. His mother had chosen propriety in her match over love. Perhaps she had been hesitant because it had worked out well in the end for her.

The duke could not say for certain that his parents ever loved each other, but they did have a mutual affection. He knew that his mother cared deeply for Isabella and wished for nothing more than the happiness of her children, but perhaps she worried that choosing love might lose its luster over time.

As a woman who had never had the chance to experience such emotions herself, it was no wonder that she could not see that such a thing was not possible. The duke was sure he would move heaven and earth for Isabella's wellbeing and happiness. That would never change over time, except to increase.

As the duke came upon the merchant front, he returned his thoughts to the problem at hand. He couldn't help but notice the freshly painted sign overhanging the entrance. It read "Baron and Smith Shipping Co." The 'and' was extremely small, making it look like Baron Smith.

It only fueled the duke's rage more to see that this man had the audacity to take from his business partner everything that Baron Leinster had, including his own daughter's reputation, and then attempt to steal his name as well.

This Mr. Smith seemed to have no honor or compassion for the dead at all. The duke wondered how Isabella's father could have been friends with such a salty character.

He knew, of course, from his time at sea that most men who employed themselves on the ocean had less than outstanding morals. That said, usually only those of good character were promoted as far as partner in a prestigious shipping company.

The duke strolled into the building with his head held high and shoulders back. Even for the early hour, the offices were already filled and busy with work. He stopped before a gentleman busily writing on parchment.

"I have come to speak with the proprietor of the business, a Mr. Smith."

The man looked the duke up and down. He could easily tell from his fine coat and exquisitely placed knot that he was a gentleman of means.

"Yes, m'lord. And who should I tell Mr. Smith is calling on 'im?"

"The Duke of Wintercrest," the duke said, handing over his card. "Though Mr. Smith is not expecting me, I wager he will be most eager to meet."

"Right away, Your Grace," the secretary said with larger eyes now and a bob to his head.

The man hurried down the hall and up a set of stairs to the main office where Mr. Smith was. The duke paced the room a few times again, making sure he checked his anger. It would do him no good to fly into a rage at the man.

He was best to face the villain with a calm and cool nature. He heard footsteps returning and reminded himself to take another steadying breath.

"He will see ya right away, Your Grace," the man said, motioning for the duke to follow.

"I thank you kindly," the duke said, walking in front of the man.

The office itself was in a shabby state. It was not uncommon for the outside of these dock offices to look rather gray from soot and salt air. The interior of the office usually fared much better. This was not the case for Mr.

Smith's workspace. It was a large, mess with dirt and mold seeming to fill every corner.

Mr. Smith himself sat behind a large oak desk also littered heavily with paperwork. He was not a very organized man, apparently. Not only was his desk out of sorts, but his person was also.

His jacket looked as if it had never been brushed and the rim of his knot and cuffs were stained with a yellow tinge. The room stank of unwashed man and tobacco.

"Please, do have a seat, Your Grace," Mr. Smith said with a blackened smile.

It was right cheerful to see the duke stand in his doorway. He knew that one way or another Miss Watts would have used her connection to others to pay for his silence. He hadn't expected it would go as high as a duke. It was more than he could have hoped for. He expected he would end the day with a yearly sum, by way of patronage, from the duke.

The duke looked down at the shabby, dirty chair across the desk from the proprietor and hesitated to sit in it. He looked around the room instead and found a hardback wooden chair against a wall. He hoped that this, at least, wouldn't soil his pantaloons.

He, in all honesty, couldn't care less for his garments, but he wanted to show Mr. Smith that he detested him and the state of his office. It would be an insult to Mr. Smith and a smooth one, at that. It would be the beginning of the game the duke was about to play.

He walked over to the chair and brought it forward. Taking a moment to remove a silk handkerchief, he dusted the seat before sitting. Mr. Smith ground his jaw in response to the duke's actions and seemed to look around the room for the first time.

"I expect you know why I have come?" the duke took control of the conversation.

"I would never presume to know, Your Grace," Mr. Smith retorted.

"Be that as it may, I am sure you are aware that Miss Watts has been in my employment over the last year."

"I was not aware in the least where the child took her vocation."

"Strange, because you seemed to have been sending an inordinate number of letters to her at my home."

Mr. Smith's face turned a little ashen at the mention of his threatening correspondence. He ran a dirty hand through the greasy mop of hair on top of his head. The man didn't even have the decency to pull back his black and grey hair with a ribbon.

"I am not sure I know what you are talking about." Mr. Smith finally said, getting control of his fear.

"I can sit here and discuss the matter with you all day until you are proven in your lies, Mr. Smith, but frankly I would rather not spend one moment more than necessary in this foul place."

"I have come to inform you that you will be publicly retracting the accusations you have made against Miss Watts and to inform you that you will never so much as speak her name again."

"And why would I do such a thing? She has stolen from me, and I only seek justice in the matter."

The duke rose from his seat in an instant. Rising to his full height, he bore down on the filth in front of him. "You will never speak such foul lies in my presence again, or I shall have you arrested."

Mr. Smith shrank back from the power of the duke.

"I beg your pardon, Your Grace, for the offense. I mean merely to say that there are amounts that must be paid and can only be done if the sum is given me."

"I suspected you hoped that would be the case in today's meeting. I am well aware of what you did with the sum taken from the late Baron Leinster's estate. What an unfortunate gamble you made," he added with a tsk. "I am willing to give you the amount of fifty pounds for you to publicly retract your statement against Miss Watts."

"Fifty pounds ain't even half of what I owe," Mr. Smith blurted out, clearly disappointed with the proposition.

"Yet it is all you will get, and it is a very generous offer. I shouldn't give you a single copper, but I will, because I am a gentleman."

"And say I refuse such offer, Your Grace. Say I choose to have Miss Watts thrown in debtors' prison instead."

"Then you would have no means to pay back even a portion of your debt."

"Aye, but I would get the satisfaction of seeing that girl in rags behind bars."

Mr. Smith was playing his only card. He also knew it was a good one and that the duke would have no choice but to submit to any terms he deemed fit to silence him.

The duke paused a moment and seemed to think the matter over as if it had never crossed his mind in the past. "I suppose you could do that. I would have no means to stop you."

"You could pay me more, Your Grace," Mr. Smith blurted out, so hungry for the money.

"I could, but I won't," the duke stated bluntly. "Please, let me clarify why you will be taking my offer and, in fact, thanking me for it."

"You may not be aware, but before I inherited my father's title, I was a Captain in the Royal Navy. I couldn't help but notice that a very significant portion of your exports last year dealt with Naval contracts, exporting goods all over the British Empire."

"I don't know how you know any of that information, Your Grace, but I don't see how it will serve your proposal to me."

The duke smiled at this. It was a simple game of cat

and mouse, and he had just cornered Mr. Smith. "I saw that most of these contracts were produced by Admiral Brown. No doubt, he was a good friend of Baron Leinster?"

"That is correct," Mr. Smith said, as he desperately tried to find the end of this conversation.

"I know the gentleman well. He captained my first ship. In fact, he was also great friends with my father and came to visit us often when I was a child. One might say he was the one who inspired me to join the naval service in the first place."

Mr. Smith narrowed his eyes at the duke.

"I would assume since most of your profits over the years came from such arrangements with Admiral Brown, that it would be devastating if he were to take his business elsewhere."

"And you are trying to tell me, Your Grace, that if I don't accept your amount and retract my statement, you will remove said client from my business?"

"All it would take is a simple letter," the duke ended. He folded his hands in front of him and sighed as if this meeting was becoming too boring for him.

"How do I know you are not just making this up?"

"Well, there is the little fact that, unlike yourself, I am a man of my word. But if that isn't enough proof for you, I suggest you test my word. Sure, you may land Miss Watts in prison, but you, too, will be following her there shortly, when you're unable to pay back any of your debts, and you will lose your business."

"I am offering you something vastly more generous than I should," the duke continued with another sigh. "I don't have to offer you a sum in any amount. I could simply inform you that if you do not retract your statement, you will find yourself out of business by the end of the year."

Mr. Smith's eyes widened as he considered this fact inwardly.

"I am a very generous man to give you something at all. So, I suggest you take my offer before I change my mind," the duke added in a warning tone.

"I 'spose I have no choice but to take your deal then," Mr. Smith finally grumbled after thinking it over for some time.

"Wonderful, the funds will be delivered to you as soon as you sign this letter stating that you made the whole thing up to tarnish Miss Watts' name and that you, yourself, took possession of all of Baron Leinster's estate."

The duke put parchment on top of the pile covering the desk. He stood tall above the man while he waited for the signature.

"For your information, this letter will also be published in The Morning Chronicle," the duke added, taking back the letter. "I have heard that you are quite fond of that particular paper, are you not?"

"Yes, I 'spose so, Your Grace," the man grumbled back.

"Now, I believe it doesn't need to be said but just to be sure, if you ever so much as speak Miss Watts' name again, even in the privacy of your own home, I will make good on my promise to remove all business associated with any and all colleagues at my disposal. I can promise you that my hand reaches far past the Admiral."

Mr. Smith nodded sullenly. The meeting hadn't gone at all as he had expected. The duke, on the other hand, was feeling a vast weight lifted after having the signed letter back in his coat pocket.

The duke deposited the discussed amount in a leather bag on top of the desk.

"Do try and be a little bit wiser with your money," he said before donning his hat and leaving the room.

He paused at the door and turned back around, "There is one more thing I need from you before I go."

40

*I*sabella spent most of the night, after Mr. Jenkins visit, doing her best to find a way to stave off her own issues with Mr. Smith before the Duke of Wintercrest could get involved. There was just one answer that she saw in her mind and she dreaded the thought.

The only way to appease the scoundrel and save the reputation of the duke and his family from having any more part in the matter was to go to the man himself and give him what he wanted.

She would stand before the horrid man and beg him for mercy. She finally resigned herself to it. It would most likely not cause him to retract his words, but satisfied that he had completely ruined her, he might just leave her alone.

Only then would she finally be able to pick up the shattered remains of her life. Perhaps she could get a new governess or teaching job somewhere far in the country, where such things about her were not known.

When Lady Louisa arrived home that night, she told her all that had transpired, as well as her plan of action. Lady Louisa wasn't supportive of Isabella going to such drastic measures, but was unable to produce an alternate solution.

"Let us both just sleep on it this night," Lady Louisa had said, "and perhaps, in the morning, something better will come."

Perhaps it was the little sleep that Isabella got that night, but no other solution ever presented itself to her. By morning at breakfast, she was determined to her cause. She would go to the docks, confront the blackguard, and stop all of this before it got any worse for the Wintercrest family.

"Do you suppose that later this morning I might borrow a carriage?" Isabella asked Lady Gilcrest over their toast and jam.

"Of course, my dear. Do you have plans to go somewhere?"

"Well, I must go on an errand of sorts." Isabella wasn't sure if she wanted to share her plan with the rest of the family. A proper young woman prostrating herself before her villain wasn't something she guessed the Gilcrests would be happy with.

"I hope it's to buy a pretty new bonnet that you will actually wear," Lord Dunthorpe said with a wink.

Isabella laughed nervously at the joke. She looked over at Lady Louisa from across the table. Lady Louisa was pleading Isabella with her eyes to change her mind.

"I'm afraid it isn't a bonnet," Isabella said finally, more toward her friend then Lord Dunthorpe. "I must do something, and if I don't do it right away, I will lose the nerve altogether to do it."

The whole family looked at Isabella questioningly. Even the Earl dipped down the corner of the paper that he had begun to read to inspect her. To the others, she most likely sounded mad, rambling in such a way. She knew that her dear friend, whom the words were meant for, had understood.

As the family was finishing their meal and preparing to go their separate ways for the day, a groomsman came into the room.

"I beg your pardon, my lord," he said to the Earl. "There is a gentleman caller come to see Miss Watts."

"So early in the morning?" Lady Gilcrest responded in a bit of shock.

"I am sure it is Mr. Jenkins again," Isabella explained. "He has been giving me vital news, pertaining to my situation, as soon as he gets it. I apologize for the early hour, but would it be alright if I saw him in the small drawing room?"

Lady Louisa's sorrowful brown eyes now lighted in

hope. If the lawyer was here again, perhaps there was new information that could prevent her friend from her current course of disaster.

"Of course, dear," Lady Gilcrest said, understanding the need for urgency. "If Mr. Jenkins is in need of a morning meal himself, have Julia here send in a tray for him," she added as an afterthought.

Isabella walked down the hallway to the drawing room where the lawyer was told to wait for her. She found herself thinking about the goodness of the Gilcrests. Even Lady Gilcrest, presented with an unfashionably early guest, only thought of her guest's well-being and comfort, enough to offer him a plate of breakfast.

She knew she was truly blessed to have found such a good friend as Lady Louisa. Even more, to have been adopted as part of the Gilcrest household since coming back to London.

She smoothed out the folds of her soft white cotton morning dress and fixed a loose curl at the side of her hair. It was more out of habit than anything else. Mrs. Mason had instilled in the ladies of her school the habit of always making sure they looked their best when hosting a guest.

Isabella opened the door and only took two steps into the room before freezing in shock. A gentleman figure stood before her, his back to her. He was leaning against a window and looking out on the street below as he waited for her arrival. It was not the thin, gangly silhouette of Mr. Jenkins, however.

"Christian?" Isabella blurted out without even thinking.

Like a dream, the duke turned around, noticing that he was no longer alone in the room. He looked over Isabella one time as if he was drinking her in for the first time all over again. Isabella couldn't help but feel the catch in her throat, as she did the same in return.

"I don't understand, Your Grace?" Isabella said, finally coming to her senses. "The groomsman said..."

"Yes, I apologize for the small fib. I was afraid if he told you I had come to speak with you...well, that you would not see me."

"Not because I wouldn't want to," Isabella said, admitting to the truth, "but for your own sake."

The duke crossed the room in three easy steps and took both of Isabella's hands in his own. He relished, for a moment, the closeness he had missed so much over the past month. He opened his mouth to speak but before he could, a hurried voice called from just outside the still open drawing-room door.

"Isabella, look what Father saw," Lady Louisa said as she came hurriedly into the room.

Lady Louisa stopped, frozen in place, recognizing the duke at once.

"Your Grace," she said with a small curtsy.

"Well, I was going to tell Isabella the news myself, but I

suspect I should give you the honor, Lady Louisa, since you seem to have the article in hand."

"What article is that?" Isabella said, looking between the two.

The duke gently tugged on her hands and guided her to the sofa. He made sure to sit down right next to her. Lady Louisa also came into the room and sat in an opposing chair.

"While Father was reading the paper he found this," Lady Louisa handed the newspaper over to Isabella.

Isabella looked at the duke, who relaxed back in his seat as he waited for her to look at the paper in front of her.

To her surprise, an entire page was completely void of any news except one piece of information. It was a letter-written, signed, and sworn to be authentic, by the Duke of Wintercrest, no less. It was a letter from Mr. Smith claiming that all his charges against Miss Watts were, in fact, false. It even went on to explain Mr. Smiths failed venture and his reasoning for the whole hoax.

Isabella couldn't believe her eyes as she read over the words again. Not only had her name been cleared, but it was printed in such a way that every single member of the town would see it very obviously.

"When did you do this?" Isabella asked, confused and finding it hard to speak.

"Just this morning. I saw Mr. Smith a little after dawn.

From there, I went straight to the papers and then to this house."

"But how? Why?" Isabella continued to stammer.

Though this didn't completely erase what had been said of her in the past, it was just about as close as she could ever expect to get. A public retraction on this level would be the talk of the town and, for once, in a good way about Isabella.

When she asked these bewildered questions of the duke, he sat up from his spot. He looked at her intently with his dazzling blue eyes.

"I think you know why," he said in a deep, husky voice.

The room got very silent for a moment as the two exchanged a look.

"Your Grace," Lady Louisa said, distracting their attention, "you must be starved. I will go and see that some proper refreshments are brought to you."

"Thank you, Lady Louisa," the duke said, knowing she was taking the opportunity to give them privacy.

Both waited till Lady Louisa had left the room before looking at each other again. The duke took both of Isabella's hands into his and softly rubbed the naked flesh.

"Christian," she said softly, looking down at their joined hands. "I appreciate all that you have done for me, I truly do. As much as I want this, I could never ask it of you or your family."

"Don't think on them," he said, cupping her face and

raising it to look at him. "Both Abigail and Mother have said that they would support any decision I make."

"And you would have me now, in this state?" Isabella asked as tears welled in her eyes.

"I knew, the moment I walked with you down the lane in the dark that first night, that you were like no other. Your kindness, your love for my family, your ability to think and act in consideration of others, these are all things that I love about you," the duke said, full of sincerity, as he gently stroked her cheek.

"I care not for titles or what others may think of us. You are the one that I have chosen. I want to be by your side, and have you by mine, through the rest of my life. That is, if you will have me?" The duke raised a brow at Isabella. She knew that he was teasing her.

"Yes," she said as a single tear escaped down her cheek. "I will have you."

The duke leaned in, lifting her chin slightly, and paused right before her lips.

"I am hoping that means you will allow me to kiss you now," he breathed against her lips.

Isabella smiled at him and tilted her head up just a bit to encourage him to finish the movement. He smiled brightly before allowing a soft tender kiss to pass between them.

The duke kept one hand cupped at her face as he slipped the other around her waist, pulling her closer to him. Looking down at her, he kissed her again and again. Finally, she leaned her head on his chest, breathless.

"How do you feel about going to Gretna Green tonight?" he asked with a wicked grin as his chin rested on the top of her dark locks.

Isabella gave his tease a tsk. "I suspect we have quite enough gossip generated by us already this day."

"Well, then I suppose I must wait for a proper wedding. Oh," he said leaning back from her and reached into his jacket pocket, "I almost forgot."

Isabella watched as he shuffled around in several pockets before finding what he was looking for. He pulled out his fisted hand. Taking Isabella's, he laid inside a cold metal object. As he removed his hand, Isabella saw that it was her locket.

"How did you ever? I was certain that Mr. Smith would have sold it the moment he got his hands on it."

"Turns out, he fancied to keep it as a trophy."

Isabella noticed that there was an added object on the chain hidden behind the locket. She flipped it over to expose a delicate gold ring with a simple green emerald placed in the center.

"Oh, it's beautiful."

"It was my mothers. She gave it to me this morning before I left."

"And she knew who you intended it for?" Isabella said, a little unsure if she should have it.

"Of course she did," the duke said with a deep chuckle. "Both Mother and Abigail are waiting very expectantly for me to return home with you on my arm."

"They are?" Isabella said, again surprised.

"And Jackie," he added.

Isabella's face lit up and she stood in an instant.

"Let us go now," she said hurriedly as she tugged at the duke's hand. "I would like to see Jackie right away."

The duke chuckled before getting out of his seat. He wrapped his arms around Isabella and kissed her softly on the lips again.

"I suppose my breakfast must wait, then. I have been bewitched by your siren song and am liable to follow you anywhere you lead. To my family's home or rocky shoals, I care not. As long as I am with you."

EPILOGUE

*I*sabella fidgeted with the folds of her dark blue silk dress. She was riding in the carriage along with the Gilcrest family to the Wintercrest ball. It had been the talk of the whole season and, with what Isabella knew of the preparations, it was set to be talked of for many months after.

The dress she wore; the duke had insisted she have made for this night. It was a silken navy blue with an iridescent sheen to the fabric. The hem was trimmed in the finest white lace that Isabella had ever seen and was finished with a thick white ribbon at her waist and in her dark hair.

"You look wonderful, Izzy," Lady Louisa said, sensing her friend's concern. "You will enter the ball this night a princess."

"Mm, I don't know if you would quite do for a princess," Lord Dunthorpe teased from across the carriage, "but I suppose you will do for a future duchess."

Isabella wrinkled her nose playfully at the Viscount as their carriage came to a stop. She took another steadying breath before allowing the Viscount to help her out.

The Earl and Lady Gilcrest arrived in their own carriage just ahead of them and together with the two siblings, they filed in to be introduced into the lavish townhouse.

Isabella couldn't help but notice that behind them came the Earl and Lady Cunningham with Lady Lydia. Her stomach did a flop inside her. She worried that they might make a scene. Instead, Lady Cunningham called out to her as they all filed into the front gate of the exquisite home.

"Oh, Miss Watts, I am so happy to see you here tonight," Lady Cunningham said graciously. "I was so concerned about your well-being when I heard the awful news. I hope I did not harm you by writing to Lady Winter-crest about it."

"It was startling, at first," Isabella said kindly, "to hear such horrible things spoken of me. But it also gave me the chance to correct them, so I think, in the end, you did some good."

"Oh, I am glad to hear it," Lady Cunningham said with a sigh. "I have been ever so worried that you might hate me over it."

Isabella could tell that the woman had meant no harm in her doing. It had caused some of the most considerable heartaches that Isabella had ever experienced. Maybe, at the time, she could not say so, but now she knew she could truthfully say she forgave Lady Cunningham all that had transpired.

Lady Lydia, who was standing just behind her mother, looked thoroughly disgusted by Isabella. Although the official announcement of their engagement wouldn't be until tonight, Isabella suspected that, with the close friendship of the two mothers, Lady Lydia already knew of their arrangement.

"That dress is divinely beautiful on you tonight," Lady Cunningham complimented Isabella, now feeling sure there was no animosity harbored.

Isabella thanked the lady graciously and went to join her own party as they made their way into the home.

The London home that the duke had inherited was not of the normal variety in London. It was vastly more extravagant and even boasted its very own grand hall for dancing.

Isabella filed in behind the Gilcrests as they were all introduced down the line of the hosting family. Isabella's eyes fell immediately on her betrothed.

He was looking even more dashingly handsome than usual. He wore a similar navy blue velvet jacket with black pantaloons and high boots. His knot was tied in a crisp

Windsor and his hair shined a radiant red against his matching navy ribbon that held it back.

As Isabella stood before him and curtsied, he lifted her white-gloved hand to his lips. He watched her with his crystal eyes as he bent over her hand, wicked smile ever-present on his lips.

"And how are you this evening, my love?" he asked just loud enough for the Cunninghams, standing just behind, to hear.

Isabella suspected that the shocked look on Lady Lydia's face was the whole reason for his extravagantly romantic salutation. His eyes fell to the locket that was replaced as a permanent fixture around Isabella's neck. Next to the pendant was still the beautiful emerald ring that the duke gave her.

"Are you ready for tonight," he asked. Though he lowered her hand, he still held tightly to it.

"I hope so," Isabella said nervously. "Do I look alright?"

"You look as perfect as you did the day I met you. But if you are nervous, it is not too late to make our way for an elopement."

"Nice try, Your Grace, but you cannot get out of a ball that easily."

"Too right," his mother said beside him. "You have a great many more guests to welcome. Stop embarrassing your poor bride and hand her over to me so that I may welcome my future daughter-in-law."

The duke gave a final wink at Isabella, lighting her cheeks with a rosy blush, much to his delight, before finally releasing her to his mother.

The evening continued with great success. All of Lady Wintercrest's hard work over the months was apparent in the lavish decorations and delicious meal provided. When the time came for dancing, the duke first stood upon the little stage before the crowd to make his announcement.

Isabella feared still that, with all that surrounded her these past few months, the reaction to their engagement would be disgust or at the very least quiet whispering. She was pleasantly surprised that, instead, the entirety of the house burst into uproarious cheers.

She spent the remainder of the evening at the duke's side as person after person came before them to congratulate them.

"I think it might be time to get some fresh air," the duke said, after a very long congratulation from the Earl and Lady Cunningham.

"Would you join me outside?" he asked of his future bride.

"I suspect you have a very wicked intent in mind," Isabella said, while wrapping her arm in the crook of his.

"I am very sure I do, as well," he said with a soft chuckle.

They made their way through the rooms full of guests and around the group of dancers in the great hall to the large doors that opened up to gardens behind the house. Unlike the property of most London houses, this one boasted a large lot with a long veranda that stretched the entire length of the ballroom.

The duke walked with her on his arm all the way to the far end of the veranda, in the seclusion of very little light from the windows.

"You always seem to find ways to get me outside, alone, and in the dark," Isabella said in her own teasing fashion.

"Well," the duke said, wrapping his arms around her waist and bringing her close to him, "how else am I to steal a kiss but in these circumstances?"

"I suppose you are right," Isabella said, looking up at his face glowing in the dim light from inside. "Though, I cannot say it is stealing when I seem to give them so freely to you. Perhaps I should try harder to resist your charm."

He paused for a moment and seemed to think her offer over. "Oh no," he finally said, dipping his head down toward her, "I don't think I like that idea at all."

.   .   .

He stifled her giggles with a soft kiss.

THE END

Did you enjoy *Falling for the Governess*? Check out the story of *Abigail* and *Colton* in *Saving Lady Abigail* here.

If you want a Bonus Scene of this book visit the link below (or just click it): https://abbyayles.com/aa-003-exep/

SAVING LADY ABIGAIL

Preview

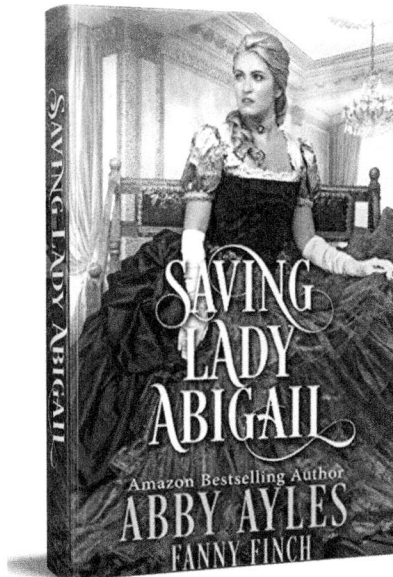

Read it now!

When Colton Gillchrist returns from war, he is not the man he once was and not the man that Lady Abigail Grant remembers and is so keen to reacquaint herself with. Sporting a gash on the side of his face and walking with a stick, Colton is rude and abrupt and prone to angry outbursts, and she is at once put off by his manner.

An incident at one of the season's finest balls only serves to make matters worse and Colton leaves hurriedly, then hides himself away, refusing to leave his home.

As his sister, Lady Louisa, and the Duchess of Wintercrest try to help him come to terms with what has happened, Abigail starts to get closer to him as well, while still attending balls and becoming involved with a charming new Lord.

But no matter how hard the women try, Colton cannot be shaken from his malaise and it takes an incident with Abigail's new suitor, who isn't what he first appeared to be, to shake him into action.

. . .

Can he save the woman he loves, but cannot admit to it, before she is forced into a marriage she does not want? Or will he remain forever imprisoned within his home and his mind?

If you like engaging characters, heart-wrenching twists and turns, and lots of romance, then you'll love "Saving Lady Abigail"

Buy "Saving Lady Abigail" and unlock the exciting story of Abigail today!

Also available with Kindle Unlimited!

Read it now!
http://abbyayles.com/AmBoo6

PROLOGUE

"I just don't understand how you could have done this without discussing it with me first," the Earl of Gilchrist said to his only son.

"I am twenty-six years of age, Father; I wouldn't need your permission to purchase a commission," Lord Colton Frasier, the Viscount Dunthorpe, responded.

"But how could you have possibly purchased a lieutenant's commission on the allowance given? I understand that it would quite normally be rather sufficient, but you are so often spending yours at the gentleman's club or on races."

Lord Gilchrist was not the type of man to be angered or raise his voice. The biggest sign of emotion he ever showed to others was the furrowing of his soft blonde brows and declarations of the impossibility of an action he didn't agree with.

"As you said, Father, my allowance is sufficient. I have grown bored with both the tables and the races. I want to experience some of life. I would have thought I chose a noble course."

"Noble? Are you not aware that we are in the midst of a war with Napoleon? What is so noble about my only son dying on the battlefield?"

The Viscount softened his demeanor. He certainly knew this announcement to his father would stir up mixed emotions. He had yet to tell his sister or mother. Lord Dunthorpe would have liked to at least have his father on his side before that time came.

"I am aware of the battle, Father. I can assure you that as a lieutenant, as well as with an earldom in my future, I will be sure to take the proper cautions."

Lord Dunthorpe got up from his leather seat and paced his father's office.

"I want to see some of the world, Father," he said waving his arms around him. "I want to have experiences and adventures. It is not fair that such things should be taken from me purely because I am your only son. Had you another son, it would not have mattered what adventures I wished to employ my time with."

"But you are my only son, and very dear to me for that matter," his father retorted, still seated behind his desk.

Lord Gilchrist knew his son was a spirited man, always hungry for the next excitement. He somewhat wished he was more like his sister, Lady Louisa. She was perpetually quiet and reserved. Where Lord Dunthorpe jumped before he thought, Lady Louisa always profoundly considered before she even spoke.

"I suppose what is done is done," Lord Gilchrist said, laying his weathered hands upon the oak desk in front of him. "I will never say I agree with this choice but, as you said, you are a grown man and liable to make your own decisions."

Lord Dunthorpe sat down in relief. Perhaps with his father now surrendered to his choice it would be easier to tell the rest of the household.

"I thought perhaps that I might announce it to Mother and Louisa this evening at dinner."

"Why so soon?"

"I leave at the end of the week, Father. There is a great need at this time for willing and capable men."

Lord Gilchrist gave out a long sigh. He would have rather liked some time to adjust to his son's new course in life.

In all honesty, Lord Gilchrist rather hoped that Colton would be forced to consider the choice he made before going straight into it. So often, his only son was prone to making rash decisions, but he would soon see rational reason if given the time.

"I suppose you hoped that with coming here and telling me first in private, I might ease the blow to the others," Lord Gilchrist said with a shuffling of papers on his desk. "I cannot promise that will be the case."

"But think of Mother," Lord Dunthorpe said with an ease of charming manipulation. "She will be so frightened at the prospect. If you support me, she will be assured that it is safe. I would ask for your agreement only for the sake of her nerves."

"You are only using the delicate nature of a lady to support your own devilish devices, and I don't think I particularly like that," Lord Gilchrist retorted.

He softened into a smile, however. There was much of himself he saw in his son.

"But because I do care so dearly for your mother and her constitution, I will give in to your demands."

Lord Dunthorpe eased into a smile. He had overcome his first hurdle. With his father now on his side, the next would be much easier.

Lord Dunthorpe was well aware that his father, and no doubt the rest of his family, would see his choice to join the regulars as a rash decision. He, on the other hand, found it to be the most promising course of action he had ever taken in the whole of his life.

He knew that the time would soon come for him when he would have to settle down, take a wife, and continue the legacy of his father's earldom. He had enjoyed the prospects of the peerage and the social discretions that came with it.

He was now finding himself a grown man, no longer fancied by the artless pleasure of a gentleman's life. He wanted to have some importance attached to his life. The constant vicissitude of seasons at his family's country estates no longer seemed worthwhile or meaningful in Colton's mind.

That evening at dinner, Lord Dunthorpe tried his best to be a perfect son for the sake of his mother. Anything to help ease the blow he was about to give was worth the sacrifice.

"Mother, I have just received a letter from Isabella. I can scarcely believe the words she wrote," Lady Louisa Frasier said to her mother across the dinner table.

"Oh, does that mean she has given birth? Do tell me quickly! Are both Isabella and the baby doing well?"

"Well," Lady Louisa said, not usually the one excited to be in the limelight. Her news, however, was just so fantastical that it made her forget her normally timid demeanor. "She told me first that everything went wonderfully and that she is recovering very quickly."

"She also reported that not only did she have a healthy baby boy," Lady Louisa paused for dramatic effect, "but also a beautiful baby girl."

The Countess of Gilchrist raised both hands to her face in shock.

"Twins?"

Lady Louisa nodded in the affirmative.

"She also inquired if we all might be able to visit her at Wintercrest Manor at our earliest convenience. Wouldn't it be wonderful to go and see both beautiful babies?"

"How very exciting. We will have to find the time to go before the winter storms settle in. It is already very near to autumn."

"I am sure she would be more than happy if we stayed the whole holiday season through," Lady Louisa added.

"What do you think, Lord Gilchrist? Shall we all go up north to see the duke and duchess' new babies?"

Lady Gilchrist turned to her husband at the other end of the table. His eyes flickered on each member seated before saying anything.

"I think it would be a lovely diversion to spend the holidays up north," Lord Gilchrist agreed.

The Frasier household rarely left their London home, all finding it to be comfortable and inviting. From time to time, as it suited their fancies, they would spend short periods of time at their country seat. It was along the western coast of the country and boasted beautiful views of the Bristol Channel very near to the fashionable retreat town of Bath.

"Colton, you must come with us as well," Lady Louisa said, turning to her brother. "I know you and the Duke of

Wintercrest got on very well. He will no doubt be most happy to have your company."

Lord Dunthorpe and his father exchanged a nervous look. This was no doubt the right window of opportunity for Lord Dunthorpe to tell his sister and mother of his alternate future to that of Wintercrest Manor.

"It seems like a charming diversion, but I'm afraid I won't be able to join you," Lord Dunthorpe said, doing his best to ease into his own arrangement.

"Why ever not?" Lady Louisa said, raising one of her mousey brows as she lifted some cured ham casually to her mouth.

"I am afraid I have my own announcement to make. The cause of it will keep me detained for quite some time."

"Don't tell me you bought another racing horse," Lady Gilchrist chimed in. "The last time you got one, you spent a whole year with the trainers and we scarcely ever saw you."

Lord Dunthorpe thought fondly back on that diversion a few years back. He had grown tired of just watching the gig races and wanted to try his hand at it himself.

Lord Dunthorpe was never one to do something half-way. For that reason, he searched the whole country over for the most outstanding racing horse stock and the fastest gig. Then he spent every waking moment training with his horse and buggy.

He had to admit it did pay off in the end. He had won almost every race. While at first it was entertaining, winning continually quickly soured Lord Dunthorpe's taste for racing. What was the point if there was no fear of losing?

"I have not purchased a horse. In fact, I can promise you that I won't even be attending any races for quite some time. I have bought a commission."

He looked back and forth between his sister and mother. Poor Lady Louisa held a boiled potato mid-air, with her mouth agape unable to move.

"I don't understand," Lady Gilchrist finally said.

It was enough to wake her daughter, and Lady Louisa set down her fork, suddenly put off from her meal.

"I will be joining the regulars, Mother. I have bought a lieutenant's commission and will be doing what is necessary for the king and crown."

Lord Dunthorpe couldn't help but hold his head up high as he said these words. It was not for pride, but to show that he was confident in his choice.

"Did you know about this, Lord Gilchrist," the Countess said, turning significantly pale as she faced her husband.

"He informed me earlier this afternoon in my office, my dear."

"And you are in agreement with it?" she struggled out.

The Earl of Gilchrist looked between his wife and son. He would not lie for one, nor would he willingly bring more unease than necessary on the other.

"I am settled to the fact. Colton is old enough to do

what he wishes with his own life. If this is the course he chooses, I will not stand in his way."

"But Colton," Lady Gilchrist said, with a visible shake to her voice, "what of the danger?"

"I promise I will be very considerate of my actions, Mother."

Lady Gilchrist promptly excused herself from the table, too overcome with emotion to stay much longer.

The room turned silent as she left. Soon after, Lord Gilchrist went to console his wife. This left the two siblings alone in the dining room.

"You are very set on this, then?" Lady Louisa finally asked.

Colton felt his first pang of regret. Their whole lives, Colton had made it his mission to take care of and protect his younger sister. She was not only younger than him, but of a very meek nature. Due to this and her moderately plain-featured looks, she had often been an easy target for a cruel miss.

"I am very set on this," he said softly.

"Then will you promise to write to me often?"

Lord Dunthorpe and Lady Louisa may have had a few years of age between them, but they were still very close. Lady Louisa had counted on him on a number of occasions to be her champion in times of distress. Not only that, but he had also brought much light and laughter to what have might otherwise be a very dull life for her.

"Of course I will," Lord Dunthorpe said, reaching across the table and taking his sister's hand. "Every day, if you wish it. So much, in fact, that it will be as if I am still here and you wish me gone."

Lady Louisa gave a soft smile of relief at this promise. She had been at her brother's side for the biggest part of her life, and she feared how she would go on with him away. What brought an even colder shudder to her was the thought that this endeavor might result in losing her brother permanently.

Read it now!
http://abbyayles.com/AmBoo6

1

"*J*ames, you little rascal. Where are you hiding?" Jackie called out down the long hall of Wintercrest Manor.

She took her slippered steps very carefully with her little cousin, Elisabeth, in her hand. They paused for a moment, as Jackie was sure she heard a giggle.

Sure enough, the sound came again. It was the soft laughter of a three-year-old who couldn't contain himself. Elisabeth gave her own toddler laugh in reply, covering her mouth with her free cherubic hand.

"We've caught them now," Jackie said to her partner.

Jackie slid open the door to what seemed like an empty bedroom. She could, however, hear the rustle of bedding.

Jackie put a finger to her lips and pointed under the bed

for Elisabeth's benefit. They both snuck over and got down on their knees before the long bed covering.

With a swift movement, Jackie lifted the bedding to reveal Elisabeth's twin brother hiding under the bed.

"Got you!" Elisabeth called out to him.

"Where is Aunt Abigail?" Jackie asked as she helped pull the three-year-old from under the bed.

It was a room that was rarely used, and so his clothes and dark hair were now covered in a light coating of dust.

James promptly sneezed as Jackie attempted to brush it off. Mrs. Murray wasn't one to rise to a temper, but she would be very unhappy to see the boy in such a state.

Elisabeth decided to search the room as Jackie did her best to brush her brother off. She knew her Aunt Abigail couldn't be far away from her hide-and-seek partner.

"Found you, too," Elisabeth called out as she poked behind a privacy screen.

There, she did find her Aunt Abigail, much too old for silly games, but still happily playing with her two nieces and nephew.

"Oh, dear. I thought I really had you fooled this time," Lady Abigail Grant said as she was led by the hand from behind the curtain.

"Aunt Abigail couldn't fit under the bed," James said with a giggle.

"I could so fit," Lady Abigail retorted with a hand on her hips. "I just didn't want to get all dusty like you."

The children happily laughed with their aunt before she returned them all to the nursery. It would soon be time for Lady Abigail to dress for dinner.

"May I come down with you too, tonight?" Jackie asked.

"I am afraid not. We are to have Captain Jones and a few of his officers from the militia with us tonight."

"But I am almost twelve years old. Certainly that is old enough," Jackie retorted.

Lady Abigail knew that her niece was now at that age where she no longer wanted to be treated as a child left in the nursery. She had struggled with the same frustrations as a young girl.

"I know it doesn't seem fair now, but you would not want to come anyway.

"Captain Jones is an ancient and very boring man. I fear you would fall asleep in your first course and never want to come to dinner again," Lady Abigail tried to add, by way of making it seem less enticing.

"I don't care, I still want to go," Jackie grumbled.

"I know, my dear. Very soon you will and wish you didn't have to."

Lady Abigail would have been more than happy to stay the night in the nursery with the twins and let Jackie go in her place. Not only was Captain Jones incredibly unentertaining, he was also very long-winded.

It was going to be a very long night of pretending to be interested. Lady Abigail's only hope was that at least one of the three lieutenants that would be joining the captain would be of some interest.

Lady Abigail was now nineteen years old and of a marrying age. She thought the prospect of finding a gentleman who would interest her to be very unlikely. They all wanted a quiet, prim, proper lady. That was not Abigail at all.

She much rather fancied the idea of marrying an officer instead. Though he might not have been one of the peerages, he was undoubtedly considered a gentleman. Men of this social standing would also be less likely to be put off by a less than gentle manner.

Lady Abigail had of course been bred to be an entirely proper lady by her parents, the Duke and Duchess of Wintercrest. However, they had also given her the freedom to grow into her own personality.

Lady Abigail hoped to marry someday. She wished to find the love that seemed to defy any barricades of social standards, as her brother, the now Duke of Wintercrest, had done when he met his wife, Isabella.

She, however, did not want to marry solely because social graces dictated that she do so. If she did marry, she had long ago determined it would be with someone she loved dearly and who would care for her just as she was.

Sadly, Lady Abigail was sorely disappointed with the night's dinner guests. Captain Jones had brought with him three of his lieutenants and a colonel. The colonel was much too old for Lady Abigail's liking, two of the three lieutenants were already married, and the third betrothed.

Lady Abigail half wondered if her brother had purposefully only invited the otherwise unavailable gentlemen to dinner that night.

The duke often had the high-ranking officers from the militia come to dinner when they were in the area. It was a gesture of high importance to him, that it also allowed him to feel nostalgia of his own days in the Royal Navy.

The duke was aware that Abigail was now of the age when courtships became pressing and engagements were on the horizon. He was rather overprotective of her when it came to opportunities of meeting gentlemen.

"You know he did it on purpose," Lady Abigail said softly to her sister-in-law after dinner.

The whole party was now seated in the drawing room. The men were by the fire talking politics while Lady Abigail, Isabella, the Duchess of Wintercrest, and the dowager duchess played a game of cards.

"I am quite certain he did do it on purpose," the duchess agreed.

"What a rotten thing to do," Lady Abigail said, setting down her cards rather exaggeratedly.

"What is it you two are whispering about," Lady Abigail's mother asked over her own hand of cards.

The dowager duchess was now deteriorating quickly in age. Lady Abigail suspected, with the loss of her husband a few years back, her mother had since lost much of the light in her.

Lady Abigail's parents could not have been more opposite creatures. Not only were they different in manners and personality, but there was a very vast age difference. If an outsider were to look in on their marriage, it would have been assumed that the arrangement was made for practical matters.

It was a well-known fact, however, by all of the late duke and dowager duchess' children that their parents did, in fact, have a deep affection for each other.

"Abigail is not very happy to see that the gentlemen invited tonight are not of her preference," the duchess explained to her mother-in-law.

"Your brother hopes better for you than a common militiaman," Lady Abigail's mother explained.

Lady Abigail didn't like this response, nor did she look forward to the idea of her overly protective brother choosing dinner guests in the future.

"Don't worry," the duchess said, taking her sister-in-law's hand and patting it softly. "Soon, the season will be upon us. You will have more suitors than you know what to do with."

It was an accurate statement that, due to Lady Abigail's beauty, she caught many eyes during her time in London each year. What was upsetting to her was that, so far, no one had caught her eye in return.

Lady Abigail brushed a rust colored ringlet back from her shoulder. It was an act of irritation that both the duchess and Lady Abigail's mother knew well.

"I have to say, I am surprised that His Grace is allowing you to go at all," Lady Abigail said with inference on her brother's proper title.

The duchess patted her belly that was beginning to show the swell of life beneath.

" I have plenty of time before this little one comes. I have been away from London for so long, I could not bear to spend another season away. And as for the duke," she said with a raised brow, "I did not ask. I merely announced my intentions."

All three ladies laughed at this. They had become quite a close trio with all the time they had spent together over the last four years.

Although up until now the duchess had chosen to remain home with her young children, Lady Abigail and her mother had still attended the season at their lavish city house. They always came home in time to spend the remainder of the year with the duke, duchess, their ever-growing family, and the late Lord James Grant's daughter, Jaqueline De'belmount.

"You will give my best to my sister, won't you?" Lady Abigail's mother asked after they all contained their rather girlish giggles.

"Of course I will," Lady Abigail assured her mother.

Lady Abigail rather looked forward to her time each year in London, less for the prospects and more for time with her favorite cousin, Lady Fortuna Rosh. She dearly loved this extension of her family and, in times past, spent many weeks visiting with her uncle and aunt, the Marquess and Marchioness of Huntington.

"I do wish you would come though, Mother," Lady Abigail added.

"I am not feeling at all up to it this year. Moreover, with all three of my grandchildren staying here at Wintercrest, I dare say I will be much happier to have them about than the ladies of the town."

"I must confess, I am also happy to have you here with them," added the duchess. "It will be my first time away from the twins. I didn't think I could do it but knowing you will be with them brings me comfort."

"Remember you said that, my dear, for when you return, you may find them entirely spoiled," Lady Abigail's mother said with a happy glow around her aging face.

Lady Abigail couldn't help but notice that, despite the wrinkles that now curled around her brown eyes and the large amounts of silver hair that glowed in the light of candles, her mother was still a gorgeous woman.

Read it now!
http://abbyayles.com/AmBoo6

2

"I still don't think it's a good idea for you to go," the duke said the following night as the whole household sat around the fire.

"Don't worry, my love," the duchess reassured her husband. "I will be able to go to town and return home at the end of the season all before this little one is even ready to come out."

"But the twins came early. What if that happens again?"

"It has only been two months since we discovered the pregnancy. I can't imagine that this child will make its debut so vastly early as to arrive in London."

"Still, all this traveling in your condition makes me nervous," the duke said, taking his wife's hand and kissing it gently.

"I don't want to go to town just for myself, but also for

Abigail. With your mother not feeling up to it this year, she will need a chaperone."

"I can be her chaperone," the duke retorted.

Isabella had to smile at this idea. Protecting Lady Abigail from having her brother as her chaperone was what she had meant. She loved her husband dearly, but he was far too protective of his younger sister.

Not to mention the fact that there would be many instances where Lady Abigail would be in need of a female chaperone to make her way among afternoon parties with other ladies. Finding your place was just as much dependent on these social gatherings as on the more commonly thought balls and large evening events.

"I think it will be more to her comfort if I am there with her," the duchess tried to explain as efficiently as possible to her husband.

She watched the fire glow reflected off his red hair as he swiveled his look from his wife on the couch to his sister sitting at a distant table with the twins. His angular face darkened as he tried to make sense of her meaning.

"I am not that horrible," he said once all the lines connected in his head.

"My love, were you not there at last night's dinner party? Could you not have invited at least one gentleman for Abigail to have found even an ounce of interest in?"

"She is far too good for a militiaman," the duke retorted.

"I didn't mean for her to marry, though I would be happy for her no matter what vocation the person she chooses to marry has. She is young and in want of some excitement. I fear, with just you taking her to London, her whole season would be much like that dinner party."

"It's just hard for me. She is my little sister after all."

"I know," the duchess said softly, touching her husband's cheek. "I fear the day that Elisabeth becomes of age. Even Jackie, for that matter," Isabella added with a smile.

The duke looked at the whole of his family in the drawing room. Although Jackie was his niece, he had treated her as if she was his own daughter and not just his ward to take care of. He could scarcely imagine his own behavior when the time came for either Jackie or his darling little Elisabeth.

Lady Abigail couldn't help but sneak a peak at her brother and his wife as they spoke on the couch by the fire. Although their relationship had begun on unsure waters, it had blossomed into something wonderful.

As Isabella ran a soft hand along her husband's face, Lady Abigail felt that pang of wistfulness deep inside her heart. She wondered if she, too, would ever find someone that she could look upon with such love and admiration as her sister-in-law did on her brother.

"Lord James, Lady Elisabeth," the children's governess,

Miss Smith, called from her seat. It is just about time to retire to bed."

The announcement woke Lady Abigail from her wishful thinking. Her young niece and nephew's governess was a very time efficient lady. Everything seemed to run on an exact schedule.

Lady Abigail expected it was a necessity when dealing with two children of the same age. Not only did that mean double the mischief, but they also seemed to have a unique connection between them that often led to more trouble.

Miss Smith had taken over the task of education of Miss Jackie after the previous governess had found a better situation. That, of course, was the Duchess of Wintercrest. Though the twins were still too young for formal education, Miss Smith had happily taken on the task of including them whenever possible.

"Aunt Abigail, will you read to us before we have to go to bed?" James asked in his sweet voice.

Lady Abigail saw that Elisabeth already had a book in hand for her to read to them.

"We only have but a moment. I would hate to make Miss Smith cross," Lady Abigail said, taking the book from the little hand.

"Do come read it over here, so we may all hear it," Lady Abigail's mother called from her seat close to the fire.

Lady Abigail did as she was bid. With a child on either side, she walked over and sat before the fire.

Jackie, too, who was at first playing the piano, also stopped to come and listen. She happily took the spot next to her grandmother.

Sitting on the floor near the warm glow of the fire, Lady Abigail began to read. It was an enjoyable pastime that the family participated in each night.

The twins, and even Jackie, though she felt herself now too old to admit it, loved when Lady Abigail read to them.

She always did it with the most animated of voices and emotions that it quite nearly brought the stories right off the pages of the book.

By the end of the week, matters between the duke and duchess were all settled and the pair, along with Lady Abigail, were setting out on the long journey to town.

The duchess tried her best to hide her tears as she kissed her children goodbye. Although it was a very usual thing for a duchess to leave her children to see to social duties, it was not something Isabella did.

Even though the duchess knew that her children would be more than well-cared for in the hands of her mother-in-law and Jackie, she was still torn by the thought of leaving them. The added emotions that came with her pregnancy didn't seem to be of much help to the matter.

"I received a letter from Fortuna yesterday," Lady Abigail said once they were all seated in the carriage and away down the road.

Lady Abigail hoped that some exciting conversation

might help distract her sister-in-law from her sorrowful feelings.

"How lovely," the duchess said, doing her best to put on a brave face. "Did she have anything of interest to say?"

Isabella was happy for the distraction, just as much as Lady Abigail was for giving it.

"They have already arrived in London. With the weather being so warm, they went early this year."

The duke and duchess both looked out their windows at this, almost to confirm that it was, in fact, unusually warm for the time of year.

"Aunt Amelia has invited us all over for dinner at our earliest convenience."

"That was very kind of her," Isabella responded. "I have been looking forward to meeting these relations that I have heard so much about over the years."

"You will really like Fortuna, I think," Lady Abigail continued, now falling into an ease of conversation. "She is very much like Lady Louisa."

"How so?" the duchess asked, intrigued.

They spent the remainder of the day describing every last detail of the relations that Isabella was soon to meet. The duchess was always happy to meet her husband's family, as she was very limited on her own.

Lady Louisa Frasier and her family had often taken Isabella under their wing as her only family, since her father, the Baron Leinster, had often been away attending to business before his passing. The Frasiers were the closest thing that Isabella had ever had to family dynamics.

When she and the duke had married, she was joyous to find that she was welcomed with open arms into not just his heart, but the whole of his household and family.

"Perhaps we should plan our own event," Lady Abigail said, after a time. "We could invite Lord and Lady Gilchrist, as well as our aunt and uncle. I think we would all get along on such a happy party."

"I think that would be a splendid idea," the duchess agreed.

"It seems to me," the duke, who, for the most part, had kept to the scenery as they went along the road, "that it might be a lot of work for someone who promised to take it easy."

The duchess waved him off as a silly man.

"It will give me something to occupy my mind with."

For the next three days, as the trio traveled from the estate up north to the prestigious house in London, Lady Abigail and the duchess were hard at work making plans for a beautiful dinner party.

Upon finally arriving at their destination, both women could honestly say they would be happy to never sit in another carriage. They made their way into the home already opened and prepared for their arrival, ready for a peaceful day of relaxation and recuperation.

"Perhaps both of you ladies should retire early for the

night," the duke said as the carriage arrived at the house at dusk.

"I promised Louisa I would send her a note as soon as I got here."

The duke didn't like his wife's answer to his suggestion, but allowed it nonetheless. He, therefore, had some tea brought into the evening sitting room so she could write her letter and regain some energy from the refreshments.

"I thought I might call on my aunt tomorrow," Lady Abigail said between sips of tea. "I'm sure she would be happy to see you, Christian, and meet you, Isabella, if you're feeling up to it."

"Well, I think after talking about them for three days, I can't bear to go much longer without meeting them," Isabella said as she finished her letter and folded it for a servant to deliver.

Regularly, Isabella would have just waited to put it with the post, but since Lady Louisa seemed most anxious to know that Isabella was safely in London, she thought it best to have it taken to the Frasier's house right away.

"And perhaps we could take a walk around the park," Lady Abigail added.

"Perhaps it's best to stick to one event at a time," the duke admonished.

"You're a ball of fun," his sister retorted back in a teasing fashion.

"Yes, well you know how much your brother loves to

spend the season in town," the duchess added to the jeering.

"Well, I would guess that you just want to catch the next gig race," the duke retorted to his sister with a raised red brow. "I am not at all certain that it's a very good idea for you."

"Why, because ladies should be abashed by such behavior?" Lady Abigail retorted.

"No, because I fear you might climb into one and show them all up. Then I would have to write to Mother and explain why her daughter is now a pariah."

"You wouldn't do that, would you?" the duchess asked Lady Abigail.

It was not at all shocking to hear that Lady Abigail wanted to attend a race, but to be a part of one seemed like an even more drastic line to cross than she could imagine for her sister-in-law.

"I may have done it, once before. But that was at Fortuna's house and in a basket, not a gig," Lady Abigail corrected her brother.

"Yes, well, things are different when you are in London. You are also a very prestigious member of the ton, whether you want it or not, and that comes with more judgmental looks."

"This is not my first time, Christian. I am well aware of the conduct I must follow."

" I don't think you do fully understand," the duke

retorted. He should have said it in a reprimanding tone, but instead, he wore a smirk of pride.

The duke detested the time in town because, unlike his sister who still had a bit of leeway to enjoy herself, he was expected to act exactly the way someone of his social status should.

"Do try not to make too big a spectacle of yourself this year, Abigail," the duke finally sighed.

"Of course not, dear brother. Plus, Isabella will keep me in line, won't you?"

It was right that, of the three, the duchess was the one keenest to sensibility and propriety. She sincerely hoped that she could install some of those values on Lady Abigail without disrupting her free spirit too much.

Read it now!
http://abbyayles.com/AmB006

SCANDALS AND SEDUCTION IN REGENCY ENGLAND

Also in this series

Regency Loves of Secrecy and Redemption

Forbidden Loves and Dashing Lords

Fateful Romances in the Most Unexpected Places

The Mysteries of a Lady's Heart

Regency Widows Redemption

The Secrets of Their Heart

Lovely Dreams of Regency Ladies

Second Chances for Broken Hearts

Trapped Ladies

Light to the Marquesses' Hearts

Falling for the Mysterious Ladies

Tales of Secrecy and Enduring Love

Fateful Twists and Unexpected Loves

Regency Wallflowers

Regency Confessions

Ladies Laced with Grace

Journals of Regency Love

A Lady's Scarred Pride

How to Survive Love

Destined Hearts in Troubled Times

Ladies Loyal to their Hearts

The Mysteries of a Lady's Heart

Secrets and Scandals

A Lady's Secret Love

Falling for the Wrong Duke

ALSO BY ABBY AYLES

The Keys to a Lockridge Heart
Melting a Duke's Winter Heart
A Loving Duke for the Shy Duchess
Freed by the Love of an Earl
The Earl's Wager for a Lady's Heart
The Lady in the Gilded Cage
A Reluctant Bride for the Baron
A Christmas Worth Remembering
A Guiding Light for the Lost Earl
The Earl Behind the Mask

Tales of Magnificent Ladies
The Odd Mystery of the Cursed Duke

A Second Chance for the Tormented Lady
Capturing the Viscount's Heart
The Lady's Patient
A Broken Heart's Redemption
The Lady The Duke And the Gentleman
Desire and Fear
A Tale of Two Sisters
What the Governess is Hiding

Betrayal and Redemption
Inconveniently Betrothed to an Earl
A Muse for the Lonely Marquess
Reforming the Rigid Duke
Stealing Away the Governess
A Healer for the Marquess's Heart
How to Train a Duke in the Ways of Love
Betrayal and Redemption
The Secret of a Lady's Heart
The Lady's Right Option

Forbidden Loves and Dashing Lords
The Lady of the Lighthouse
A Forbidden Gamble for the Duke's Heart

Falling for the Governess

Saving Lady Abigail

Secret Dreams of a Fearless Governess

A Daring Captain for Her Loyal Heart

Loving A Lady

Unlocking the Secrets of a Duke's Heart

The Duke's Rebellious Daughter

The Duke's Juliet

A MESSAGE FROM ABBY

Dear Reader,

Thank you for reading! I hope you enjoyed every page and I would love to hear your thoughts whether it be a review online or you contact me via my website. I am eternally grateful for you and none of this would be possible without our shared love of romance.

I pray that someday I will get to meet each of you and thank you in person, but in the meantime, all I can do is tell you how amazing you are.

As I prepare my next love story for you, keep believing in your dreams and know that mine would not be possible without you.

With Love, Abby Ayles

PS. Come join our Facebook Group if you want to interact with me and other authors from Starfall Publication on a daily basis, win FREE Giveaways and find out when new content is being released.

Join our Facebook Group

abbyayles.com/Facebook-Group

Join my newsletter for information on new books and deals plus a few free books!

You can get your books by clicking or visiting the link below

https://BookHip.com/JBWAHR

ABOUT STARFALL PUBLICATIONS

Starfall Publications has helped me and so many others extend my passion from writing to you.

The prime focus of this company has been – and always will be – *quality* and I am honored to be able to publish my books under their name.

Having said that, I would like to officially thank Starfall Publications for offering me the opportunity to be part of such a wonderful, hard-working team!

Thanks to them, my dreams – and your dreams — have come true!

Visit their website starfallpublications.com and download their 100% FREE books!

ABOUT ABBY AYLES

Abby Ayles was born in the northern city of Manchester, England, but currently lives in Charleston, South Carolina, with her husband and their three cats. She holds a Master's degree in History and Arts and worked as a history teacher in middle school.

Her greatest interest lies in the era of Regency and Victorian England and Abby shares her love and knowledge of these periods with many readers in her newsletter.

In addition to this, she has also written her first romantic novel, *The Duke's Secrets*, which is set in the era and is available for free on her website. As one reader commented, "*Abby's writing makes you travel back in time!*"

When she has time to herself, Abby enjoys going to the theatre, reading, and watching documentaries about Regency and Victorian England.

Social Media

- Facebook
- Facebook Group
- Goodreads
- Amazon
- BookBub

Printed in Great Britain
by Amazon

44838876R00249